COSMO

SPENCER GORDON

Coach House Books, Toronto

first edition

Published with the generous assistance of the Canada Council for the Arts and the Ontario Arts Council. Coach House Books also acknowledges the support of the Government of Canada through the Canada Book Fund and the Government of Ontario through the Ontario Book Publishing Tax Credit.

While some of the characters in these stories take their names from real-life personages, their personalities and behaviour should be read as entirely fictional – they bear no resemblance to the persons whose names they share. Everything in this collection is a product of the imagination of the author.

LIBRARY AND ARCHIVES CANADA CATALOGUING IN PUBLICATION

Gordon, Spencer, 1984-
   Cosmo / Spencer Gordon.

Issued also in electronic format.
ISBN 978-1-55245-267-7

   I. Title.

PS8613.O735C67 2012   C813'.6   C2012-905208-6

Cosmo is available as an ebook: ISBN 978-1-77056-331-5.

Purchase of the print version of this book entitles you to a free digital copy. To claim your ebook of this title, please email sales@chbooks.com with proof of purchase or visit chbooks.com/digital. (Coach House Books reserves the right to terminate the free digital download offer at any time.)

TABLE OF CONTENTS

OPERATION SMILE

This is authentic, Crystle thought. The turquoise scrubs, the sky-blue smock. The military watch and the brush cut. The man spoke slowly, deliberately, gestured emphatically with his hands. She noted the fine polish of his fingernails, his trimmed cuticles, the skin softened by constant scrubbing. *This is a man who cares about his appearance*, she thought. *That's refreshing; I could talk to this man.*

It was significant that Commander Kubis didn't seem nervous. Most men were nervous or jittery around her. It didn't matter that they fought wars or made policy or saved lives, worked with living tissue, bore immense responsibilities. When confronted by all that beauty and poise, most were reduced to stammering, wide-eyed children. The only men who weren't usually nervous were the actors and millionaires, because for them, she assumed, beauty was simply functional, like furniture.

'Take a look around you,' Kubis said, smiling. 'And don't be afraid to get a bit close and cozy. Even on a day like today, there's lots of work to do.'

Commander Kubis (Kenneth, she remembered) was director of Surgical Services. It was a title that carried a certain weight. *Maybe I can interview him after the tour*, she thought. *Document his struggles, his motivations, record his climb to seniority.* She had to profile common, everyday sort of people as well as the celebrities, the big names. It was good to think about the book, the future, now, because she would have trouble remembering it all later. *These* stories, *this* journey: it was what would distinguish her manuscript from others, what would elevate her work in the eyes of publishers. She understood that distinguishing herself was vital, that such a chance would not come again.

Crystle Danae Stewart, Miss U.S.A. 2008, stood six feet from Commander Kubis aboard the USNS *Mercy*. She was on the far right of a small semi-circle of women, flanked on her left by Jennifer Barrientos, Miss Philippines; Samantha Tajik, Miss Canada; Simran Kaur Mundi, Miss India; and Siera Robertson, Miss Guam. Crystle knew only their first names. In her opinion, they were five of the most attractive girls in the competition. They were all brunettes, and tall, their average skin tone being a dark caramel. It was refreshing to be away from America's monopoly of blond hair and blue eyes, the expectation to be vivacious yet neighbourly, if a touch naive.

If they could only just shut up, Crystle thought, *these girls could be the A-Team*. Aside from Miss Canada, the other three suffered from typical sorts of ESL problems: twisted vowels, torturous locution. Jennifer's accent was so horrendous that it was almost funny, and Guam (though wisely quiet) was so obviously taking a day off in terms of cosmetics and wardrobe that Crystle was embarrassed for her. She resented Guam for wearing the ridiculous *Mercy* baseball hat, the worn-in jeans. It was an all-too-easy trick, and one Crystle knew well: trying to look like you aren't trying, trying to look like the girl next door. Like those bubble-gum girls in her stadium-sized classes at the University of Houston, taking Consumer Science and Merchandising, their hair tucked back through designer baseball caps, wearing snug-fitting sweat pants and immaculate lip gloss. Who were they trying to kid?

Stupid girls, Crystle thought. *Stupid Guam. This isn't a day off.*

She was confident that Commander Kubis appreciated her attention, her smart questions and well-timed nods. And, surely, her flattering and respectful attire: a sleeveless black silk blouse, professionally pressed khaki capris. Tasteful gold-hoop earrings, makeup applied with a light touch, hair straightened and tied back. He must be secretly pulling for her, hoping she'd bring the crown home. She was an American, after all, and this was an American military vessel; she felt a small but noteworthy swelling of pride. When he looked in her eyes, she flashed her teeth.

They had been aboard the *Mercy*, docked in the Nha Trang harbour in southeastern Vietnam, for thirty-five minutes. The five contestants were on a tour of the colossal ship to showcase the altruistic commitments of the Miss Universe competition – a taste of things to come for the winner, who would be obliged to be an ambassador of goodwill and human rights around the world. They had been informed earlier, in a droning summary by a considerably less charismatic shipmate, that the *Mercy* was acting on behalf of Operation Smile, part of Pacific Partnership 2008: a four-month humanitarian deployment involving a host of nations, staffed by both military personnel and civilian NGOs.

'We have a total of one thousand beds,' Kubis said, emphasizing the point with sharp, karate-like chops of his hands. 'That's our total patient capacity: a thousand beds. Our wards are ranked by severity of need and degree of care. We go by intensive, recovery, intermediate, light and limited. This room here – this is intensive.'

Crystle watched the other girls gaze blankly over the sky-blue sheets spread taut over the reclining surgical beds. There was a surprising amount of clutter for an OR – cords and wiring, wheeled workstations, fire extinguishers and arcane naval gadgets that simultaneously fascinated and frightened her. It was strange, too, that in sections the floor was dark and carpeted – what about spilled fluids? It felt as though she wasn't on a ship at all, but shuffling along the glossy floors of some giant metropolitan hospital, complete with swinging double doors, lofty ceilings, passing gurneys, even elevators. Descriptions of GE turbines, maximum speeds, information from the National Steel and Shipbuilding Company, basic dimensional summaries – such tedious detail was straining her concentration, making her wary of possible questions or quizzes. All that specialized naval jargon – the raised forecastle, the transom stem, the bulbous bow, the extended deck house with its forward bridge – made her long for a cool shower, the clean white linens of her four-star Diamond Bay Resort hotel room and the guided-meditation tapes she'd forced herself to listen to, if only to calm her nerves. In any case, soon they'd get to the more intimidating stuff: the burn ward, casualty reception, the morgue (which she hoped they'd pretty much skip).

'The *Mercy* is basically a mobile surgical hospital,' Kubis continued, his smile widening. 'If we were engaged in battle, we'd be providing medical and surgical support to our Marines and Air Force units. These days, we lend a hand in humanitarian and disaster relief – we're still busy, even in peacetime.'

It was a hokey, generous smile. Commander Kubis exuded a sort of calm and trustworthy radiance. Obviously a projection of his personality type, she noted. From what she could tell, he was a fine example of her personal philosophy: the alliterative principles of *Persistence, Patience* and *Perseverance*. And simply by repeating these three words, Crystle was able to conjure all the familiar comforts of home: sitting in the backyard of her parents' modest bungalow in Missouri City, listening to the dry winds rattle the high wooden fence and the cicadas sound their motorized whine, a tall glass of iced tea or lemonade sitting nearby on the arm of her deck chair. No thoughts of outfits or makeup or rehearsed responses, simply family time, the heart of 'Team Crystle': her homespun support network of friends and co-workers who made the early mornings and the dieting and the exercise less isolating, less liable to break her spirit. *Spirit* was a concept they'd discussed often, reclining in the backyard on those humid afternoons, her father with his blue Oxford shirt and slippers, her mother clutching at her chest, both of them hanging on her every word, every setback she listed or every doubt she had of her own worth. *Spirit* was her parents' hard-working ethos, equal parts secular stick-to-it-iveness and no-nonsense Christianity. *Spirit* meant character and charity, something to see her through the long haul of the year, the move to New York City and the posh new apartment, the new life of charity balls and careful public appearances. Crystle was reminded daily that *spirit* meant you were beautiful on the *inside* – that a person can't be pretty on the outside and have rotten guts. And even when everything seemed unreal and the world of photographers and journalists and actors swarmed her, she could feel secure if (and only if) she remained a strong, *spiritual* woman. She had a 'big responsibility to fulfill,' her father would add, being such a 'trailblazer,' because she was the first 100 percent African-American to hold the title (Chelsi Smith being biracial and Rachel Smith being *tri*-racial, after all).

Days of discipline, she remembered, of uncertainty and promise. A strong dose of the Bible, Crystle riding in the back seat of their suv every Sunday and Wednesday to the Emmanuel Pentecostal Church near Murphy Road and Avenue E, standing tall, shoulders thrust back, as the choir unrolled its hymns of judgment and redemption and the oak rafters shook with the sound. Sitting alone on her bed in the quiet hours after the sermon, planners and pens before her, silently reviewing her six steps to achieving goals, the words of advice from her interview and locution coaches who championed the need for preparation and lists – organizational tools that were like bread crumbs lining paths through strange woods. Woods filled with wolves she and her team dubbed *biters*, old friends and colleagues who suddenly weren't so enthused when her name was flashed across the front pages of newspapers across Texas or the nation, or when churches and schools congratulated CRYSTLE STEWART! on their billboards, proud of their hero who would take the crown in Nha Trang. Biters: people who hated her success out of envy, the fact that she could be rich soon and leave them to obscurity forever, because that's how things happened – it was bad enough to leave Missouri City for Houston proper, but she had left the entire South behind for downtown Manhattan, which might as well be another country.

It will all go in the book, Crystle thought, as more smocked hospital workers and photographers filtered into the OR. She'd already thought of a title: *Waiting to Win*. It was perfect.

Kubis had moved on. She snapped back to attention. 'Before we were a floating hospital, the *Mercy* was an oil tanker. In those days, the ship was called the ss *Worth*. But since 1984, we've been entirely dedicated to military support or humanitarian efforts. And with our nine-hundred-person staff, including three hundred health experts, we can do almost everything that a standard, on-land emergency room can.'

Kubis glanced up, nodding at someone over the heads of the women. Turning on her heels, Crystle caught the eye of a younger man standing behind them, sporting the same brush cut, his hands clasped over his belt buckle. He wore pressed khakis and a dark-ribbed naval sweater, embroidered gold bars at his shoulders, no smock. He was clean-shaven and blond and obviously quite relaxed.

'I'd like to introduce you to Lieutenant Coby Croft,' Kubis said. 'He's the head OR nurse on board. He'll be explaining how Operation Smile is making the difference for so many children in the region.'

The girls turned. Miss Canada raised her hand and wiggled her fingers.

'If any of you've heard of *Nurse TV*,' Kubis added warmly, now speaking to their backs, 'you may recognize Lieutenant Croft. He did a great job of showing off the ship during their tour.'

'You can find me on YouTube,' Croft said, chuckling and rocking back on his heels, instigating some general tittering and exhaling among the crowd.

Crystle held up her chin, maintained eye contact and tried to look attentive. But inside – inside something trembled. The word *YouTube* rang like black magic, a sinister *open sesame* to some sealed chamber inside her. The very mention made her face tingle, her lips sting, and while Croft unclasped his hands and began rehashing a summary of medical supplies, surgical preparation, the extent of the *Mercy*'s health care capabilities, *YouTube* rumbled down into her intestines, causing a barely audible gurgle and pop. She brushed her hands against her midsection, quelling the sudden surge of discomfort.

Not here, she thought. *Pay attention and forget it.*

'If I can have you all follow me,' Croft said, passing his left hand toward a set of double doors and striding across the room. Crystle kept her eyes locked on his polished heels, letting the other girls fall into a makeshift line behind him. Taking the rear, she rubbed her exposed forearms, already feeling cold.

The video was uploaded to YouTube almost immediately after the incident. Within hours, the Video Response function was disabled; comments were so nasty, so stridently political, that deleting all racist or sexist posts would have been a tremendous undertaking. Disabling the comments, however, did nothing to halt the clip's skyrocketing popularity. By the time Crystle was aboard the USNS *Mercy*, the video had surpassed its two millionth viewing.

The scene begins in long shot. The floor, the backdrop, the lights – everything is blue, overwhelmingly so, shades wavering between sapphire and denim, giving the impression that the auditorium is resting at the bottom of the sea, that viewers are being given a glimpse of some deep Atlantic twilight. Stage lights pulse in time with the beat of an extended edition of Sean Paul's 'Give It Up to Me' (ft. Keyshia Cole), the serpentine, dance-hall rhythms of the track assuming the shudder and thud of chain-mine detonation, shipwrecks. The stage floor is glossy and dark, reflecting the glitter of plastic sequins hung as immense curtains, while a massive grid-like structure, divided into equal-sized compartments (reminiscent of *Hollywood Squares*), dominates the backdrop. A short flight of mirrored steps connects the structure and the stage floor. In each square (or cell) is the silhouette of a woman dressed in evening wear, as if posing in a display case or red-light brothel window.

The camera sweeps toward the stage, panning to the right. Closer, it's evident that only the ground level of the anterior display case contains real women; the upper squares are stocked with evening-gowned mannequins. The focal point of the shot, though, is a solitary woman standing centre stage: an incredibly slender, olive-skinned girl with wavy, treated brown hair that reaches down between her shoulder blades. She is incredibly pretty, glowing like some phosphorescent anemone. Like the women behind her, she wears a glamorous evening gown: something slinky and black, form-fitting, blooming in a bell shape around her ankles. It's also sparkly and reflective, much like the dark blue floor and pulsating backdrop.

As viewers get a clear view of her face, her dark eyes and white teeth and the shimmer of her earrings, a caption appears at the bottom of the screen beside the NBC peacock: *U.S.A., Rachel Smith*. Rachel begins to walk toward the camera, her arms loose, her hands brushing the sides of her hips. A woman's voice, enthused and emphatic, calls out the country – *U.S.A.!* – triggering a swell of cheers and applause from the unseen audience.

It happens between her sixth and seventh step. It takes roughly three seconds: first, the shudder of her thighs, the slight pivot of her waist. Her upper body buckles, her right ankle tilts sharply and her heels lose their grip on the glossy floor. Then: *kerplunk*, Rachel goes down, hard on her ass, palms at her sides to soften the blow. But she's up again in astonishing time, climbing on her heels with practiced dexterity, turning on cue with her right hand on her hip and smiling big for the camera. Three seconds of a forty-three-second film clip, featuring close-ups and multiple poses, a consistent smile. So practised is Rachel's poise, so polished is her resolve to continue, that the show goes on as if there had been no error, no failure at all.

By the time Crystle was aboard the *Mercy*, she had watched the video ninety-four times. On one evening in early May, while Crystle was home for a visit, her mother snapped a photograph of her watching the clip. The camera caught Crystle in profile, chin resting heavily in her upturned palm. Her fingernails were manicured and white, her lips pursed, free of lipstick, puckered in a fake kiss. When Crystle found the JPEG on her parents' computer, she immediately deleted it: the image of herself, bent over at the desk in the dark, her eyes wide and watchful – it made her sick to see it, sick to see how far things had come.

It began at a Missouri City roadhouse, back in the blurry nether-time before her move to Manhattan; Crystle drank two daiquiris and two glasses of water and waited for the 'celebratory' night to end, her flight to New York scheduled for the day after the next. She and her friends bumped into an acquaintance – an ex–Elkins Knight football player, bloated with confidence from four years of throwing balls and the night's several Budweisers. And only passing by, hitting on one of her friends, giving her the expected congratulations before trying to be funny and reminding her of the obvious, of what she already knew: *Hey, don't fall now, that last girl fell on 'er ass!* Crystle rolled her eyes and turned away, got caught up in another conversation about what Donny and Marie Osmond had been like in person (*amazing*, she'd said). Of course, like anyone even remotely associated with the competition, she'd already studied, scanned and memorized Rachel Smith's fall; it was *the* great tragedy of last year's pageant. Miss U.S.A. falling down? Old news. But there was something weird about hearing the warning in such a non-industry, non-threatening environment, coming from the last person she expected would remember. Hearing it there hammered home just how notorious the event had been. Made her realize, coldly, and for the first time, just how many people were watching – even beer-bloated footballers, it would seem. Before bed she found the clip on YouTube and watched with her fingers laced together over her eyes, rigid, as if she were a scared little girl watching a late-night thriller on TV.

Soon, watching the clip became part of her nightly ritual, before the laborious process of removing her makeup, scrubbing her face, applying revitalizing creams unavailable in North America, sent in small white boxes from Northern Europe or the Middle East. Before donning her ice mask or applying tea bags or even Preparation H to tired, dark-circled eyes. Before her *Focus on Success!* meditation tapes and the extra crunches she'd added to her routine, even though she was at her breaking point in terms of weight training and cardio. It was what she watched before bed, before her stomach calmed and her thoughts could drift. Sometimes she'd take a Gravol, sometimes two; sometimes it was Alka-Seltzer, sometimes Pepto-Bismol. As the months slipped by – those gloriously cool months in Manhattan spent jogging through Central Park, days slinking toward July and her booked flight to Vietnam – she switched to sleeping aids: Nytol, Sominex, sometimes Unisom (always over-the-counter, never prescription – she wasn't about to gamble with her reputation). The video invariably upset her stomach, made her anxious and on edge. Or it set her thoughts turning, locking her into winding circles of insomnia: fears of potential repeat performances in Nha Trang. The thought of slipping, hitting the hard stage floor. Having to hold a smile throughout the rest of the botched walk, only to collapse in the wings, knowing everything was finally, chillingly over. Or having to endure the remainder of the competition, knowing any recovery was futile, that victory was stolen away with the petty twist of an ankle.

Anxiety, butterflies in the stomach, stage fright: these were nothing new. She'd slogged through six years of semi-finals, four years being first runner-up (or best loser, she thought) to some evidently 'superior' (i.e., Caucasian) competitor. It was plain fun and excitement the first time around, way back in 2002, when she strutted out as Miss Fort Bend County, winking at her friends and feeling like she was simply testing the waters and playing a role – no long-term investment, no deep attachment to some paltry win. When she'd made the semi-finals, though, things got serious, and fast. As soon as she figured she actually had a chance, giddy excitement gave way to deep, bowel-churning anxiety. In the intervening years of intensity, she thought she'd conquered disquiet and despair, being first runner-up to Lauren Lanning two painful years in a row, 2005 and 2006, only to repeat the double set of losses to a different girl, Magen Ellis, in 2006 and 2007. And she thought she knew anxiety's secret name, its trembling guts, its icy sweat and stink of fear, as she clasped hands with Brooke Daniels at last year's Miss U.S.A. competition, final round, and Donny and Marie Osmond cruelly cut to commercial after an agonizing stretch of silence just before the awful judgment came down. Posing in her bikini before the intimidating celebrity panel, hoping the extra panty tape was keeping her swimsuit in place. Yes, she thought she'd faced fear, chased it off cowering and defeated. But the video struck like a rattler in the Texas grass, a black widow in the unshaken shoe. And it was unspeakable, where all the other challenges could be talked away, shared with Team Crystle, or worked out of her system with huge, heaving sobs.

Some nights Crystle would slow down the footage, pausing the screen at the precise moment Rachel loses her balance. By pausing and scrolling, she managed to isolate and expand the aching split second of film when everything turned to shit – Rachel's beautiful smile suddenly transforming into a wide, O-shaped distortion. Crystle stared into the pixilated void of Rachel's gaping mouth, seeing an automatic muscular reflex, seeing supreme shock and disappointment, seeing it all as dark fortune: it could happen to anyone, the stage floors were glossy, the cameras were bright and the flash of bulbs could disorient or even blind, and some of those high heels were absolutely treacherous. Who's to say it wouldn't happen again? Who's to say it wouldn't happen to *her*?

Later in the evening – the Miss Universe Competition 2007, held in Mexico City in May – Rachel Smith (miraculously) managed to clear the hurdles of the general competition and was selected to compete in the semi-finals. Despite her fall, the judges were suitably impressed by her overall talent, her petite figure and flawless skin, her unique ethnic composition and her obvious intelligence. But the live audience thought differently. When Rachel was called upon in the question round, the auditorium erupted in boos, hisses, profanity. Crystle knew this was more political than personal – the Mexican audience probably believed the show was rigged in the American's favour (it was Trump's project, after all, conducted in English, and Miss Mexico – who calmly cleared the evening-gown competition without incident – tellingly didn't make the semi-finals). But, politics aside, it disturbed Crystle to the core: the look of humiliation on Rachel's face, the shame of having to slog through her answer before such a withering, high-decibel chorus of disapproval. Crystle could read the defeat, the clear signs of surrender. Had Rachel expected mercy, sportsmanship, support from the crowd? What a twist of the blade, Crystle sympathized, to realize that she wasn't encouraged, wasn't liked, wasn't even tolerated, but *hated*.

It could happen to you, Crystle told herself, staring at the screen. *It could happen to you, black girl, southern girl, American*. In the line at the supermarket, at the bank, turning in the dark in her queen-sized bed, the thoughts sent her squirming. In interviews with the press and in pep talks with her parents. *It could happen to you*, she thought, even on the *Mercy*, as Lieutenant Croft pointed toward some strange, ominous machinery meant to suture ruined skin.

Lieutenant Croft turned to speak before pushing through the doors. Crystle found her rehearsed expression. She stopped rubbing her arms and found a spot beside Miss India, her skin the smoothest espresso, beaming at a near-ecstatic Vietnamese photographer who snapped her picture from three feet back. Croft's mouth was opening and closing, but it would take her a few more seconds to catch his drift. When thoughts of the video returned, her attention was always compromised. Things would refocus shortly. Until then, she assumed an expression of genuine fascination.

'So if I could have your attention, we'll get on –'

She hadn't always felt so empowered, so in charge of her bearing. Indeed, there was a time when the thought of being a professional model – let alone who she was today – would have been ludicrous. Thinking about the three P's, the quiet afternoons in her parents' backyard, could sometimes bring a glimmer of those truly distant memories, of a time and place and self she now hardly recognized. Coursing through the gleaming hallways of Elkins High School, a freshman, a stack of binders pressed protectively against her chest, avoiding the squash and rush of unselfconscious faces as they slammed against their lockers and laughed. Watching a crowd of girls her age flirting with a group of seniors – Elkins Knights, all of them, tall and smooth-skinned and loud – and feeling the familiar twinge of discomfort, the pang of envy at the grace with which her peers could josh and flirt with men three years their senior, who were undoubtedly experienced in sex, in things done in cars and at parties, at hooking up. Feeling a sharp divide in confidence even though it was clear that Crystle was the one always getting the stares from the older guys, the guys who thought scoring a freshman made them studs, calling her *bangin'* behind her back, simulating doggy style with swaying thighs to the laughs of their jeering crew. Crystle pitied the less-fortunate-looking girls, the too-skinny ones who were hollowed-out and fragile, ribs and shoulders poking through cotton like they were made of sticks, or the big, bloated girls, pale asses like dump trucks, losing a sense of possibility in the prospect of boys and romance. Who'd want to rub up against their bones, their flat chests and butts, at formals or post-game parties? She dialed up her locker number, felt enchanted (saved from such a horrible fate, but nevertheless cursed with what she thought was a kind of survivor's guilt: having to be responsible for her God-given excellence, having to protect what was important) and looked down, down into the rest of her afternoons: cutting across the gym floor with the blue and gold Castle of Champions banner overhead, making her way across the parking lots and streets to work another shift at the Kroger pharmacy squatting mercilessly off Highway 6, its field of carts scattered haphazardly between the road and the sliding doors.

But the months and years snuck by, and in small, tentative trickles she let herself accept what she could no longer deny: the attention, the fawning, the advances on the phone, the boys handing her red plastic cups at parties, wrapping their hands around her waist when the gym was dark and shaking with hip hop. The second-hand whispers of *he likes you, he's into you*, and Crystle's cheeks flushing with blood and the most delirious embarrassment (*of course he likes me*, she thought, *has he seen those other girls?*). Slowly, she affected a kind of swagger, done with thinking too hard of other, less attractive girls, her eyes rising from the bottoms of lockers and spiral-bound notebooks to watch the sun slant across her afternoon classrooms with something like joy. Soon she could take time off from studying in her spare periods because she was already smart; she could run circles around the girls who were known as straight-A achievers. And how sweet the springs became when her head was dizzy with sunlight and pollen, and the lark sparrows and goldfinches sang, and she drove with her friends in her parents' car to Houston, feeling the warm air blowing over her bare skin while they sang the lyrics to whatever song was on, didn't matter if it was any good. Those dark, pitying feelings had been blown out by the sun and by vodka at parties and by the wet lips of boys her age or older, whose hands slipped down her back and squeezed what they could get away with. *Screw it*, she thought; she was desired, popular from day one without feeling like she'd donned a mask, and the A's rolled in and soon college loomed so magical. And so it was a quote on a scrap of paper that suddenly made things snap together: *the race goes not to the swift but to the one who endures*. Hadn't she endured? Hadn't she endured those evenings in the lunchroom of the Kroger, with its rank scent of wax cardboard and carrots while the dance was thumping at the school? Or being rejected by the 'smart girls' just because she was gorgeous and they were not, or snubbed by certain so-called popular girls who turned to catty bitches whenever Crystle caught the eyes of their boyfriends? She'd endured – endured so much that victory, truly *winning*, was now only right.

But the leap from pretty to *supermodel* was still slow in the making. Crystle couldn't remember the moment, couldn't pinpoint an instant. Girlfriends offered their admonishing jabs when she felt ugly, or too skinny, or just plain dull: *What are you whining about?* they'd ask. *You're one to talk. Ugly? You're perfect, you're gorgeous, like no one I've ever seen.* When she was comic and self-deprecating like her father, or when a boy didn't return her gaze or her veiled flirts: *It's 'cause he's scared, girl. 'Cause he ain't never seen something like you.* First it was walking through the mall and one day catching sight of herself in a mirror and not recognizing who she saw. Then it was whole rows of men turning their heads in theatres, in church pews, in restaurants. Pimpled gas-station crews having to focus on the hood of her car, windshield wipers soapy and dripping in their hands. Buttoned-up waiters trembling with memorized menus. Door-to-door religious witnesses suddenly forgetting why they'd come calling. *They done broke the mould*, or *My oh my, I remember you when you was just a little*, or simply *Daaaaaamn*, a drawn-out eruption from a passing window, the collective sighs of Missouri City falling to worship this mature, tall, full-lipped woman, neck so long it could reach the clouds that capped the city in its flatness. Suddenly she was *the* Crystle Danae Stewart, name recited by ninth-grade boys as they scanned the graduating photos of 1999, thinking ahead four impossible years, baffled that anyone so beautiful could have sat in their seats or stared at the same blackboards, doodling or dreaming their afternoons away.

Snap back. Pay attention. Crystle gave herself a shake. It was a strange adolescence, she thought, something she recognized as at once unbearably conflicted and sickly sweet. It made her hurt, ache, with nostalgia to think of it; the only way not to tear up was to imagine today as the logical fulfillment of all that promise. *Pay attention.* From beyond the next set of doors came the abrupt rush of voices: the rising, nasal twang of several women chatting rapidly in Vietnamese and breaking into full-throated, giddy laughter.

Croft tugged at the hem of his sweater and continued. 'Our main mission in the past few months has been to perform reconstructive surgery for children born with certain facial deformities, such as cleft palates and cleft lips. Since 1982, Operation Smile has provided surgical care to over 135,000 children around the world, from over fifty countries. The *Mercy*'s been proud to lend a helping hand throughout the entire South Pacific.' He paused. 'Does everyone know what I mean by a cleft palate or a cleft lip?'

The circle of contestants murmured and nodded, looks of concern and compassion breaking out on five troubled brows. Crystle caught Miss Guam's eyes for a fraction of a second. Was that confusion, incomprehension? A glimmer, anyway. *Oh, Guam*, Crystle thought, mentally *tsk*'ing and feeling more or less back on the ball.

'Rather than give you more of a tour – which, I gotta admit, must have been boring,' an admission receiving some relieved laughter, 'now we're going to give you the chance to meet some of our patients. Through these doors are several children who've been through the final stages of their surgeries and who're now receiving their concluding assessments. In other words, after today, they can go home for good. This has been a long and difficult process, but our doctors and nurses have been able to give them a fresh start in life. Now these kids'll be able to eat, speak and interact the way they've always wanted to. And I'm sure they'll be thrilled to meet you!'

Croft opened the doors with his shoulder. Beyond the OR was a long, hall-like room, partitioned at a dozen points by white plastic curtains. Positioned according to some ship-based logic were half as many stainless-steel bed frames, topped with white mattresses and familiar blue sheets. The room teemed with activity, hummed with conversation: Vietnamese civilians, women, alone or in clusters, sat on black folding chairs or stood at the ends of the various beds, some bouncing small children in their arms. A baby bawled, its face muffled against fabric. Some of the closer women stood and scooted their chairs away from the doors, edging nearer to the beds. On each sat a child, wearing street clothes, shorts and T-shirts, sandals or running shoes. Crystle avoided looking at the kids too closely, afraid that staring would be rude. When she didn't focus, their healing lips were reduced to smudges, a blur around their mouths, any scars mercifully indistinct.

She found herself standing somewhat awkwardly at the rear of the group, holding her palms against her thighs, scanning the ranks of Vietnamese mothers and grandmothers, their floral-patterned blouses and chestnut skin and thin black eyes summoning visions of the street she'd left behind only forty minutes back in the crazy sunlight and sluggish humidity of the Nha Trang harbour. Little reminders that this was no ordinary hospital, that they weren't gathered on the upper floors of a walk-in clinic on some mundane street of Houston. Again awash in that sharp, utterly incomprehensible dialect, Crystle felt a painful stab of home-sickness. She felt their eyes roaming over her limbs, inspecting her wardrobe, her sash, her figure, the long curve of her neck. Imperfect grins

– some with yellow or broken or missing teeth – forced her to return the expression. Like so many of her public days of meeting and greeting, today demanded an unnatural amount of smiling. If it went on much longer, she'd have to duck into a restroom and apply some Vaseline to her teeth. She forced herself to return the women's smiles for only a second before looking away, trying to orient herself in this swirl of activity, the sudden hush that fell as the locals noticed that a tour was underway – that a seemingly extraterrestrial quintet of striking, richly garbed women had entered behind one of the *Mercy*'s most senior officials.

Croft addressed the room in a slow, careful-sounding Vietnamese. Immediately the women applauded, shifting excitedly in their chairs, rising to their feet.

'I've just let them know who you are,' Croft said, above the claps.

The girls waved back modestly, but with a certain magisterial practice.

'Many of these women speak English,' Croft said. 'I'll let you visit with the children; I'm sure a quick hello would brighten their day. They'd love to get a picture with you, too.'

Crystle watched Croft drift toward a woman and get assaulted with hugs, a quick peck on the cheek. The girls were left to mingle and meet with the recovering kids, looking uncomfortable for only a cold snap of a second before they broke apart and attended to the various groups. Crystle found her stomach and bearing, feeling for the right mixture of sympathy, the right expression of interest. Closest to her sat a woman in her late twenties, holding a bald baby in her lap. Crystle approached and bowed. On the nearby bed sat a boy wearing a Spider-Man T, drawstring shorts, tiny Velcro sandals. He was about nine, small and thin, his knees scraped and scabbing. Faced with no other choice, Crystle really *looked*, and saw his mouth puckered with a swollen red line of stitching running at an angle to his right nostril, the right and left sides of his upper lip fused in an uneven stripe.

'Hello,' Crystle said, after a beat, drawing out the *o*.

'Hell*ooh*,' said the woman, imitating her tone. Crystle counted a few seconds, unsure of what to do. The woman reached beneath her seat and pulled up a manila folder, which opened to reveal a large glossy picture of the boy on the bed, obviously pre-surgery: his face rent by a massive, disfiguring hole in his palate, yellow baby teeth crowding around the gap in the bone and skin. A successful surgery, then, Crystle guessed.

'Wow!' she said, nodding, looking up at the boy. 'It's so wonderful ...'

'This Huyhn,' the woman said, 'my son.'

'Hello, Huyhn,' Crystle said, reaching out to touch the tip of the boy's sandal. 'My name is Crystle. It's nice to meet you.' The boy smiled.

It really is incredible, she thought: the boy wouldn't have been able to eat or speak or have a girlfriend – so many things would have been withheld. She felt a genuine sense of pity, worried suddenly that she had cringed. How cruel God could be, she thought, considering the boy's fate. How many people born into ugliness, into misfortune. But improving this depressing turn of mind – this wide and irreconcilable gulf between her life and his, between her life and those of her Missouri City peers, the fat and forgotten – she felt again a sense of pride, not for who she happened to be or from where she came, but for what she was representing. If these were the sorts of missions she'd be asked to represent or promote as Miss Universe ... well, she could live with that. Watching the United States, the nations of the First World, operating for a force of peace. Curing children of maladies – it was almost too good to be true. Humanitarian work held a subtle but not insignificant allure; she considered the ways in which her motivational work – that burgeoning business plan she'd carefully set out back in Texas, the crowded churches she knew she could pack with people who would listen to her story of sacrifice – could be the bridge between her education and what her mother told her was the Lord's work, the *spirit* they were so eager to remind her of. It would have to be a substantial section of *Waiting to Win*, this personal and national obligation to those less fortunate. She never expected that merely days before the competition's end she would be feeling this much warmth and pride for her culture, her people, what the block-lettered *U.S.A.* on her sash could stand for.

'Can you take picture?' the woman asked her, holding a disposable camera with her free hand.

'Sure,' Crystle replied. She was shuffled toward the side of the bed, made to pose beside Huynh, who sat looking happy but scared, smiling his scarred and uneven smile. A few shots were taken, then a few more standing beside Huyhn's mother, who flashed the peace sign. Then it was time to sign autographs on ruled paper, using the Sharpie she carried in her purse. It was still surreal to be famous, but never a chore: all you had to do was show up, be there and smile, and suddenly you'd brightened and blessed someone's humdrum day. She gladly signed autographs or posed for pictures, losing that sense of awkwardness by doing what was now routine. If this was what these people wanted, then she would humbly oblige.

Before she could move on to another bed, saying goodbye to Huyhn and his mother, Lieutenant Croft emerged from the noise and confusion of the room and sidled up beside her. *Finally*, she thought, *one of these Navy boys has come to talk to Miss U.S.A.*

'How're we doing here?' Croft asked, rubbing his hands together.

'Just wonderful,' Crystle said, waving again at Huyhn, who now seemed distracted, speaking slowly and obviously painfully to his mother.

'That's great. I mean, chances are these kids will remember this day for a long, long time. It's been such a hard road, after all.'

'Oh, I can only imagine.'

'But you've probably had a hard road yourself. It must not be easy being Miss America!' Croft laughed, a wheezy exhalation.

'No, it's not exactly all fun and games,' she said, but then remembered, 'but a complete walk in the park compared to what these kids have been through.' *A good answer*, she thought, and true, but it would be gratifying to talk to someone like Croft, or Commander Kubis, about how hard it actually was. All the things she couldn't say, the things no one wanted to hear.

Croft nodded, frowning. 'Yeah, no doubt. But still, it must be hard for you. In a way. The travelling, the exercise, the dieting. I'm only guessing, though ...'

Crystle felt good hearing this. It was probably his halting attempt at hitting on her. It was charming. He sounded edgy, a little off his game. *Let him go on*, she thought.

'... but you must have to pay, like, real close attention to how you dress, all the little details. The discipline. What you eat ... even how you talk, uh, saying the right things ...'

Sure, Crystle thought. *You're just scratching the surface, pal.*

'But then again, I have no idea. I mean, I can't imagine what it must be like. Some kinda stress, huh?'

She laughed and nodded.

'I mean, you could get a question you aren't ready for, or you could fall down or something, like last year?' He laughed a bit, as if in apology.

'Oh, of course, of course,' Crystle said rapidly, her throat feeling pinched, squeezed down to a straw. 'Yeah, ah, I just ...' *Of course I could*, she thought. *I could fall.* She was blushing, feeling the familiar needles tickling her cheeks.

Croft grinned. He seemed aware of the red rush of blood to her face, staring at her in a way that suggested he was delighted by her blushing. Then he said something else, and touched her arm just below the elbow, grazing the tips of his fingers against her bare skin, but the sound of his voice seemed so cloudy and flat, as if she'd been dunked underwater and was now trying to listen to a radio playing above the surface. Was someone playing music? She had the distinct impression that there was music playing somewhere. Why would they have a radio in a hospital? She turned from Croft, or she thought she did, dizzy now, her mouth fixed in its frieze of geniality, of polite conversation, and caught the eye of a boy a few feet away, maybe four or five years old, peeking from behind one of the curtains separating the beds. A brief, passing image of a child, his mouth blown to pieces by a monstrous cleft: pre-surgery, this one, for some reason mingled with the other patients. Like he'd been snuck into the group to remind the cured children of how far they'd come. *Unfair*, she thought. Why was this baby here? Why were they letting this happen? His mouth opened and closed in silence, revealing his pink gums, his grotesque jaw. They weren't prepared to see this. They weren't prepped. He was crying. The baby was crying.

'–rry, are you okay?' Croft said, his voice sharpening to reach her, fingers still hovering over the sensitive patch of skin below her elbow.

Crystle snatched her arm away. Croft was too close – she could smell his sweat through his deodorant, the fabric softener on his sweater. She pulled her purse farther up onto her shoulder and took a short step back. No, that wasn't the right move. Her pulse felt out of control; she felt a crazy vein wriggling in her temple. The baby had disappeared, moving behind the curtain. She stepped forward again, smiled, and reached out and touched Croft in return, tapping the left side of his ribbed sweater. She batted her lashes and looked into his eyes and asked, in as soft a voice as she could manage, 'Lieutenant Croft, is there a rest-room I could use?' Her voice surprised her: it was full of the old Texan drawl she'd been trying so hard to vanquish in New York.

Croft looked boyish, hurt. 'Uh, sure thing, yeah, of course ... just let me show you ...'

Then there was a nurse by her side, a white woman in her late forties, her head a grey skillet of tightly cropped hair, slightly overweight, leading her back through the laughing ranks of Vietnamese women and the double doors and then along another hall. Crystle knew instantly that she was utterly lost on board the ship; she'd need a guide to return to the tour. She felt girlish and uncoordinated, being led by an adult who seemed infinitely more composed. She wondered if any of the other girls saw her being led away, if they'd raise an eyebrow, speculate aloud if she was okay – some fake gesture of concern that would ultimately fuel the fires of gossip. They reached a washroom.

'Take all the time you need, hon,' the woman said, but didn't smile.

The washroom was enormous – over a dozen stalls arranged in uniform, factory-modelled succession. Beneath the harsh light of fluo-rescents, Crystle dropped onto the lid of a toilet, door locked, unspooling a roll of sanitary paper and dabbing at her eyes. The tissue came back dry; she wasn't crying. She wrapped her hands around the back of her neck, massaging, breathing in the sharp smell of disinfectant. *All right, all right*, she thought. *When you're worried about something, you see it everywhere. You notice it more often because your brain is* fixated *on it. It's natural. You're just hearing something your brain* wants *you to hear.* She blinked. 'Get a grip, baby,' she whispered, bent over, kneading the flesh of her neck.

She sat on the toilet for what felt like a long time (or time passed in an odd, weightless way: the feeling of time not passing at all, her eyes tracing along the minute seams in the fabric of her capris). But she knew she had to get moving – she didn't want the chubby nurse or the other girls to think she was sick, or making a BM. Her heart was thumping too furiously, though, to chance getting up and risking another attack. An *attack* – that's what it was. She wasn't stupid; she'd seen enough pre-pageant meltdowns (girls hyperventilating into makeup bags, crying hysterically, bent over with dry heaves or calling their mother or boyfriend or daddy saying, *I can't do this! I can't do this!*) to recognize a full-fledged panic attack when she saw one. It was the first of its kind; all other moments of disorientation paled in comparison: those flapping butterflies or seizing chills or losses of concentration. This time she'd completely lost track of what was being said to her, thought she'd heard music, got angry over a misfortunate baby. It was like she'd blacked out. There were anxious unknowns: what had she said to Croft? Where did that nurse come from? Her heart still squirming, Crystle rose and pushed through the door, emerging from the stall and forcing herself into composure out of sheer embarrassment. She stood before the steel sink, the flawless mirror, dabbing at tiny beads of sweat that had gathered at her hairline. She was careful with the folded toilet paper, worried that the sweat would start a chain reaction of frizz that would explode in the outdoor humidity. Then she sucked in a great gulp of air, puffed violently, slapped her cheeks and left the restroom.

The nurse was standing in the hall, hands on her thighs. 'Ready to go back?' she asked.

'I am ready,' Crystle said. There was that southern drawl again – as if she were slipping back into that easy, seductive way of speaking, as if she'd hadn't been working so hard at firming up her r's. *Get a grip*, she repeated.

'We've had to move everyone forward,' the nurse said, after they'd entered the intensive-care ward. 'You'll have to catch up with the group.'

'Oh, I'm sorry for slowing things down ...'

'No, it's no problem. It's just that – uh huh,' she said in confirmation, opening the doors to the room in which Crystle had met Huynh, still boisterous with children and attending mothers. A quick scan revealed that the other contestants were gone. 'We'll have to get a move on,' the nurse continued briskly, even snottily. 'I'll get you there in a jiffy, though.'

The nurse moved ahead, leading her back through rooms she'd passed earlier in the tour. A column of Vietnamese civilians lined the wall of one wide and crowded corridor, each adult and child wearing a white hospital mask and looking impatient. She could sense them watching her as she passed. She felt under an immense pressure. Those eyes. She fought down deep to find her usual comportment, right hand gripping the straps of her purse, staying three steps behind the scurrying nurse.

Now Crystle recognized the main entry point to the ship: an access area jammed with people, card-carrying crew members scrutinizing a stream of mask-wearing locals. She'd been here an hour ago. She spotted Commander Kubis among the crush. As she approached, he turned and smiled at her: that warm and generous smile, his composed appearance. In a few more seconds she was approaching the massive port, getting flashing glimpses of the blinding bay.

She shuffled with the line past a pair of tarpaulin curtains, crossing the threshold from shade to light and slipping on her sunglasses. She was outside now, in the heat. Blinking, a hot gust fluttering her blouse, she held the crown of her head with the flat of her hand, gazing eastward across the bay and into the smudged horizon of the South China Sea. She looked out past the jutting hulls of passing yachts and the hotel's scuba boats and the stiff canvas sails of local fishing vessels, out to the limits of vision: the meeting between the flat azure of the bay and the cloudless, boundless blue of the July afternoon. Then she turned toward the shore, eyes sweeping across the jade sandbar, hearing the cry of gulls in the air, the sound of unseen flags rippling in the wind above her, smelling the salt in the water, watching distant bathers wading before the warm and shallow reef. She could spot the reclining, tricoloured beach chairs of her Diamond Bay Resort. All those drinking, lounging tourists, playing in the sand, waited on by a fleet of diligent, uniformed Vietnamese with their broken English and lisped French. And in the distance the green and blue watercolour hills of the jungle, a serene and unchanging backdrop to the apartments and government buildings of Nha Trang: all that raw energy, car horns and confusion.

There was a long ramp. The long ramp she'd climbed to board over an hour ago, excited for the tour, the photo ops, was made of corrugated steel that was searing and dazzling in the sunlight. Nurses and crew filed ahead of and behind her, loose scrubs rippling in the wind, flanked on either side by hip-level railings sloping down toward the docks of the harbour. A mass of bodies crowded the waterfront: half of the group leaving, half arriving, a mix of *Mercy* employees and brightly clothed Vietnamese, the tops of their heads uniformly black and gleaming. In seconds, she spotted the four girls, wearing sunglasses and looking up. *They'd be hard to miss*, she thought. Jennifer was waving, her brown arm a languid noodle in the glare.

They needed Crystle to move, to fall in line with the march of legs and shoes, right hand wrapped loosely around the rail, and step down the long ramp to join them. They were beckoning to her, laughing, making it all a game. Or were they laughing *at* her? Thinking her ditzy or incompetent? It would take her thirty seconds, striding in time behind the blue-smocked nurse ahead of her, avoiding stepping on her heels, while the mask-wearing Vietnamese, adults and children, filed by her left, climbing up and into the *Mercy*, headed toward reunion or diagnosis, calamity or relief.

She'd left Commander Kubis behind her in the shelter of the ship: a last, smiling vision of the assured and confident officer, a final wave of his polished hand. *I've forgotten to ask him questions*, she thought, now on the platform at the lip of the ramp. *I've forgotten the interview*. But it was too late: she couldn't wait or turn back; she was a servant to the queue; she was late. They needed her to reach the bottom so they could board another minibus, be shuttled down the shore of the city to their various destinations, the hotel room at the close of day. She couldn't hold up the production, even by a few meagre minutes; they couldn't leave without her. She looked down.

And while walking she saw another ramp, separated from the present by a handful of precious days and nights, as clear as the corrugated steel before her. There were similarities: there were groups of people waiting for her to walk, people invested in her ability to think and act and perform. There were colossal expectations for her to move, and move well, to accomplish the easy task of walking. To smarten up and meet them. To go out, ten steps forward, and turn to the left. Hand on hip. Smile. Turn again, and walk the long ramp. Stop, hip thrust. Walk away from the crowd, the roar. Stop again. Look over the shoulder. There were colossal expectations. But where one ramp was bright and on a decline, the other was dark and level and glossy. The other was in the Crown Convention Center of the Diamond Bay, the largest arena of its kind in the country. She'd stand in the wings in a line of other contestants, waiting for the production staff with their impatient clipboards and headsets to wave her forward; it was all a quick snap of judgment and paying close attention to your cue. Recalling rehearsals. Jerry Springer or Mel B, one of the hosts, would announce her time onstage over the in-house loudspeakers: *U.S.A.* and *Crystle Stewart* would flash along the bottom half of television screens in Missouri City, in Houston, in Manhattan, in living rooms and in bars and restaurants, and those watching in public places would stand and lift signs and whistle and blow into dollar-store noisemakers, clapping, cheering. Her mother and father, ecstatic, Team Crystle, ex-classmates and teachers from the University of Houston, from Elkins High School, even the biters. This was their girl, about to glide across the slick floor, past the tiki torches and vertical fronds, the imitation waterfalls and horizontal red and black lights that suggested a lake at sunset, the tropical exoticisms of contemporary Vietnam. Immense columns of Romanesque stone like a tiered display case, the arched wall of a coliseum. American voices, celebrities, judges, performances by Lady Gaga. An extended edition of Robin Thicke's R&B hit 'Magic.' Springer and Mel B zipping onto the stage on a moped. This was the moment. This was the evening-gown competition, late in the pageant, and it meant sink or swim. It meant poise and sophistication, conjuring a collective notion of classical, mid-century beauty. The dresses reached the floor, were meant to glide effortlessly with the walker. Heels were mandatory. This is what she had trained for: the endless hours of preparation, one chance at execution, one chance to impress. The channelled pain. Psychic training and teeth-grinding concentration and pain. A mind turning on its body, transforming it, moulding dumb flesh into purpose, through routine and repetition, ironing out its weaknesses, conquering fatigue and fear. *The race goes not to the swift*; it was Crystle's turn to walk. She took a step, and another, and then it was lights, the great star-like spotlights of the theatre, and out in the gloom of the primeval audience, where thousands of Asian faces smiled and watched, Crystle saw her name written in code. A script for the recorded television broadcast, saved and uploaded as a file meant for public consumption. *Crystle* and *Stewart* becoming keywords, allowing searchers to find the video, to sift through the mass of moving pictures to find her performance. Her body transformed to pixilation, out and above the void of the arena, already electronic, leaping from flesh and decay into endless repetition, playback, memorization. Her practised movements now able to be slowed, paused, sped up and repeated. Embedded. Saw it clearly, the code that would hold her ageless and unchanging, perfect.

She took another step.

A piece of corrugation, a bullet or bump in the metal, the sunlight over the water, the wind, and suddenly Crystle was falling, *falling*, it was all real, reaching for something, anything –

A hand caught her left arm, steadying her. She looked up, her heart skipping. She was held by a boy, fourteen or fifteen, Vietnamese, distant puffs of cumulus forming a halo over the crown of his head. She translated experience: she'd tripped against a bump, lost her balance, fell, but was caught and steadied by a boy before she crashed against the ramp. She was outside in the heat and the raw wind, the seashore, the present. She felt the boy's rough fingers on her wrist. She clutched at his T-shirt. Saw the smooth skin of his neck.

Then she saw his mouth: his upper lip curled up into one wide, distorted nostril, central incisors lost to a carnivalesque deformity. He was smiling – she could tell from his cheeks and eyes.

Crystle yanked her arm away, repulsed, and grabbed the railing. She looked away, again at the sea, heart continuing its pounding dance. There was another hand on her shoulder, from behind. She let out a squeal and wrenched her body forward, straining away. In her flailing she pushed the nurse ahead of her, causing her to stumble and turn. Crystle wrapped both hands around the railing and crouched, shaking, clenching her eyes.

Hands were on her exposed back and shoulders, clasping hands that were gentle and supportive but unwanted, violating, as if reaching past her quivering skin and touching something sensitive and painful inside her. One hand was gloved with smooth latex; another was the rough palm of a civilian. She squealed again, head tucked against her chest, ponytail flying in the wind.

Now she'd have to face them, no hiding the marks, the evidence of her breakdown. Knowing what was coming – the judgments, the smirking, the glances – made her want to cower and dig, collapse in a jellied mush, be forcibly removed by strong hospital workers, attached to an IV drip and sedated. She'd scream if she had to, if it got the right attention, if it got the job done. She imagined, with a seismic and despairing longing, being airlifted via helicopter from the entire offending province, then boarding an airplane that would spirit her back to Los Angeles and then home, to Texas.

'I'm not ready,' she said, bursting forth with tears. 'I'm not ready to *walk*.'

There was a scuffling halt to the line, the boat crew attempting to stop the flow, to allow Crystle her space. The hands withdrew, leaving her to tremble and sputter. In a few dizzying seconds she was completely aware, self-conscious and humiliated, touching at the dark streaks of mascara that stained her cheeks with a folded tissue from her purse. She looked up, and through occluding tears saw Kubis staring back from the *Mercy*. She wrenched away, mortified, dabbing at her nose and sniffling, a last image of his concerned face looming out of the ship's cool shade. On the docks below her, she saw the girls and their minibus driver edging closer to the lip of the ramp in a glimmer of light.

Of course, there'd be no screaming tantrums. She breathed. There was no turning back or running home. She was locked into a summer camp without end, without the succour of family or friends. She'd have to face the music, the dim arena, the rehearsals, the final walk in her evening gown before millions of viewers. Be pixilated and formatted and saved, regardless of the outcome. She trudged down the ramp, heels clanging on the corrugated rivets, looking up from out of her glazed insecurity as she reached the dock, prepared to weather the girls' collective scrutiny. She breathed.

In a second she was embraced by Guam, Crystle's chin resting surprised between her neck and shoulder, Guam's chin and mouth buried against Crystle's collarbone. India was next, followed by Philippines and

Canada, the girls standing in a huddle and obstructing traffic. Philippines was dabbing at Crystle's cheek with a fresh tissue, and Canada murmured, 'You poor thing,' amid a chorus of *It's okay*s and *Don't worry, honey*s. Crystle floated on the supportive cloud, away from the water along the docks, dodging photographers, the minibus driver and other suit-wearing pageant attendants and security staff barking at gawkers and journalists. They walked along the promenade, up a flight of stone stairs cracked by centuries of use, and ducked as a group into the long grey minibus, tinted windows rolled up and the air-conditioning system blasting and beautiful.

'We saw how affected you were by the little kids on the ship,' said Miss Canada (Samantha, she remembered), when they were all seated and buckled up. 'It was moving for all of us. So hard.'

'You're just not used to seeing children like that,' said Simran, Miss India. 'It gets easier as time goes by. Not that it ever gets really, truly *easy*.'

'You've got such a big heart,' said Guam, who reached out and squeezed her knee.

'I'm sorry,' Crystle said, sighing, pinching her purse between her thighs. She breathed. 'I didn't mean to hold all y'all up. I'm just a crybaby. Those kids were so brave.' She felt the tears edge back, perilously close to making a return. She let her drawl out, heavy and slow and the way she imagined all wise and holy people spoke. 'And I felt so honoured ...'

She didn't have to finish her thought; the girls understood. They said it was something they'd hold in their hearts, this time spent visiting and spreading joy. They said it was an experience that would draw the five of them closer, make it easier to hope for one another; that no matter what the outcome at the Crown Convention Center, with the whole world watching, they'd have each other's backs. The A-Team, they joked. They were rooting for each other, hoping for happiness despite the near certainty of a loss.

Perhaps there was still hope in the end, Crystle thought – a glimmer of something unforeseeable and moving, like the orange glow of Heaven spreading its storybook light over a redeemed world. That's how she envisioned Heaven, anyway: something to save in the back of her mind, a reward for a hardworking life that came as a welcome surprise. Not much to think about now, but something foggy and distant – something to look forward to. Maybe that's how all this would turn out. All she needed was the right kind of spirit.

JOBBERS

Amid a pile of paper plates, pizza boxes and the crumbly remains of breakfast, I stare down at the July '91 edition of wwf *Magazine*. Jake 'The Snake' Roberts glares back from the glossy cover, his cocked brow just oozing evil. wwf *Magazine* is a regular sight in our house. Eddy, my eight-year-old brother, saves all his change to run down to the convenience store every month to grab the new edition. He has me read the articles to him. On this month's cover there's a headline about The Ultimate Warrior – Eddy's favourite wrestler – and his ongoing feud with The Undertaker, who's one of the most feared heels in the World Wrestling Federation. To Eddy, wrestling is literally life and death, especially when the Warrior is involved. Of course, as his big sister, I know better – I know it's absolute horseshit.

From where I sit at the table, I can hear Gorilla Monsoon – black, hyperactive poodle, bought for forty bucks two weeks ago from a retired steelworker on East 22nd Street – whining non-stop in the spare bedroom. Gorilla isn't properly housebroken. Mom and Uncle Keith (not really my uncle – he's Mom's boyfriend, most recent and longest lasting) are throwing a party tonight. They want Gorilla locked in the bedroom because if we let him run around the house he'll piss and shit all over the floors, and for now it's just too hot to keep him out back, especially with all that black fur. Gorilla's so spastic that neither of them wants to deal with his jumping and barking, so his prison sentence extends until the end of the bash. Knowing Gorilla, and knowing Mom's parties, the puppy will be yelping until three in the morning.

Eddy's outside knocking spiders into a Cheez Whiz jar behind the tool shed, so he can't hear. If he could, he wouldn't understand – the whimpering would drive him crazy, make him cry or complain, so it's better to keep him occupied. Eddy's got a dirty-blond mushroom cut and jar-thick glasses, a soft stomach and white, flabby arms. He's got some real serious mental problems – *head trauma* according to Mom, *retardation* according to Keith – but everyone around here is used to it. The kid needs constant supervision at school, loping around and holding hands with the guidance counsellor.

I've got a growing list of tasks that I use to keep Eddy busy. This spider-collecting gig is totally new; I'm trying to see how long it'll hold his attention. I told him that every black spider he plops into the jar equals ten minutes of playtime with me later on. I figured it would give him a real thrill; the shed is crawling with those leathery bastards. That's basically my summer job: keeping my brother busy, creating distractions. I don't get paid.

'But I don't like the black spiders,' he whined earlier, looking sideways at the Cheez Whiz jar and rubbing his crotch.

I clucked my tongue and flexed my biceps, as if to say *no pain, no gain*. He got the hint and stepped out into the flat, smoggy heat of our north Hamilton summer. Just in time, too, because Gorilla started up his whimpering just a few seconds later.

Mom's at work down at Robin's Donuts, past all the drooling pit bulls tied to front-porch lattices, past all the little flower gardens and dried-up lawns. She works days, preferring the fat people on their motorized scooters to the drunken teenagers at night. She gets home at 6:30 and brings us boxes of doughnuts. Or doesn't.

Just as Gorilla starts going absolutely bananas, Uncle Keith crashes down the stairs. I start humming what I think would be his WWF entrance music, if he were ever on the card: Hank Williams's 'Kaw-Liga.'

'I'm gonna cover this,' he says to me, smirking, holding up a chipped block of wood and chewing on a cigarette filter. He doesn't mean the song: Uncle Keith has a small pile of wooden blocks near the shed, and he's determined to cover each block with beer caps before the end of the summer. Keith stands shirtless and barefoot in the doorway, his gut sagging hairy and swollen over his yellow swimming trunks. He's really tanned, loves to sit out in the sun, pounding bottle caps onto blocks, bitching about things like the puppy, like the food Mom doesn't cook him, like Eddy and me. He's got a serious black moustache and a cleft, a scar, on his jaw.

I wish he *was* a wrestler, always on the road and working out, sending letters reminding us to take our vitamins and say our prayers. Sometimes Keith watches wrestling with us, but I don't think he gets it; he spends two-thirds of every *Saturday Night's Main Event* chuckling into a Pilsner, telling us how dumb we are to be watching. He keeps saying, 'It's fake. What the hell, it's fake,' as if I could be seventeen years old (old enough to drive! almost old enough to vote!) and not know this.

'Don't let the dog out of the bedroom. Don't go *near* the bedroom. The dog's got shitloads of food and water up there.'

'I'll take him for a walk,' I say, 'I'll take him to the park.'

'Like hell you will.' He says this in a way that means business, like he's cutting a mean pre-show promo. He says this like Hulk Hogan would say, 'Whatcha gonna do, brother?' but without all the cartoon goofiness, the reminders to exercise and stay in school – his version of Hogan is pure aggression. Keith hates the Hulkster, thinks he's all water weight and juice. He hates all the good guys. He prefers the heels, like Sgt. Slaughter, or Big Boss Man, or Mr. Perfect – guys, he says, who 'just don't give a fuck.'

'You ain't goin' nowhere. You see that list?' he asks, pointing with the block at the refrigerator. There's a yellow strip of paper stuck to the door with a Hamilton Ti-Cats magnet. It's covered with Mom's cocka-mamie scrawl: a list of chores that I'm supposed to finish before she gets home. There's only three hours left to go.

'Yeah,' I say.

'Well?' Then Keith pushes open the screen door and walks into the backyard. It's clear that he's won the match, retained his title as King of the Ring (King Shit, I call him). I'm just a pale and flabby jobber, laid out on the mat. I imagine 'Kaw-Liga' blasting from secret speakers as Keith makes his exit. I hear him grab the extension cord, plug in his paint-stained stereo and fumble around with his Hank Williams cassette. I hear him haul the green garden hose from around the side of the house and hear the hollow crash of cold hose water filling up our Aqua Nova kiddie pool. I listen to him pull up his lawn chair, dunk his fat feet into the water and hammer a bottle cap onto a block of wood. The first strains of 'There'll Be No Teardrops Tonight' blast out trebly and flat and the puppy starts to howl.

Eddy pounds into the kitchen, almost tearing the screen door off its hinges. The jar's crawling with black spiders, his eyes filling with tears.

'Gorilla Mon*soon*,' he says, little chin trembling.

So Eddy and I watch the wwf on our tint-distorting tv. Eddy's hunched forward in a Maple Leafs jogging suit, an empty McDonald's carton in his lap, with the last few McNugget crumbs caught in a thick smear of plum sauce. He breathes heavily, his mouth open, playing with the spit between his tongue and his lips, blowing tiny bubbles.

Today The Ultimate Warrior is wrestling a nobody, a total jobber. The first notes of his entrance music send the audience into a frenzy. A very blurry and purply Warrior sprints to the ring. The Warrior wears red spandex trunks, shimmering tassels tied around his boots and his elbows, and bright yellow, almost *tribal* face paint. His gimmick is hard to follow: he snorts a lot, speaks in outrageous grunts about mystical powers and the harmony of the spheres, and says things like, 'Now you must deal with the creation of all the unpleasantries in the entire universe, as I feel the attention of the gods above!' People love him; he's a huge face.

'WARRI-OR!' Eddy yells. He thrusts his fists into the air, imitating the huge, oiled body on the screen. He's so excited over his Warri-*or*, or the tv's so loud, that he doesn't notice the dog's whimpering. I do, but pretend not to; instead, I act like I'm interested in the match. Jake 'The Snake' Roberts has been helping The Warrior face the dark side lately; it's the only way he'll ever defeat his current enemy, The Undertaker, who's still undefeated by pinfall or submission. When the 'Taker defeats other wrestlers, he crosses their arms over their chests. Sometimes, if he's wrestling jobbers, he drags their unconscious bodies into body bags, zips them up and carries them out of the arena. Nobody knows what he does with them, but kids like Eddy suspect that he buries them alive.

A few months ago, The Undertaker ambushed The Warrior and sealed him inside a casket. While we watched, a host of inept backstage attendants spent precious minutes fiddling with the casket's locks before they could finally crack the lid. Once they got it open, they had to perform CPR on The Warrior to revive him – he was apparently unconscious from a lack of oxygen.

Being such a mark, Eddy was accordingly traumatized. He screamed in a kind of agonized warble, sat on the ground and started rocking his head in his hands, back and forth. You'd think he would've seen this type of shit before, but for some reason this was different. Mom stormed in from the kitchen and screamed at us to 'Turn that faggoty shit off, it'll give him nightmares,' so I had to shut off the TV before Eddy could witness the happy ending: The Warrior being lifted from the coffin – unconscious, but alive.

Today, things seem fine, or forgotten. Eddy loves the good guys. He loves Hulkamania and Macho Madness. His top three favourite things in the world are wrestling, Gorilla Monsoon and Chicken McNuggets. Eddy's least favourite things are Halloween (rubber masks specifically), needles and nightmares – nights when he wakes up with a head full of dreams, eyes open, talking strange and scary like he's still seeing the witch who lives in the basement, the witch with icy fingers that curl around his neck, who whispers hate and nonsense into his ear – though one night he confessed to me that sometimes the dreams weren't about a witch at all; they were about Mom, or Keith, usually naked, grabbing and holding him down, about to do something to him that's painful and loud and in slow motion.

Eddy jumps from his end of the couch with his elbow aimed at my stomach. I'm ready for him; he collides with my knees and arms. I grab him, outweighing him by twenty, thirty pounds, and press his arms behind his back. Then I wrestle him giggling through the den and out the front door. When we step outside, heat hits us like a spear tackle. We sit gasping in the sun's glare on the concrete steps of the porch. A dozen

Malaysian and Filipino children run screeching toward the intersection, daring each other to throw rocks at cars or windows, to whip friendly, sleeping cats with sticks. I can't stand the neighbourhood kids, but occasionally I feel for them. Some mothers throw loaves of bread from second-storey windows: that's food for the day. Some mothers throw luggage and blue jeans and shoes onto lawns: that means an uncle or a friend or a father is leaving. Sometimes a magazine or a newspaper is used as toilet paper – you'd be surprised at how many kids think it's reasonable to squat and shit beneath a cedar.

I unfold the note from Mom, smoothing the yellow sheet against the step.

'What's that?' Eddy asks, mouth hanging open, glasses sliding down the flat bridge of his nose.

I keep smoothing. 'This is a note,' I say. 'From Mom. We have lots to do this afternoon.'

I glance up to see Eddy massaging the back of his neck, staring at the bright blue sky. His glasses gleam in the sunlight.

'I know,' he says, resigned. 'I know. I know.'

'Like hell you do,' I say. 'Listen to me. We have to clean the house before Mom gets home at six, so –'

'Why?' he asks, a little shrilly.

'I thought you said you knew. Don't lie to me, shithead. And don't interrupt. It's because Mom and Keith are having a party and they don't want a messy place.'

He keeps staring at the sky like it will tell him something.

'So you're gonna go around with me today and help me clean. See?' I show him the note, force his face down to read it. 'It says: "do the dishes, take out the trash, wipe the counters, sweep and mop the floor, pick up Eddy's toys" – that's you, *Eddy*, you see that? – "vacuum the rug and dust off the shelves." Think you can do that, *brother*?'

Eddy wipes his lips, sighs. 'Where's Gorilla Monsoon?' he asks.

I take a deep breath. He's already forgotten, but that's normal.

'He's upstairs in the spare room. We gotta keep him there today 'cause otherwise he'll piss all over the floor, and that'll just mean more to clean.'

'It's lonely up there,' he says, looking up.

For a second, I think he's talking about his brain – I get this image of a warehouse filled with old, broken-down machinery, dust-covered gears. 'It's just for the day. It's just until tonight, until after all the people go home.'

'But that's so *long*.'

'Too bad,' I say. 'Life sucks. Dig it?'

'Life sucks,' he echoes. Cicadas wail like tiny motorcycles.

'If you're good,' I say, steering an ant away from a sandy hill, 'we'll have a match tonight. You can be The Ultimate Warrior. I'll be The Undertaker. We'll set up the ring in your bedroom with the mats. It'll be like WrestleMania. Mom and Keith won't care 'cause they'll be in the backyard. We can do a whole match.'

Eddy closes his eyes and smiles. 'WARRI-OR!' he screams, fists in the air. And just as he lets loose, two boys about his age walk past on the sidewalk, turning to stare with big, stupid grins, catcalls and insults poised on their lips. But I stand up and stare at them like The Undertaker, hands wrapped around our shitty iron railing.

'Say something,' I say, staring with the 'Taker's dead eyes. 'Say one fucking word.'

They keep walking. They're obviously the smarter type of neighbourhood kid: a real rarity. But by minding their own business, they've managed to avoid a bloodbath. There've been so many I sometimes lose count: shitty, rainy afternoons when I'd find a huddle of smiling children circling Eddy on the playground. How I'd find Eddy on his muddied ass, his mouth full of black dirt and half-chewed worms. The Halloween of 1989 when kids locked Eddy in a storage closet at our school, surrounded by the mannequins from the drama department, their smooth faces concealed by horrible Mummy and Werewolf masks. How I sat on the other side of the door waiting for the teacher's key while Eddy wept. You should have seen his eyes when he got out.

Thing is, Eddy's likely to run up and give a big, caring hug to anyone who's just dunked his head into a toilet or made him drink piss. Even the smallest act of kindness can instantly turn a heel into a face, a villain into a hero. Just like the wrestlers he loves who're constantly switching sides – one day mortal enemies, the next best friends. I'm not so eager to let go, forgive. 'Don't be such a jobber,' I keep telling him while walking him home from school. Looking after Eddy is like working hundreds of tag-team matches held in countless house shows across the city, with your partner not even aware of the fight.

I can't stand the heat any longer. I tell Eddy it's time to clean the house. I get *The Wrestling Album* blaring on the living room tape player, drowning out the pathetic squeals coming from upstairs. Eddy dries while I wash, holds the dustpan while I sweep, collects his toys and crayons and colouring books and puts them in his room. I work up a shiny sweat, scrubbing counters and vacuuming the den, sucking all the bread crumbs, dog hairs, staples and clumps of calcified snot from underneath the couch. The sun cuts across the sky while we work, pushing the air outside into a level of heat that's killer.

'Land of a Thousand Dances' shakes the thin walls of the house. Eddy leaps onto the freshly vacuumed sofa, holding my old T-ball trophy for a microphone, and belts out the first verse. I hear his squeaky whine trying to keep pace with Mean Gene Okerlund, 'Rowdy' Roddy Piper and all the other wrestlers McMahon forced into recording this brutal cover. I join him during the long, ridiculous chorus, chanting out the repetitive stream of *na*'s and strumming on the vacuum shaft like it's an electric guitar. Uncle Keith reappears, his hands clamped over his ears. His sunburnt chest looks like a giant hickey. I resist the urge to give him a knife-edge chop right across his sagging bitch-tits. He's got a stupid, exhausted look on his face, and mumbles something to me about taking a nap, barely audible over the grating roar of the vacuum and the cassette player, and then plods up the stairs to pass out. This means he hasn't finished cleaning the backyard. This means Mom is going to be royally pissed. But for now, Eddy and I have some fun. I rush into the kitchen, open the freezer and stick my head inside. The cold air is delicious. I grab four grape freezies and a pair of scissors, head back into the living room. Calmed, Eddy and I suck and chew on the thin packages of sugary ice, our chests slowing down. We sit side by side, the evening and its consequences still a million miles away, as the last words from 'Land of a Thousand Dances' shake the floor beneath our feet.

Mom comes home from work smelling like metallic coffee grounds and burnt toast. She's in her typical flurry of post-shift exasperation, complaining about the pervert customers who ask about her menstrual cycles or turn-ons. Before she's even thrown her keys onto the kitchen counter, she asks me if the chores are finished, if the list was followed. Judging from her narrow-eyed gaze across the living room, her survey of the kitchen and her slow, satisfied nod, I figure Eddy and me are off the hook. Then she asks about Keith, who's still upstairs, asleep, even though *The Wrestling Album* is still blaring.

'King Shit's all tuckered out,' I say, then realize it's high time to run down to the convenience store to buy some pop and chips, and take our time doing so, because shit is going to *soar*.

By the time we're back, Keith has managed some sort of miracle: Mom, somehow, seems okay. We find them unfolding lawn chairs in the backyard, hauling up coolers and bags of crushed ice from the basement. They have case upon case of Coors Light and Canadian and tons of pop for mix. They both seem excited, or drunk.

'This is gonna be a real shaker,' Keith says, unfolding a plastic chair and sweating through a CHCH News T-shirt from '89. Mom laughs. She's rosy and clean from the shower, still wearing a bunched towel on her head. Seeing her like this is always a supreme relief; whenever she's happy the walls seem to radiate calm, as if the plaster and brick of the house were somehow hard-wired to her fluctuating moods. Despite all of Vince McMahon's insistence that wrestlers like Hogan or 'Macho Man' Randy Savage are *the* most electrifying superstars of our day and age, none of them can come close to matching Mom for her intimidation, microphone skills and thunderous, static-charged aura.

I barely have time to shower or change clothes before the backyard party gets going. The guests arrive earlier than I figured, filing through the door or staggering around the side of the house. Jim and Danielle O'Brien, with their strange talk of star signs and crystals and alien energies, Jim's wild paintings of the 'elder beings' he wants to show Mom. Swingers, acid-poppers, hippy-dippies – plain creepy, with glazed looks in their eyes and frizzy hair. Keith's old garage buddies Don and Pat and Mike, with their rank smell of gasoline and butts, their dirty fingernails and high-pitched hoots, lugging two-fours and already carving up Keith over his gut (not that I mind – they remind Eddy of The Bushwhackers, give him a laugh). Mom's hyperactive friends Gail and Tyler, women who chain-smoke cigarettes and go to bingo and talk about things like the lottery and the weather and how they can't handle standing in lines. And of course Aunt Deb and Uncle Frank, drunk and high respectively, but thankfully without their brood. What a tag team: Uncle Frank sitting stoned in his dank basement, lost in the Nintendo Mushroom Kingdom, only peeling himself off his moist couch to work another night shift or to spark a J from his crappy marijuana crops. Aunt Deb bellowing from her backyard, bursting out of her blue bathing suit, letting her kids know that they're in deep shit. With *six* kids, no less, all of whom have teased or tortured Eddy and aroused my wrath. But that's the way she goes – we've known them so long, they're sort of like family.

With the dog's whining drowned out by the guests, Eddy and I get called into the backyard to say our hellos. Uncle Frank asks me if I have a boyfriend while his eyes go up and down my body. Don and Pat get Eddy to chug a can of Sprite, despite my glances at Mom. By the time it's nine o'clock, there's gotta be twenty, thirty people in the backyard, friends of friends, old boyfriends and girlfriends and married people, and everybody's drinking and hollering; the noise becomes a bass hum through the walls of the house. 'It's like the Royal Rumble,' I say to Eddy, jabbing him, making him stutter and laugh, spitting Sprite. And Keith gets his stereo blasting Night Ranger and Journey and Rush: the worst bands in the world.

After most of the guests arrive and the party is in full throttle, Eddy plunks himself down outside the door to the spare bedroom with a bag of sour-cream-and-onion chips, singing lullabies to a door-scratching Gorilla. I'm relaxing on my own bed, flipping through *Rolling Stone*, an article on Guns N' Roses I've been meaning to read. So far, so fucking amazing; Slash is the sexiest monster I've ever seen, and so much hotter than the New Kids' 'Step by Step' nonsense that the girls get wide-ons over – it's not even a contest. It's almost peaceful: the door closed, a tall glass of ice water on my night table, *Appetite for Destruction* in the tape player. I close my eyes for a second, begin to drift to the sounds of 'My Michelle.'

The door flies open. Eddy's standing there with the Cheez Whiz jar in his hand.

'Holy shit, what do you *want*?' I ask him, groggily.

He walks over and puts the jar on my bed. It's jammed with spiders, squirming over each other, one mass of legs and fangs and swollen abdomens.

'Get it away!' I yell, curling up.

'There's fifteen spiders,' he says, taking it back. 'One bit me. You said –'

'Fuck, I know what I said. Just give me some peace and quiet.' But Eddy's got that look on his face – I can tell that he's been waiting, biding his time. That he's bored out of his skull.

'What do you wanna do?' I ask him, defeated, closing my magazine.

'You said we'd have a *match*.'

I stand. 'Okay then,' I say, sighing. I roll over and hit PAUSE on the cassette player. 'Let's have a match. But this is going to be *the* match – the match to end all matches.'

Eddy starts getting excited, hopping from one foot to the other like a cartoon character. I start issuing commands. There's a lot of stuff to do before we're ready to rumble.

Eddy and I fold all the sheets on his bed and put them in his closet. We do the same with mine. Then we drag my mattress out of my room, across the hall and into his. It takes longer than you'd think, involves lots of sweating and cursing and Eddy almost crying on more than one occasion. We push the two bare mattresses against each other in the middle of his room. Even when they're flush, they take up almost all the floor space, so we push Eddy's trunk and baskets and other crap into the hallway. Meanwhile, we can hear Gorilla getting revved up, like he can sense there's gonna be some real crazy shit going down. I turn to Eddy and nod.

'Get changed, superstar,' I say.

Eddy runs to his closet and starts rummaging through his stuff, humming the *Saturday Night's Main Event* theme music. I walk back to my room and start changing into a black button-down blouse and a pair of tights. I go down the hall to Mom's room and find her old leather gloves, a bright and brassy shade of violet. Then I find Keith's ridiculous Stetson hat and one of his grey striped ties. Using Mom's mirror, I tuck in the blouse, tie up the tie and don the hat. It's the closest approximation to The Undertaker that I can manage without applying white face paint or drawing dark circles under my eyes. For a moment, I stand and pose, rolling my eyes back into my head.

When I'm back in Eddy's room, he's already in his Warrior getup. He wears his red Speedo and red knee-high socks. He's tied multicoloured wrapping-paper ribbons around his elbows, in the crooks of his arms. And he's tried to apply the Warrior's distinctive face paint – obviously using red and blue ballpoint pens, and ending up with something that makes me want to howl with laughter and beat him senseless at the same time.

'You idiot,' I say. 'Don't use Bic pens on your face. They won't come off.'

Eddy growls and charges me, head down, butting into my stomach. It hurts; the little shit almost knocks the wind out of me. I push him back down onto the bed.

'You *bitch*!' I say, before leaping on him. From there, we start laying into each other, but this is no ordinary match – I don't give him any quarter. Eddy gets a thorough beating: DDTs, clotheslines, backbreakers, spinebusters, armbars – the works. At first it seems as though he's died and gone to heaven, squealing and giggling. I guess he assumes it's okay if he hits me with force behind it; the kid doesn't know his own strength. So I retaliate, hurting him, smacking him in the crotch a couple times before smearing his face against the mattress, pulling him up for air just before it seems he'll burst into tears. I grab him around the neck, squeezing hard, about to perform The Undertaker's signature chokeslam. He starts kicking my shins, spitting, punching me in the gut; he's desperate, terrified. But gravity and height win out, and I lift him off his feet and send him crashing down onto the mat. Then I cross his arms over his chest, sit on his stomach and count *one, two, three*, as Gorilla screams through the wall.

'How do you like that, huh?' I ask him, expecting him to flee the room sobbing. But after a few seconds Eddy sits up, looking as though he were just asked to do some advanced math problem. 'Holy *crap*,' he says, smiling big. And then he's on his feet, flushed, the ink smeared and sweaty on his cheeks. He rubs his hands together like he's warming himself over my body, like I'm some sort of crackling fire.

'Again,' he says. 'Rematch.'

'Okay,' I say, catching my breath, shaking my head. 'Just gimme a minute. And no rough stuff. That was way, *way* too rough.' I prop myself up on my elbows. 'So The Ultimate Warrior lost,' I continue, thinking about how we can get through this without killing each other. 'There's a rematch coming, of course, but the last thing we want is a repeat of last time – which, I've gotta say, was a total *debacle*.'

'A total de*bac*le, yeah,' Eddy says, grinning.

'Don't smile. I was gonna rip your head off. Anyway, how're we gonna make it different? How're you gonna win?'

Eddy stares straight up. 'Train hard,' he says, eyes on the spidery cracks of the plaster ceiling.

'Right,' I say, edging closer. 'Train hard, but The Warrior is already in peak physical condition. You can't get any stronger. You've seen your muscles – your veins are like bungee cords. But you're not up against a physical adversary – this challenge is emotional. Spiritual, even.' I curl my fingers and drop my voice to the 'Taker's gravelly baritone. 'You're up against an opponent who wants more than your body – he wants your *soul*.' I roll my eyes up into their lids. 'Just like with Jake The Snake, you're going to have to face the dark side, face your fears, before you're ever gonna be ready to pin the Demon from Death Valley.'

Eddy drops to all fours, staring me in the eye, his bangs falling sweaty over his brow.

'How must I face the demons?' he grunts, in his totally inaccurate imitation of The Warrior.

'Just pretend I'm your spirit guide. First things first: let's determine, exactly, what scares you most.'

Eddy backs up until he's up against the door. 'No ...' he whispers, still in character.

'Yes ...' I say, holding my gloved hand toward him. 'And I'm not gonna give you the satisfaction of naming your own fears. I'm gonna decide for you.' I think for a minute. 'First one, since you've already told me today how much you don't like them, *spiders*.'

Eddy rubs his face, looking at me like I've just pronounced his death sentence.

'No, I'm not ...' he says, breaking *kayfabe*, breaking character.

'Yes,' I say. 'Second. Second is ... the skull mask.'

Eddy whimpers. The skull mask is an old family legend: a rubber Halloween mask that has a long history of being strangely, horribly magnificent. It was, and is, an ancient and evil threat: a distorted mass of puckered white skin made to look like bone, fringed with a foul-smelling lion's mane of wispy grey hair. We used to hide the mask in drawers and cupboards where we'd keep bleach and other poisonous chemicals, just so Eddy would keep his distance. This'll be cool, I think – whether Eddy can deal with the mask is a real point of interest. A few years back, it would have been impossible.

I start thinking about the next challenge. As the third and final hurdle it'll have to be the ultimate experience in terror. I think long, weighing my options, Eddy looking pale and small against the door.

'The casket!' I say, finally. 'The casket.'

Eddy frowns, his mouth open.

'Remember the trunk? The tickle trunk?' In our basement – the cold, concrete cellar, Keith's rarely used 'workroom,' where we store our old winter coats and boots and Keith's garage jumpsuits, with the boiler standing dusty in the corner and the single bulb swaying on its chain – deep in the far corner is the *tickle trunk*. The trunk's four feet long, about two and a half feet deep, and navy blue. I figure the trunk will be an adequate stand-in for the real casket they used to seal up The Warrior last April on TV.

'Yeah ...' Eddy says, cautiously.

'Well, that's gonna be your final test. You get what I'm saying, Warrior?'

He gets it, all right; tears spring to his eyes.

'Think about it. After you finish, you'll never be afraid of the basement again. It'll be bullshit fairy stuff to you. No more nightmares. You'll be able to go down and bring us up some Cokes or grab a beer for King Shit. Who knows? Maybe Halloween won't be so fucking scary – maybe you can come trick-or-treating with me this fall.'

'Can't we just wrestle?' he asks.

'Sorry – but if you wanna beat the 'Taker you're gonna have to pass the tests. Face your demons. Become a true warrior.'

'How long?' he asks.

'Not that long. Thirty seconds,' I guess, knowing he won't make it much longer. 'And I'll be there with you the whole time. You've got nothing to worry about.'

'There's so much, though: spiders, skull masks …'

Somebody drops a bottle outside. Manic laughter ensues.

'How about this: we do it all at once. You hold the mask in one hand, the jar of spiders in the other. Then we close the lid. You wait thirty seconds and it's all over, we can have that rematch and you can pin me, fair and square in the middle of the ring.'

He still looks unconvinced.

'Okay, fine,' I say, taking this further than I know I should. 'Final offer. We can let Gorilla out. Just for a bit. We can carry him downstairs.'

Eddy considers this, his face brightening. 'Can I play with him for an hour?'

'Sure,' I say. 'But if he gets outside we're dead.'

'Can I use a chair in our match?'

'All right.'

'Can I jump off the dresser?'

'No, but you can jump off the desk.'

He thinks about it. 'Okay,' he says, his voice low. 'Let's fucking do it.'

I'm about to tell him to watch his mouth, but I find myself so seriously proud of him for going along with the plan, I decide to let it slide. But then I think, what kind of babysitter, sister and tag-team partner would I be if I did?

So I don't.

'Watch your fucking mouth,' I say, and help him to his feet.

We edge open the door to the spare bedroom, making sure the puppy can't squeeze his way through. And while Eddy sits and plays with Gorilla, who squeals and licks and runs circles around him, ecstatic for the company, I clean up the two neat piles of shit he's left on the carpet. We fetch his leash and then slink down to the basement door, making sure the coast is clear before heading downstairs.

Our house is pretty new. It's a townhouse built about twenty years ago. There are no ancient, creaking floorboards or sealed-off attics, no threat of Indian burial grounds or eighteenth-century hauntings. You're more likely to find a bucket of KFC bones than a leering human skeleton. Besides, Eddy's old enough not to be so shiveringly, pathetically afraid. His fear of the basement puts all similar chickenshit bedwetters to shame. His affliction should be studied and monitored, recorded in some scientific journal as the Most Ridiculous Fear Ever. Maybe if Eddy could face his fear of the basement, of the dark and of his dreams, he'd be tougher at school. Baby steps, I think. First conquer your fear of the unknown, of the stuff that can't actually hurt you, and then move on to the stuff that *can*: the bullies, the swirlies, the insults. One day Eddy will stand up for himself and move on to singles competition; one day we won't have to be jobbers.

I make sure the lights are on, that there are no 'witches' waiting for Eddy before we head downstairs. Eddy waits on the main floor with the dog on his leash and the spider jar under his arm while I investigate the basement for monsters or murderers. From outside, we can hear a male voice yelling *Don't give me that! Don't give me that!* followed by repulsive peals of laughter. We haven't seen Mom or Keith in a while, so they're obviously having a wild time, which is good news for us.

'It's ready,' I say, taking the leash and holding his free hand as we descend the stairs. His palm is warm and clammy in mine.

First, I push past swaying grease-monkey jumpsuits, locate our old box of Halloween costumes and dump the contents onto the floor: silken robes and scarves, clown costumes and party hats and Ninja Turtle masks, fake fangs and a plastic scythe. And, of course, the skull mask, as twisted and grotesque as I remember it. With the mask tucked under my arm, I go after the tickle trunk, clearing a few other boxes off the lid and cracking it open. It's hot inside; it smells like stale bread and stage makeup. I dust it out for insects or webbing or mould. Then I drag the box across the ground so it's yawning before Eddy, who stands before it in his Warrior costume.

'Not backing out, are we?' I ask, crossing my arms, letting the skull mask dangle.

Eddy looks at the trunk, the Cheez Whiz jar of spiders, the mask hanging limp and ghoulish in my hand. Something turns, clicks, in the clogged machinery of his mind.

'All right. Now. Now,' he says.

'Spoken like a true warrior. Every victory begins by conquering *yourself*.'

He gazes into the open box. Slowly, cautiously, he steps inside, one foot after the other. He hands me Gorilla's leash, and I scoop up the shivering dog and hold him against my shoulder. Then Eddy's crouching, sitting, finally turning on his side and drawing up his knees. It's a tight fit for Eddy's excessive flab. After a bit of wriggling, he's found a comfortable enough position, his arms wrapped around his shins. I hand him the sealed jar of spiders. Then I place the skull mask under his chin, just to see if he's got the guts. He's got his eyes closed tight, starts breathing rapidly.

I wait a moment, enjoying this show of bravery, this potential for change. This little kid in a Speedo curled up in an old chest.

'Rest ... in ... *peace*,' I say, and close the lid.

After a second I hear him puffing, gasping, making this low weird noise from the back of his throat.

'It's all right, Warrior,' I say. 'You know I'm right here.' The ceiling light flickers, still wobbling from when I knocked it while dragging the chest. 'There's nothing to fear but fear itself.'

'*Warri-or!*' I hear, muffled, from inside.

'Here, just so you know I'm close, I'm gonna sit down on the lid. You can hear me tap on the roof, know that I'm just inches away.' I hear a faint shout of approval. I ease down on top of the trunk, straddling it, my legs banging against its clasps, holding Gorilla in my arms. Then I wrap my knuckles on the top, humming The Ultimate Warrior's entrance theme. From upstairs and outside, I can hear the foggy sounds of the party, still in full swing: that distant funhouse of mingling conversations, scraping lawn chairs, clinking bottles, the screen door whacking open and shut. I look forward to the quiet that will eventually settle on the house, for the humidity to finally break. Sleeping in on Sunday morning and heading out, not having to look after Eddy or babysit a yapping dog. Driving around in Shannon's dad's car, messing around with her video camera. Going to the bonfires, drinking, flirting with the Grade 13s. Not having to talk about wrestling. I've earned a break, I figure. I've been so goddamned good.

It's been about twenty-five seconds. I start a countdown for the last five. 'Okay, you ready? Five, four, three, two and … you're free!' I yell, sliding off the box and setting Gorilla on the ground. Then I open the lid.

Or … I don't. Or, I move to open the lid and something stops me. I'm not lifting it right, I think. I spread out my arms and yank from both ends.

Nothing. It's gotta be the gold latch, I think. It's been knocked down to the locked position. But since there's no lock, no key, all I have to do is flip it back. The latch swings up easily, and again I pull on the lid.

Still nothing. I shake the trunk a little. 'What the fuck,' I mutter.

'Lemme out,' Eddy says.

'Hold on.' I walk around the other side of the box and start pulling. I try to jam the tips of my fingers into the crevice beneath the lid. I attack it, yanking, jostling, rubbing my fingers raw in about fifteen seconds.

Eddy's moaning something, but I'm not paying attention. I stand up and give it some distance, scowling. There's gotta be something, something I'm miss–

Then it hits me – hits me like The Warrior's running boot to the gut, and yet just the outline of a memory, from two years back: Keith cutting a promo about using the trunk for certain 'supplies.' That he wanted to figure out a way to keep the lid locked, so Eddy or I couldn't get inside. 'Man's gotta have a place to keep his privates,' was what he said, rubbing that damned cleft in his jaw. Said – and *oh god*, I think, remembering – that if you put enough weight on the lid, if you pressed down on it harder than normal and waited until you heard a certain *click,* then it would …

I whistle in amazement. My head, my chest, my stomach – everything starts vibrating. I have to piss, have to drink some water, have to lie down.

'Please, please,' Eddy's moaning. Then, before I can say a word, say something reassuring or comforting, he starts to scream. His first scream is probably involuntary; it's short and surprised, but the sound of his voice ricocheting back to him in that tiny casket, in the black – it's all too much. He starts screaming wildly, crazily, hiccupping through sobs, like he's being tortured, like he's been buried alive. Gorilla Monsoon

begins barking in a frenzy, sprinting around the box and scratching the sides. And I stand there, lips still in the shape of a soundless whistle, bare feet frozen to the concrete floor.

'Eddy,' I say, finally able to speak. I don't think he can hear me. He's gurgling now. Thinking quickly, I throw the end of Gorilla's leash beneath the trunk, Eddy screaming harder as I lift the edge. 'Sorry, sorry,' I say, and then sprint up the stairs, careful to close the door on my way out.

I pass a man and woman standing close in the kitchen, their arms entwined, who instantly back away from each other as I rush past them. Then I'm through the screen door, bursting out into a circle of lawn chairs surrounding the kiddie pool. The stereo's blasting the Cars and I wheel around, trying to find a familiar face. Luckily, I spot Keith first, standing close to the door, smoke in hand, sipping a beer. Moths and other winged insects bash against the porch light over his head.

'Inside,' I say, breathing hard. 'You need to come down into the basement.'

'Why?' he says, lips glistening from the bottle. Mike, his old work buddy, stands beside him, drunk as hell and clearly amused by my red cheeks and heaving chest.

'Eddy's hurt himself downstairs and I need you *now*,' I say.

'Fuck,' he says, shaking his head. 'Go get your mother.'

The thought of telling Mom delivers another running boot to my gut.

'No, no, you've gotta do it.'

'What we ask you to do tonight?' he grunts.

'I know it's just – '

'Go. Get. Your. *Mother*.'

King Shit, I think. He smiles at me. And I lose it.

'Eddy's locked in your *fuck*ing trunk, you turd!' I yell, really marking out. I can feel the eyes of party guests, but happily the music is so loud that the majority of the gathering hasn't heard. Mom's somewhere else, thank god, or else by now I'd have felt an open-hand slap on the back of my head.

Keith's shoulders drop. He stares at me, and I can tell: he hates me, hates everything about me. Then his look changes a little, like he's just the tiniest bit afraid.

'Hold on,' he says casually to Mike, and walks toward the door. I lead him inside, passing the scarlet-faced couple in the kitchen (now standing a metre apart), and down the stairs. As soon as we're halfway to the bottom, Keith's heavy tread behind me, I can hear Eddy's garbled, muffled shrieks.

'Je-*sus*,' he says. 'What the fuck have you done to him?'

I stand by the trunk with my arms crossed, and finally feel the stinging threat of tears. I don't care to explain myself, or what we've done. I don't care how much Keith insults me. I just stand aside and expect him to do something about this, crack the lid, so I can calm Eddy down.

'Go up and close the door,' Keith says, squatting down. It's quiet now, the party sounding a mile away, but Eddy's screams just ratchet up a notch and set my teeth on edge.

'I'm gonna get this bitch open and you're not gonna say jack shit to your mother,' he says, and then looks at me. 'Or we're both dead.' I moan. Keith fumbles around on his disorganized, paint-and-beer-stained tool bench. He knocks through tape measures and pencils and hammers until he finds a crowbar.

'Don't you have a *key*?' I ask.

'It's safe, somewhere else,' he says. 'I'm not riskin' it. Your mother would sniff us out.'

I realize how drunk he is. Keith gets impatient and bull-headed when's he's hammered; likes the feel of heavy tools and taking direct, sloppy action.

First he pitches Gorilla Monsoon away from him, the leash skittering across the floor and the puppy yelping in protest. 'Stupid dog,' Keith mutters. 'What the hell's he doing out of the spare room?' Then he goes about tapping at the lid, trying to find a hold for the hooked end of the bar.

'Eddy!' he bellows. 'Make sure your hands are away from the lid!' Then, without listening for a response, he starts cranking on the crowbar, trying to snap the clasp. It's a slapdash performance, a stumbling act of bending, crouching and cursing. He's making a ridiculous racket, too – something he fails to notice in his hammered state. Eventually he throws the crowbar across the room, defeated.

'Fuck it,' he says, walking back to his workbench and picking up his electric drill. He's got the thing plugged in and whirling in a few more minutes, lying on his side against the back of the trunk, shakily fitting the end of the drill bit into the various screws. It's easier to listen to the drill than to have to bear Eddy's muffled wails. Gold screws begin to fall from the back of the chest, landing around Keith's gut in a small pile. Finally, after that achingly slow process, he's removed everything attaching the rear side of the lid to the trunk. Then he stands and retrieves the crowbar, going back to work. He's able to wedge the bar right in, and after a few solid thrusts the locking mechanism snaps apart in a satisfying *crunch*. And there's Eddy, his pale skin and flabby arms, the Bic pen makeup completely smeared and running with his tears. The skull mask and jar of spiders have been kicked down to his feet.

'It's okay,' I say, kneeling beside the box, offering him my hand. 'It's gonna be –'

Eddy screams and sits up, eyes rolling around in his head, looking feral. And suddenly he's up, out of the box, still screaming, and running for the stairs.

By the time I'm at the base of the steps, he's whipped open the door to the basement and run screaming into the kitchen. *Oh, shit*, I'm thinking, just as Gorilla sprints between my legs in a blur of curly black fur, up the stairs and hot on Eddy's tail. Then they're gone, the boy and his dog, off toward the back door.

I turn to look back at Keith. He shrugs his shoulders, smiles.

'Ring the bell,' he says, and finishes his beer.

A few hours later. It's about two in the morning, and Mom and Keith have been going at it for half an hour. Eddy's been sent to bed and I've tried to do some cleaning, but mostly just to eavesdrop on their argument. I keep twisting the dishcloth in my hands, forearms dunked into the sink and fingers already rubbery. Eddy pissed his Speedo in the backyard and Gorilla went apeshit.

'Oh my god, your fucking privacy. You've got all day to have your privacy, sitting on your *ass*. Who the hell do you think you are?'

'Suck my cock.'

'*I can't take it anymore!*' Mom screams, and I cringe, ripping into the dishcloth. I want this to be over, want the heat between Keith and Mom to finally fizzle, break, and Mom to emerge victorious, kicking Keith's ass to the curb in the process.

'Will you just listen to me for a second?' Keith howls.

'No!' Mom says, crying now, hysterical.

'Why?'

'Because I hate you! I fucking hate you! You're a terrible man.'

'Right, I'm so fucking terrible, looking after, cleaning up after these little shits. *Well, fuck you, too!*'

I stand perfectly still. Neither of them says a word, but Mom keeps crying. And then I hear the floorboards groaning over my head: Eddy's heavy stomp down the hallway from his bedroom. And I hear a loud thud as he drops to the ground.

'*Listen* to me. You never *listen* to what I'm saying,' Keith says.

Mom keeps crying. Then, suddenly, 'Do *not* touch me!'

'I'm not doing anyth–'

'Stop touching me oh god don't touch me.'

In the world of professional wrestling, if a wrestler accidentally lands a blow or delivers a move with full force behind it, and subsequently injures his or her opponent, then this is called a *potato*. I guess you could say that I potatoed Eddy. Sealing him inside the chest was too much of a high-spot move; I should have known better. But then again, it was all in the spirit of the game – in other words, it was an accident. A typical wrestling match follows a vague script, ending with an agreed-upon outcome. And thus a typical wrestling match is called a *work* because everyone involved is working toward the same resolution. Eddy and I were *working* today – I never meant to seal him up, make him piss his pants or drive him crazy. I'm confident that I'll be able to convince Eddy that we were only *working*, that it was all *supposed* to be fake. But the situation in the living room has surpassed the level of a work and entered into *shoot* territory: a scenario in which heat or animosity between two opponents is legitimate, unscripted. Real.

'You've got no right to touch me!'

'Oh my *GOD!*'

I lift my hands out of the sink, dry them with the towel and walk as quietly as possible to the living room entryway. From where I stand, peering around the corner, I see Mom and Keith standing beside the coffee table, Keith's meaty hands wrapped around Mom's wrists. She's staring up at him with her teeth clenched, her face red and mangled in anger. Keith stares back, jaw slack, eyes glassy with booze. Eddy sits cross-legged at the top of the stairs, shaking his head from side to side, making his blond mushroom cut flash clean and white in the amber glow of the hall light. He's shaking and nodding robotically, his palms clamped over his ears, his fingernails digging into the skin of his scalp. Whenever he gets like this, you've got to hold his head in your hands to make him stop; you've got to hold your hands over his and say *please, please,* in a near whisper – you can't be impatient because otherwise Eddy might be rocking for hours.

'Just *go!*'

'Where the fuck am I going to go?'

'Find somewhere, anywhere, just get out.'

'Would you just *listen* to yourself for once?'

I've got my fingers wrapped around the door jamb. Anything could happen, and each low blow or ripping yank they trade keeps me riveted in place. I wipe the tears from my eyes. I don't want to watch anymore, but I can't resist an ending, even a dark one, that's so close. There's no wrestling match that can forgive this. No bout to make sense of it. All the cartoon heroes flicker out, light to dark, the TV gone black.

They're in each other's faces, screaming nonsense, when Keith bangs his knees against the coffee table. In a split second he's off balance, and then falling, hands still wrapped around Mom's wrists. She follows, tripping against the sharp edge of the table, hands grasping at Keith's crotch. And they go down, Keith dragging Mom to the floor. Cups and plates and cans fly in the air as they hit the surface of the coffee table. The table – cheap, shoddy wood – snaps down the middle. It's an incredible noise, Keith splitting through the wood and Mom following after, sharp splinters and four table legs spiralling away across the room. Keith lies still, eyes fluttering, grip released on Mom's wrists, as she tries to scramble to her feet. From the doorway I can see a spot of blood forming on Keith's forehead, and from the way he lies there, groaning, I figure he's gotta be at least partway hurt. Mom's so drunk she can't find a handhold, can't get to her feet, so she lies there panting atop his hulking belly.

Please be over, I think. *Please be finished. Let this be done.* But there's no logical end to this, no one to raise a victor's hand in the air.

But then there's Eddy, out of the corner of my eye, on all fours on the carpet. He must have crawled down the stairs while they were grappling each other. Mom looks up with tears in her eyes, spotting him, her face tormented and ugly. 'Honey,' she's trying to say, but Eddy drops to one elbow, his legs splayed out behind him, and raises his right hand in the air.

No, I think ...

Eddy slaps his hand down on the floor. 'ONE!' he screams, then raises it again.

And I close my eyes. I close my eyes and imagine Mom blowing the hair off her face and starting to laugh. She laughs so hard that she rouses Keith from his groaning daze, and he screws around his head to stare at what's so funny, and seeing Eddy there on the floor counting them out, well, it sends Keith into hysterics, too. And I laugh with them from the doorway, and when Eddy's finally finished pounding the floor he looks around, confused, but then that grin ripples over his lips as he sees real smiles and real laughs around him, and he leaps up and sprints over to Mom and raises her wrist in victory, points at her with his other hand, and this just kills everyone, and the joke gets bigger and fuller and richer because this was a work after all – that after the bloody performance we all find ourselves in the locker room slapping backs and swigging beers, giving respect and love for the broken bones and pulled muscles, for everything sacrificed and offered up in the middle of the ring, all the fake animosity and hatred for a common cause. And Mom kisses Keith, still on top of him, and they stand and Keith lifts up Eddy into his arms for the first time and swings him around the room while a big rock song plays for our victory.

And I keep my eyes shut, seeing it all work itself into happiness. Eddy goes to school in the fall and gets help from the counsellors and gets changed to a different school where he gets the kind of classes and therapy he needs, the kind of meds his fucked-up brain is thirsting for, and he grows up to be one of those kids who're popular even though they're challenged and the high school jocks defend him and give him rides and the girls kiss his cheeks in the halls and the teachers all love him because Eddy's heart is fucking pure and simple, and one day he goes to work for a local wrestling show maybe selling popcorn and sweeping up the aisles (even if it's just some borrowed gymnasium), but he's there every night, exactly where he wants to be, watching from the stands as the indie-show wrestlers tell their minor-league stories and mirror the big guys into the next century. And I visit Eddy in his own place every weekend, and we grab McDonald's fries and nuggets together and watch old WWF reruns on his crappy TV and laugh about how we were a tag team once, how we had so many cruel opponents and never had a chance at a title but we were the people's favourites, the underdogs everyone screamed for in the dark matches of our youth, and Eddy never worked for Tim Hortons until his forties mopping floors, living without assistance, and he never had his accident on the slick stairs and he never ended up where he did, worse than ever, and I never became this crater that lies awake thinking of him, I'm back there in the living room watching him pound the carpet, I'm back there watching him in his pyjamas before the show went off the air and the bad guys won.

JOURNEY TO THE CENTRE
OF SOMETHING

I

McConaughey loved the Painted Desert for its emptiness, its flat inhospitality. He loved it for its tiny unthinking lizard brain, buried miles beneath the buttes, dreaming its quiet dreams like some sleeping, insane god. How the chalky browns and whites could explode into lavenders and coppers, glorious pinks and yellows, spilling into canyons and valleys that would never feel the tread of a boot. The heavenly shadows of mesas, the secret, life-saving nectar of cacti. As a kid he loved stories of criminals tied to anthills, of horses keeled over from thirst, of terrible yawning jaws of human and mammal and monster skulls half-buried in the shifting sands. It was the tarry smell of it, the whipping gales, the grit of rock in his mouth; how suddenly the wind could rise to freeze his blood as the sun dropped low and gory, ripping out his guts with its beauty. How easily a rattler could nip his heel and stop his heart. To boil it down: it didn't care about him. The buzzards hanging perfect and still in the painful blue sky, waiting to eat and digest and shit him down onto lonely, passing traffic. This was a place for rocks, not people. It hated his paper skin. It hated his gentleness.

Yet here he was, Matthew McConaughey, squinting over the dash of his beloved van behind tortoiseshell shades as the light seared through the glass and stuck his naked, sweaty flesh to the leather seat. McConaughey drove naked in the desert, always had – he felt entirely alone, and so why not feel the heat on every inch of his body, the raw lash of the passing wind against his temple and cheek and pubic hair as he cranked down the windows and cooked. On this summer day in the twenty-eighth year of his life, McConaughey headed south, ostensibly lost, though he knew if he unfolded the wrinkled state map at his feet he would find his way home. Soon the Petrified Forest Road would recede to a mote on the horizon, and he'd turn onto Highway 180, having then the choice of right or left, east or west – of more flat, open road or a town, a beer, a bed – the romance of solitude and small places, the blurring of identity. Before nightfall, he'd be close to Silver Creek. Tomorrow he'd reach Mexico, if he gunned it, and so he did, fine to be lost and alone in the *big empty*, curling his toes over the sooty gas pedal and kicking the map away.

The van, like all his vehicles and animals, had a name: *Cosmo*. It was his personal chariot through good times and dangerous places – hell, the whole cosmos, if his head was screwed on right. It was his key to adventure, immaturity, boyish exploration, and he loved its white base coat and slick blue stripe, its dependable, beat-up attitude (not the kind of thing you'd expect from the star of *A Time to Kill*, let alone *Amistad*). He liked to think he could count on Cosmo's curving, faux-wood walls, the soft bed for napping behind him, the captain's chair to his back draped with stained flags (of the Lone Star State and the U.S.A., over-lapped), the bead curtain separating forward from rear decks, the blue carpet beneath his sandy toes and the glittering disco ball rocking on its ceiling screws. Today, he kept the television quiet, but blared his Amboy Dukes CD – Ted Nugent's motorcycle guitars on 'Journey to the Center of the Mind' revving from six speakers, subwoofers, flowing up through his butt to hammer its way through his trembling hands.

Native American carvings and tokens – Navajo, Ojibwa, Aztec – dangled from short lengths of dental floss attached to the roof. A small brown Smoking Indian, just for the kitsch, rotated endlessly from his rear-view mirror. They were his talismans, wards against losing his path, against the demons that crowded lost roads and wayward travellers. Little pieces of the land held aloft to reassure the sleeping lizard god beneath his wheels that he came in peace, that he had prepared his offering. The ground begged for water, and in a place of such heat, human moisture was the most holy, precious gift. Clutching his penis one-handed, he aimed his stream of urine into a red plastic funnel attached to a tube leading beneath the van, sprinkling his piss along the asphalt in tiny droplets.

'You're welcome,' he said breathily to the road, to no one, swigging from his bottle of mineral water and shaking his dick dry.

Beside the Smoking Indian, attached to his rear-view mirror by plastic clip, hung his reliable tape recorder, recently loaded with two double-A batteries and an unused cassette. He turned down the Dukes and made another entry in his road diary.

'Time: 3:04 p.m. Making for the 180. And then, well, the sky being the limit, we don't know ... This *is* a voyage, all right ... And something ... *something* is *definitely* going to happen. But don't get impatient, now. Let that *something* come to you.'

He pressed STOP. Maybe that last entry was unnecessary. Just a sigh to fill the silence. So far he'd done no profound thinking, but he knew if he kept driving the thoughts would come. The muses would start speaking to him, come whispering in under the radio and dash as he let the blankness purge all mind-fucking trauma. Muses, spirits, whatever – he needed the blankness to clean out his brain, give him the cherished white page upon which he'd record some mental masterpiece, some dexterous feat of thinking to save him from his city-based, head-clutter funk. He'd done some of his best acting alone, just Matthew vs. the recorder, working out his shit, practising his accents and tricks at delivery. Indeed, he'd recorded his greatest insight on the same device: a bit of wisdom that came to him last year on a nighttime highway in northern Texas, where he realized that true acting involved the *head*, not the *heart*. Only the head could get sucked in. A mature heart would stay put, no matter what sacrifices were made, so it made no difference how deeply you delved into a persona or how methody you got pursuing a role. If you knew this, you could allow yourself to get reckless, to lose for longer periods whatever you thought was some essential *you*. He had no fear, now, about going the extra mile, or going to those dark places certain roles required. Spielberg taught him some of that. So did Joel Schumacher, and the Buddha, and his father, and Val Kilmer, but it was mostly a Matthew original, thought up while doing his roadwork, confessing for his recorder.

Here's a real confession, he thought. He hit REC.

'I don't want the day to end. I'm happy to be here.'

He let the wheels spin on the tape, recording dead air, the distant sounds of the highway and the weird whispers in the rushing wind. *Happy to be here*, he thought. *Why?* Because every city, cellphone and email meant a miniature catastrophe. Every convenience store, grocery store, pharmacy, doctor's office in every town across the country: a tabloid shot of him and Sandra, neither of them smiling, at some early-evening L.A. premiere. He couldn't remember the day or occasion, what the goddamned weather'd been like (though it was always sunny, he recalled: that one constant hurt). What could he do now but run, burrow, hide? He was tired, felt sick to death of heartache. The desert meant total erasure; it meant a fade-out to a new scene.

'Something's got to happen,' he whispered, though not entirely sure how that something would turn out. There were two irksome worms troubling his conscience: one romance-related, the other a matter of career. He'd broken out of his Dave Wooderson, *Dazed and Confused* obscurity with the John Grisham project *A Time to Kill*, feeling that the time was finally right, that his moon had lined up with some ascendant star. The re-release of *The Return of the Texas Chainsaw Massacre* merely amused him, now that he was famous; let all the mainstream filmgoers puzzle over his hammed-up role in the straight-to-video, schlocky gore flick. It amused him in the same way Cosmo could put people off, remind them he was wise to the head game of Hollywood, that he didn't exactly *want* to fit in. And then he'd scored his next big shot, one of the surefire films of the decade: *Amistad*, historical tear-jerker, December release, with Hopkins overacting as John Quincy Adams and Spielberg almost frighteningly confident at the helm. It was like winning the lottery. How could he fuck up a film with such star power, about something as unanimously cherished as abolition? Got to play another smart-sounding lawyer, too: James Baldwin, southern gentleman and estate attorney, much like in his lucky break as the southern-born defence attorney Jake

Brigance in *A Time*. All the right conditions, and he thought he'd kicked it straight through the posts: Oscars and Golden Globes, whispers of promise in the flashbulb air. Especially after his earlier summer exposure in the high-grossing *Contact*, which had him billed second to Jodie Foster and generally commended for his laid-back, soft-toned approach to playing a holy man. But what was the miserable, memorized consensus? Ebert put it plainly: he was 'not much moved' by his performance. *TV Guide* thought his accent 'unidentifiable,' his mannerisms a 'liability,' said he was still too much the 'dude from Texas.' The *San Francisco Chronicle* called his passionate exclamations 'broad gesturing,' his overall portrayal 'close to embarrassing.' There were some good reviews, sure, and thank the sleeping gods, but the split decision was pummelling, tripping him up with a hollow sort of fatigue: a hurt that kept on like a gnawing, persistent hangover, reminding him that lightning, as the saying went, only strikes once.

Then it all collapsed with Sandra: a pain that compounded the disappointments of those divided reviews. Everyone could see the honest gut-check chemistry between them. They 'sizzled' onscreen, wrote the journalists; the Deep South sexuality was like thick grease between them, coating them, slick and irresistible. They seemed powerless, innocent of design, as all the mags and TV spots started the rumours before they were even true: that Sandra and Matthew were an on-set couple, an affair in the making. He saw her as a geeky girl who couldn't care less about how she was perceived. He dug her, dug the five years she had on him, dug the way her laugh turned to a honk, dug her heavy-lidded gaze. They could play together; they could high-five, wrestle, burp. He knew she dug him back, but maybe it was all the pressure, the articles and the gossip sheets and the surreptitious snapshots, all that public certainty, that sealed the deal. Maybe. Maybe, in some other, kinder universe, it would have been better to meet away from the camera's imperious eye, to find their own pace, let things fall more naturally. In any case, it happened: they touched in trailers, they made love, they were out in public, and that was that. She'd been a rock throughout that whole crazy year, the New York and L.A. premieres of *Contact* and *Amistad*, the hoping and praying, the long periods of weariness and moping after the mixed reviews. She'd been the first ear for his fears, a *golden* ear, willing and giving and so patient it made him cry, coaxing thin rivers of tears from his eyes while he toked from his three-foot bong on Cosmo's rear bumper.

Her eyes were wet with crying, too, on the night it finally fizzled – fat, salty tears that he would kiss away, and that one-in-a-million wisdom he'd never find again. He was sweating buckets, not from the night (which was breezy and cool) but from the dread of what was coming. They pressed their foreheads together, fogging up the windows with their heat, saying they loved each other but it *just wasn't right* – that it wasn't being *in* love. And it was exactly what he'd been yearning to say, knowing through the heavy spring rains of '98 that it was doomed, drawing them toward this quiet confrontation. The urge to see her had shrivelled during their extended time apart, they were talking less and less, and soon he'd begun to believe that their love wouldn't have happened if not for the media's meddling, the public's demand for the beautiful picture of their pairing, which seemed so right. He felt a relief in voicing it, and they spoke in soothing tones, crying a little over what could have been and for the time they'd had, which he knew would stay like a damp, bittersweet chill in his bones. They kissed, slow and on the lips, the salt of her sweat beading there against his tongue. And then she slid the door open and left the van, gave a last small squeeze to his hand, called him *Matty*. He slept in Cosmo's stale sheets until just before dawn, waking to a headache, to a clutching paranoia and regret: that even if there was no more thrill, no real connective tissue, no *reason*, there was still the past, and the fanatical force propelling him to hold her and envision some impossible golden future together, denying and delaying all the fine-cutting loneliness that was waiting high above, like a hovering buzzard, falling feather-like to rest and claw at his stomach.

But that was all gone. That sun had set, and here he was. Alone. Healing.

'Happy to be here,' he said again, before stopping the tape.

He reached an intersection. A line of automobiles had stretched behind him; he realized he'd been doing ten or twenty under the limit. Dwelling on all that baggage. Journeying to the centre of something.

Sporadic cars and trucks thundered by on the 180, most heading northwest. McConaughey waited for an opening and merged, throwing Cosmo onto the road and following the main flow of traffic, instantly disappointed that he'd taken the more popular route. He wasn't *about* the popular route; he wasn't *about* going slow. He was all about trailblazing, speeding along the road less travelled. He'd turn off on the first desolate stretch that presented itself, he decided, as long as it meant plowing south, toward the heat and naked expanse that sat between him and the vigilant border: a place that would reward his loneliness, and in its absence both absorb and forgive. He drained the last drops of his water and threw the plastic bottle over his shoulder, where it came to rest amid the camp and detritus of his life.

11

Boy, you done it now, McConaughey thought. *Got yourself good and lost.* He stuck his neck out the window and sent a long Texan *whoop!* toward the dry horizon.

He couldn't explain the sense of elation he'd been feeling since he yanked the wheel left, splitting to the south and roaring down a nameless road. The Dukes were cooking and jamming up some toe-tapping, extended psychedelia, Nugent labouring a pentatonic riff into ecstasy. McConaughey slammed Cosmo's roof with his palm, another squeal of pleasure leaving his lips as the riff collapsed back into a bass-heavy, pickup rhythm. This was what he'd been waiting for: no destination in sight, no crowding presence, no phone, no email, no connection to anything but the groove of the music and the awful skyline.

There was a passage he'd read somewhere, a long time ago, that came rushing back to mind. Something about the difference between a *pilgrim* and a *tourist.* Could have been from way back in high school, maybe, or while researching a part (or was it an Aerosmith lyric?). Basically, it said that a tourist's travels were mostly physical in nature, that the roving tourist was seeing, experiencing, absorbing, but always as an outsider with home in mind. The itinerary was set in advance, and the journey gained momentum as a return, rather than a departure. McConaughey was terrified of being the tourist, fanny-packed and Tilley-hatted, visiting the brochure attractions and never once stepping outside the comfortable routes predetermined by tradition or by some expensive agency. No, when he travelled he was pure pilgrim, embarking upon a quest more spiritual than fleshy, where each step along the road was just as important as the last and no firm destination materialized to kill a sense of spontaneity. The road was metaphorical, he thought – a process of becoming rather than visiting.

He had a breakthrough. He thumbed his recorder.

'Okay. Here we go. The pilgrim travels along a spiritual path; to him the journey requires that he *become* a different dude by the end. On the other hand, the tourist walks a purely physical road, picking up bits and pieces of other cultures and peoples ... but keeping his mind set on home, on a version of himself that won't change ... And this ... this is *exactly* like acting. An actor plays all these parts, but keeps his heart safe and sound, just like a tourist remembering his home. Being on a pilgrimage is dangerous, but acting ... acting is easy ... acting's about the *head* ... and real change requires ... the *heart*.'

Hitting STOP, he felt a clarity of mind he hadn't had for months. It was rare that a trip like this would pan out exactly as he envisioned it. He imagined the stack of tapes he'd fill with philosophy before the end. He tapped his fingers at ten and two, jiggling his thighs in time with the music, letting his thoughts levitate into orbit as miles began to thread out behind him and the rocky sediment to his left began turning to a chalky, bone-like white, swirling higher now in elevation like an inverted crater, and along the empty field were scattered bleak and purposeless stones, ragged hardness, this tanned and prostrate body –

What?

Matthew whipped his head to the left and brought his foot down hard on the brakes. His tires squealed to a dusty stop on the right shoulder. *No way.* He looked again, and there it was, his eyes refusing to play tricks. *Aw, shit*, he thought, fumbling for his sunglasses. There, about thirty feet from the road: a body, *some*body, a human being, lying on his chest in the dirt, a tanned, bare ass mooning him, the buzzards, the empty sky.

'No way, no *way*,' he said aloud, more excited than scared. He was about to immediately rush onto the road to help the poor bastard, but then remembered his nudity. He pulled on a pair of board shorts crumpled under a pile of occult books and magazines. Wiping the sweat from his eyes and raking a few errant locks from his forehead, he slipped into a pair of flip-flops and unlatched Cosmo's back door, the sunlight making him dizzy.

He still wasn't convinced, even though he'd gotten a solid look from behind the wheel. You just didn't find a naked body out in the middle of nowhere, thirty feet from a nameless desert road. Or … or *did* you? Still, it was probably a rock, or an animal, a trick of that intense and ancient star beating down from the radioactive sky. Nugent and the Dukes chugged along a minor-chord progression while Matthew flip-flopped across the road, slowing his pace as he approached the heap in the sand.

He dropped to a crouch, hands clasped in the shape of a prayer over his lips. Yep, no mistaking it from this close. It was a body. Naked. And by the looks of it, recently deposited, as there were no signs of decomposition, dehydration or the telltale rips of scavengers. *What in the name of high holy fuck*, he thought, staring at the man's muscular back, his well-toned calves, his sun-kissed skin, as a drift of dust sprayed over the form.

He squinted north, feeling a hot point of heat fingering the back of his skull. No signs of life, simply the shimmer of the horizon. It was probably best to go back to the van and race toward the 180, hail down any passing car and get somebody to use a phone. Call in the authorities and let himself off the hook. But then again, he didn't want the road trip to end. His escape would be over. This day, this day of happiness and freedom, would end, and he couldn't stomach a break in his aimless itinerary.

Hell, he thought. A vague sense of fear quickly shifted into exhilaration.

He stood over the body, hands at his sides, breathing through his mouth. Then he bent his knees and pulled the guy over by the shoulder, grimacing, struggling against the dead weight, surprised by his willingness and knowing that somehow this was terribly wrong – that there was an odd feeling in his stomach, some strange timbre in the air, and that he should really just be moving on. And every hair on his body reached toward the sky; and all at once he was cold, deathly cold, leaping back from the body, hands flailing as a low gurgle came bubbling up his throat, the voice in his head screaming from some unaccountable canyon that the body wasn't just a body: the body was *him*.

As in: Matthew McConaughey. A perfect clone.

Then he was sick, neat and heaving in the dirt, the scrambled eggs and toast he'd had for breakfast and all the lukewarm water he'd sipped on the road. He spat bile, perching on all fours, staring east and straining to breathe. He couldn't think. He waited a minute, two, three, four, let his spinning head clear, let those twisting stomach knots unravel.

I am hallucinating, he thought. As he caught his breath, he reviewed the most likely of explanations. Sunstroke. Maybe one of the granola bars or eggs he'd eaten had gone fusty. Food poisoning. Something in the water. Radiation in the air. An acid flashback from '96. He coughed a few more times, blowing his nose in his hands. *Get ready*, he thought. And then he looked again, expecting normalcy to return.

But there was no mistaking a perfect reflection. It was *him*, plain and simple. He tipped back onto his ass, body trembling, staring at some version of himself, face ground into the dirt. *I've lost my shit*, he repeated to himself. *Or – or – this is just some dude who really, really looks like me. Like it's my long-lost brother or something. Has to be.*

There were stranger things in the world, after all. The wind picked up force, sending grains of rock and dust into his mouth and eyes, as if the desert were agreeing with the thought: that this had all the markings of a vision quest or major spiritual battle in the works. He didn't want to think just yet of ghosts or spirits (or demons, or devils, met along some forbidding crossroads), freezing his blood and turning him to mush. It was time to use his head, be rational and get the job done, like all his old acting heroes, the John Waynes and Humphrey Bogarts, the Marlon Brandos and James Deans. He had, for a small but surreally out-of-body moment, the queer impression that he was on a set – that lights and boom mics and cameras were trained on his reaction, and that sooner or later the director would yell *cut!* and this man, this other Matthew, would stand, peel off a mask and walk back to wardrobe. *Oh yeah*, he'd realize, rising to his feet. *I forgot I was making that cameo on* The X-Files.

It was just a moment. He was back to his radiant outdoor reality, collecting himself, trying not to be afraid, banking reasonably on the assumption that this was just a massive coincidence, that the guy was just a fantastic look-alike. Not quite as handsome, on closer inspection. Just a stupendous sort of luck to find such a convincing body double, he thought. Cosmic alignments, et cetera. And what a goddamned *story*! He'd be on *Entertainment Tonight* by tomorrow, smiling across from Bob Goen and Mary Hart, relating how he found a missing person and helped solve a mystery.

There were things to do, though, before he'd be on TV. To get full credit, he couldn't let anyone else find the body; he should transport it to a hospital himself. Besides, that way no one but the doctors would get a look at his twin's genitals, caked in coppery soil. He hadn't even checked the man's pulse. He leaned over the body and pressed his fingers against its neck, searching for a beat. Nothing. *So it's done*, he thought. Time to get it out of the dirt before the elements took it.

He sucked in a deep breath. Then he thrust his hands under the corpse's armpits and began dragging the body toward the van, trying to elevate the torso as much as possible so that only the heels and calves were touching the ground. He puffed and clenched his teeth but it wasn't difficult; he was fit, an iron man, used to running and swimming and struggling with weights. There was the threat of being spotted, of passing traffic spoiling his chance to be the sole transporter, but of course the nameless road was still vacant by the time he reached the vehicle. It (he?) was cumbersome, and scraped up from the drag, but in a few flexing seconds he had the body into the van and stretched prone on the mattress. Matthew pushed through the beads and seated himself behind the wheel, the Dukes still wailing away.

He cranked Cosmo into DRIVE, looking over his right shoulder before swerving onto the road. He had to part the curtain to get a glimpse of his double: lying feet-first toward the rear of the van, arms splayed, one leg slightly bent, penis curled demurely and sand caked beneath finger- and toenails. The body's face was his face, only sleeping: something he'd seen before in a few photographs, or whenever he watched himself close his eyes onscreen. He let the beads fall and turned back to the dash, applying pressure to the pedal.

About ten seconds later he was mashing REC.

'Okay ... bizarre thing happened to me ... found me ... found me a *body* on the side of the road ... just lying there, naked ... but turns out ... it's ... *he's* like my identical twin, or like some clone or something ... craziest ... Continuing to head south ... closest town is Silver Creek, I think ... should be there soon.

'Ha!' he cackled, fingers wrapped tight around the wheel. He felt electric, crackling. He wondered how much time had passed: ten minutes? twenty? He couldn't remember when he'd pulled over. It was like he was blurring along some speed tunnel, unable to tell what the appropriate response should be, the colour of experience smearing into his field of vision. It was funny, it was actually *funny* (which he'd love to tell Sandra, if talking wasn't something that still might open a wound).

And he wasn't another mile, the landscape just as vacant, remorseless as stone, a white and shell-like spiral of rock approaching on his left, when he saw another one. This time there was no comic double take or neck-wrenching screech. He saw it well in advance, his jaw falling slack, his hands resuming their tremble, the squashed muscle in his throat releasing a trebly *ohhh*. And without really knowing what he was doing, he crossed to the left side of the road and parked. Then he left the van and shuffled over the windy sand, kicking through scrub over the thirty feet off the asphalt to where the naked body lay crumpled almost exactly like the one he'd just picked up.

He nudged it with a single flip-flopped toe, and a silvery filament of sanity quivered in his imagination, so fine that a strong gust of wind seemed liable to snap it. He shook his head. It was another Matthew, probably dead, naked, with his cheek pressed against the ground, one peaceful, closed lid exposed to the sun.

He crossed his arms and rolled back on his heels. Well, this was certainly something. Cinematic, even. He was the protagonist in some back-roads drama, something existential, inevitably called 'quirky' and 'fun' and 'darkly comic' by the reviewers. Was his acting adequate? Was he conveying the appropriate levels of disbelief, desperation, horror? Or would his dramatic flailing be seen as too *dude*-ish? Would Ebert be 'much moved' by his performance?

He felt calmer than he thought he ought to be. It was the acting experience, he knew: the method-acting disassociation, the ability to role-play, to project. He picked up and dragged his double across the asphalt, clutching it around the chest from behind. Once inside the van, he sat it down, limbs floppy, next to the first corpse, which he managed to roll over onto its side while he leaned the second against its back, Siamese bedfellows. He climbed back into the captain's chair with a new, frigid smile stamped on his sweat-drenched face.

After a good swig of water and a stiff slap to the cheeks, he drove on, the terrain unfolding like a gaudy postcard. The sky was a vision of some pagan heaven, he felt, its worship causing a dissociative kind of vertigo: a feeling that deepened, now, to nausea-rekindling degrees, with the spotting of another body. He pulled the van over. And the feeling of sitting there, about to leap from his vehicle and collect another duplicate, somehow held the foreshadowing of routine. There was work to be done, dreadful work, but he had to act, had to attend to each mess of limbs with equal care and comportment, hefting the new body off the soil and rock, lugging it into the van and lying it down gingerly with its brothers. 'Now there are three,' Matthew said, after it was safely in and with its duplicates. He sucked air, nearly hyperventilating, feeling like some lost terrestrial janitor skipping along the highway of his splintered psyche, tidying up its errant shards. Then breaking into emotion, feeling fatherly, motherly, in the same space of breath, staring down at his three sleeping children, whose faces he covered with one of Cosmo's thin white sheets (though he felt an energy stored and patient beneath the cotton, a lonesome desire from the clones, willing more and more siblings to sprout like pods from the earth – or had *he* fertilized it? Had his droplets of hot urine leeched into the soil to produce these cabbage-patch corpses?). The sun felt too hot, too real. What was real? Was the sand on his toes real? Were Academy Awards, or was regret, real? Were buzzards? Were the three sleeping Matthew McConaugheys in the rear of his van real things, flesh and blood, or were they something else? He thrust his arm through the bead curtain, feeling the hair and scalp of one of his copies. 'Something is going to happen,' he said aloud, though now he was certain: that his prophecy was correct, and that *something* was going to break his heart.

Still in PARK, he stared at the shell-like uprising from the ground, unable to force the van farther down the road. He'd sit and wait. Wait until things made sense again, until he could think properly, use the recorder. It would all make sense. But what if the brothers kept coming? What if they kept sprouting from the ground, one after another, as if to punish him? *What if I'm in hell*, he thought.

'I'll have to leave some behind,' he whispered. And with a sudden cough, he wept.

I I I

McConaughey wrenched Cosmo toward a trail marked by repeat tire tracks and a worn and beaten feeling. He abandoned the main road because a white puff of cloud had formed what looked like a curved arrowhead, seemingly gesturing to a spot on the horizon. (He was indeed following shapes in clouds; he figured he was past the point of measured responses.) The path ran to the east, around pathetic dunes and ridges. He urged Cosmo on delicately, with only the softest pressure on the gas. He wanted to be tender, as if too much commotion might rouse the three Matthews in the back.

Relief began to bubble and blossom as he followed the trail for another mile, tires dipping in and out of gouges, crunching over the broken earth. He whined in delight with each passing rock, whispering *oh thank you oh thank you* as the path yielded only more mounds of sand and blunt nature, inch by nerve-wracking inch. After the second mile, he began to shout in happiness, punching Cosmo's roof, as if he'd just been spared some deathly sentence. He was free, maybe; there were no more Matthews along the trail.

'I'm sorry,' he groaned, to his own surprise, reaching back to stroke the sprawling arm of one of the clones. There was still the blunt irrefutability of that mass of brotherly flesh. Where would he dump them? Who was going to help him in the middle of the desert? He felt crushed; he closed his eyes and loosened his grip on the steering wheel, letting the vehicle drift beneath him. For a senseless stretch of minutes, he drove blind, Cosmo veering off the path and into untrammelled dirt. When he opened his eyes, they stung with fresh tears, as a splinter of sunlight made the windshield gleam. He took his foot off the gas completely, let Cosmo rock to a halt. He turned off the engine, leaned his sweaty forehead against the sun-heated wheel and muttered a word, halfway between *can't* and *shit*, but posed as a question. The sky was large and stupid and didn't answer.

Time passed, white. He rose from the wheel and blinked, lids cracking. What kind of so-called *acting* experience could possibly have prepared him? He was a semi-decent actor, a surfer; he liked to throw footballs and smoke bowls and read the odd Michael Crichton novel. You couldn't prep for a role like this; method acting didn't even come close. One body was doable, maybe, but *three*? And *why* three? Why not two, or five, or fifteen? He thought hard. Numbers held power – of this he was, at least, pretty sure. He'd done some reading on numerology, the power of naming. Even had a book on the topic, lost now, with a purple hard-cover, that gave him a basic rundown of things he'd already known about himself: that the combination of letters in *Matthew* translated to the number nine, which meant he was good at following his feelings and emotions; that he was inspiring to others and was well-suited to co-operative work; that he was mostly tolerant of difference, with a broad-minded perspective and compassionate heart (if a bit idealistic); and that he was naturally suited to creative endeavours, to imagination and art. If he allowed himself to falter, he'd be pegged as aloof and insensitive, selfish and indifferent to other people's problems.

From what he could remember, three was the pinnacle number, lorded over by the benevolent planet Jupiter, rich in symbolism of compassion, love and harmony. It was the Holy Trinity, the Golden Triangle and the highest good; it meant sacrifice and giving, Fame and Beauty and Happiness and Wealth, order and stability. LOVE itself, according to the number chart, equalled three. That there were *three* clones, according to numerology, could only mean good – if not absolutely terrifying – things. Matthew chewed on his cheek, thinking. Maybe there were three bodies because each was a third of his whole, just as 3 x 3 = 9. Maybe each was an equal portion of his psyche, or soul, or animus, or whatever. That they needed to be put back together. Or that he'd broken himself into pieces.

He turned up the volume on the CD player and rolled down the windows, letting the noise tear into the desert's arrogant silence. He rubbed his face violently. 'The desert was made for pilgrims,' he muttered, or laughed: serious travellers stopping at holy shrines to make offerings, penance, prayers. Stages of a journey of transcendence. He was not a tourist in this waste, but a holy soul, a lover, stopping to reflect with each recovered token. Once again, he hit REC, his voice shaking.

'This is all acting; I'm playing a role. I have three versions of myself in the back of the van. And maybe I'm picking up pieces of all the roles I've nailed … I mean, really *nailed* … because I've left too much heart, too much, like, *love* out there in the atmosphere. Too much of Matthew floating around the cosmos. Gotta pick up the pieces, recollect the parts of my *soul*. Feel like a million tiny pieces coming back together!'

This came as a surprise, the thought that his mood or depression was really a scattering, a feeling of being disassembled. Like he'd lost a sense of who he was and wanted to be, the Matthew of his imagination, the Matthew he was *proud* to be. He'd given it away to people, to agents and extras and advertisers. The media writers, the mooching groupies. He'd given a large chunk to Sandra, maybe the largest of all. There were far too many versions of himself floating disembodied in the ether, and now the blankness had responded, conjuring out of the expanse those dreadful visions of what he'd lost. He was a fool to think he was just using his head. The heart was always involved. Intimately. He nearly leapt from his seat.

'Okay! I'm listening!' he bellowed into the air, following up with a jackal-like laugh. 'I hear you! I'm a*vai*lable!' The wind made no answer. He listened to its breathy incoherence, sticking his head out the window like a panting dog. An insect flew into his mouth and squirmed against his throat; he swallowed. He imagined the relief in releasing his fear, his sorrow, his clutching attachment to trifling icons, karma and voodoo and spiritualism. Falling back into his seat, he tore the Smoking Indian from his rear-view, snapping the dental floss and whipping the brown figurine out the window. He'd rip out and discard all his paltry wards and possessions, offer them up to the void.

After all the tokens had been thrown away and his body was squelching with sweat, the sky was less of a pure, earnest blue; it was deeper and richer to the east. The sun was lower, glowing orange, the thin surrounding clouds swelling with blood. In a few hours there would be one of those dazzling desert sunsets he loved: the atmosphere thrown into indigo and violet, great bars of colour not unlike a punishing, sky-stretching rainbow. The heat had already broken.

He would have to make a decision. Something had to be done with the brothers. He reviewed his options, drinking mineral water thirstily. There was the path of covert disposal. Burial. Cremation. That was easiest; he had enough gasoline. Or, the strangest yet most sensible: drive to town and civilization, hand them over to some hospital's forensic specialist, receive a 'scientific' explanation. This – the worldly, scientific solution – would require the most courage. Perhaps it was best. Hand off the bodies, get a sliver of a rationalization, rather than ditch the clones and leave all his pain and confusion in the unresponsive wild.

As he scanned the horizon, a small variation of light caught his eye. To the south and east was a distant, ground-level glimmer. He focused and looked. It was something metallic – the fierce rays of the sun's passing lustre rebounding off a metal surface. The sudden thought of somebody, *anybody,* giving him a hand was too sweet and relieving to refuse. He was stupid to have left the road, to have followed a cloudy arrowhead. He should have rushed back to the 180 the minute he found the first body. He cranked the keys and gunned Cosmo toward the reflective surface.

The drive overland was rough, full of worry that the pile of Matthews would awaken. As he closed in, he spotted a rectangular cement structure painted a creamy yellow that made it partially blend into the landscape. The glint Matthew had followed was a bead of light reflecting off a wilted stretch of chain-link fence dangling from its connecting supports. In front of the building was a concrete, cubic block that sank into the earth. Another hotly reflective metal, which looked like a ventilation shaft, ran alongside the concrete. Cosmo bumped and jostled over the torturous ground. The main structure was two storeys, shot with perfectly square, glassless windows. It was dark inside. Someone had spray-painted a neon-green swath across the side, its original message lost to the wind's persistence. The ground swelled up to meet the base, or camp, or facility; an abandoned workstation, probably commissioned by the government. Matthew was about to hit the brakes, discouraged, and head for the highway, when he saw someone sitting on the steps of the building's vacant doorway.

The figure – a hiker, a tourist, whoever – was a calm drop of moisture in so much dryness, a salve to his cracked lips and the hot finger of heat poking the back of his skull. Matthew pressed the pedal and nosed through a gap in the diminished fence, four-wheel drive accelerating and sputtering uphill. Near the building's looming shadow, he reached behind him and freed a wrinkled Longhorns T-shirt from beneath a stone-like ankle. He stopped the van, donned the shirt and stepped onto the soil, wearing a friendly smile, a *you're not gonna believe this, but* expression. Maybe so-and-so would recognize him; celebrity could always help.

He looked and then lost his breath. It was the worst kind of recognition: as if he'd been walking with his head down, his eyes full of sleep, counting his steps on some warm and even pavement of Los Angeles, and before he could be collected and witty and put together, she was there before him, nearly bumping into him. And of course ruining him, making him blush wildly, making him curse the luck that brought him like a homer toward her through the million chancing alleys of a metropolitan city. Making him feel that something spiritual had intervened to make them meet.

He stood a few feet before the cubic slab of concrete. Sandra rose from the stairs, brushing her jeans of what the wind carried. She wore a T-shirt he hadn't seen before: an evergreen. She smiled at him across the fifty feet of soil, and the wind blew her hair into a straight line, pointing west. She looked skinnier than he remembered; he focused on her collarbone, the knobs of her wrists and hips, blinking as grit and dust cut across his bare, sunburnt face. Then she was walking toward him, the same slow stride.

He knew then that he'd stumbled into fantasy – that at some point in the remote distance of the day, waking reality had slipped into dream. Why else were there bodies, identical triplets? Though he was lucid, the direction of the dream was out of his control. He would have to be brave and trust to feeling – *like being on drugs*, he thought – you had to let the flowers bloom unmolested, allow the petals to fall as they wished. He closed his eyes until he heard her scraping footsteps before him. *Wake up*, he told himself, but the world didn't change. He opened his eyes and took in the full sight of her, standing two feet away.

'Where are we?' he asked after a beat, throat cracking with dryness.

'What do you mean?' Her voice was the same, but newer, like listening to a recording of his own.

'Ah, hell,' he said, pointlessly, catching a tone between baffled and bemused.

She kept smiling. The desert still, hushed, gathered around to watch them.

'This is a bomb shelter,' she said, as if amused by the word *bomb*. 'Cold War relic, you know. Not many people know about it.'

'You were waiting for me?'

'Why not?' She took a step forward. Matthew wanted to back away but his legs felt too heavy. Sandra curled a pinky finger around his, hanging loose and slack at his side. The finger sent a warm shock up his arm, through his neck, making him salivate. She was inches away and smelled of green things, of juice and fruit, citrus and lime. Beneath this airy smell there was the scent of rot somewhere. Her cheekbones were so defined they seemed chiselled from the ridges that surrounded them. He saw the small scar on her jaw that makeup and cameras typically covered up – a line he'd traced and retraced with his thumb, kissed. Her neck was dirty, but her sweat made long and clear lines in the soot.

'How'd you get out here?' he asked.

She looked in his eyes. Her brow knit in sympathy. 'I got a ride.'

'Ahh,' he said. He found he was smiling, too, though nothing was well. His free hand went looking for hers, tugging at her fingers. 'Ahh.'

'Want to get started?' she asked.

Matthew looked down, staring at her dusty sandals, the zipper of her jeans and her shirt's hemline. He was nodding. She knew about the bodies, the brothers. It was like someone knowing your filthy secrets. She radiated knowing. He kept nodding, conscious of the work to do, but it didn't feel right to waste what light they had by handling such ridiculous cargo. He'd driven out to the middle of nothing and found her here, after months of separation. They should be sitting together in the doorway, watching the sun descend and ravish the sky. They should be driving to Silver Creek, where there were motels and soap and clean sheets. L.A. waited for them in the west, the coffee shops and bars and restaurants where her dark eyes glowed in the dancing light of a candle. There were conversations left unfinished, the last word on every subject left hanging and deferred. He thought he was healing but the wound hadn't even closed.

He wanted to remind her of a phone call he'd made a few weeks after their breakup. It was stagey, like an audition – he was channelling all the rainy regret of the season, drunk on Jim Beam and standing against the door to his bedroom, the phone cord wrapped around his fist. It was after two in the morning and he stood whispering into the receiver, reasoning with her, bargaining for a solution. Saying maybe they'd been too hasty. He didn't want to start promoting *The Newton Boys* without someone out there waiting for him, someone who knew his secret weaknesses, someone to counsel and support him. He was drunk and weak, weaker than he'd ever felt, but she kept saying the same thing, like a chant: *No, Matty*, unwavering, despite his plea bargains, his careful arguments, his gambits and his begging. And when it was done, when there was nothing left to say and resentment rose against her tireless denials, her strength, he threw down the receiver and sunk into bed, exhausted and sick of himself. He wanted to remind her of that last conversation – how hard it was on him. He wanted to tell her that she'd never given him a second chance; that maybe if he'd gotten the reviews he deserved for *Amistad*, say, she would have acted differently. That maybe it was all about careers, in the end – their stupid, absurd careers sabotaging something so alive between them. He wanted to call her a bitch, an idiot for letting him go, cruel for blowing him off when he needed her most.

'I miss you so much,' he found himself saying, staring at the patch of earth between her feet. He waited for her to answer, clutching her hands harder than he meant. The light was changing. Then he heard her say, 'I know,' and she slid her hands up past his wrists and over the back of his arms, letting him take her into an embrace, and upon feeling the heat of her body he found himself sobbing, loud and hard against the citrusy, rotten smell of her new T-shirt, smelling her hair and her sweat, arms pawing and clutching at the fabric around her back. He watched, felt himself doing this, surprised at the show. His snot and spit pooled on her shoulder. He held her as hard as he could, whispering, 'Wake up, wake up,' still convinced that this was all made of dreams and dust.

'Please?' he asked, choking on the *l*. He knew he shouldn't have asked, knew it was useless. He pulled back.

Sandra shook her head, but not without kindness. 'We should finish,' she said firmly, withdrawing, gesturing toward Cosmo with her eyes.

Matthew wiped his nose, sniffing. 'Ah, hell,' he said again. The light was rich and fiery in her eyes. 'So what are we doing?' he asked.

'There's a place for them underground,' she said, pushing her hair over her ears, which stood out gawky and endearing from the sides of her head. 'Through here.' She pointed at the rise of concrete beside the metal ventilation shaft. There was a steel door set into the pasty yellow material. Matthew walked to the door and placed his fingers against the cool of the latch. It swung out with a stiff yank, whining on ancient, rusted hinges. Beyond were five feet of white cement floor, then a flight of stairs sinking down into absolute black, ageless and still.

Sandra stepped into the foyer of the shelter and picked up a flashlight from the floor, setting the beam on the top step, illuminating the short flight of stairs, the limits of a room beyond. Then she turned back to Matthew, smiling again: that same sad, resolved smile.

We'll do it together, he thought. *We'll carry the trio down the stairs, one at a time, and leave them there.* It was senseless, meaningless, but it was a plan. Down beneath the soil, where his three sleeping triplets could hear the whispers of the earth, the insane god beneath their feet. Where they would rot unmolested. It was what she wanted, at any rate, and he'd always gone along with her notions.

So they began. Matthew held each twin around the chest while Sandra gripped its ankles. He went down backwards, shuffling on the stairs and disturbing clouds of choking dust. They grunted and sweated, wiping their foreheads with their T-shirts and steadying themselves in the foyer before inching down the stairs. The room at the bottom was large – much larger than he'd imagined. They laid the bodies evenly and with care: head to toe, head to toe. She'd run up the stairs before him, meet him at the van, the wind rising now and then to make her flatten and rake at her hair. The sky's pallet became awful, extraterrestrial. Jewelled stars and streaks of gases appeared in the east, growing a deeper and deeper blue. He unscrewed the caps on a pair of water bottles and they drank, gulping savagely. They'd made it to the final body, staring into the western skyline and wondering what sweet brute could have made a world so organized, so painful, so generous. 'So beautiful,' he said to her, not knowing what to say, exactly, but feeling as if he could say anything in the world, leaning one arm on Cosmo's now radiant, sun-streaked door and gazing into the fading heat. And they returned to the long, back-breaking struggle, freighting the last body into its tomb.

After the Matthews were laid to rest, she ran up the stairs as before, but he didn't follow. Lingering there in the cool grave, he walked a slow circle around the square room. He could barely see, save for what was caught in the flashlight's patch of yellow. He looked at their sleeping faces, feeling the weight so heavy above him, the compact pounds of dirt and rock and cement, the fine filigree of dust that covered the world. He kneeled and took one of the heads in his hands, kissing it slow and on the brow, not knowing what he was doing, if this was right. *It doesn't matter*, he thought. *We make ourselves at every moment.* Looking around the room, seeing this kinship of flesh, he sighed, knowing this was the last look. He was okay with that. They were copies, but not essential. They didn't have his memories, his sense of humour, his heart. They could be buried, left in the dirt. He could forget.

He walked up the steps. Sandra stood halfway to the facility, hands in her pockets, staring into the boundless sky.

'So, hey,' he said, walking toward her. 'I really don't know what I'm saying. I guess I'm gonna go. It's gonna get real cold out here. You'd better come with me in Cos.'

'No, thanks,' she said quietly. 'I'm waiting on a ride of my own.'

He could have predicted as much. This wasn't really Sandra, anyway, he figured. It was a stand-in. Another kind of clone he'd discovered, or recovered, from all this waste. He took a deep, noisy breath, imagining what would happen if he stayed out here past dark, waiting for Sandra's ride. Who would be coming to pick her up. Another *third* actor. Another triangle. What nightmares in the final night, watching her climb into some weird jeep. He wasn't meant to stay and watch. This part of the story didn't involve him.

She was looking back at the sunlight. He felt less sadness now, watching her in profile. He'd meet her again, and it would be in a city, surrounded by the assembled regiments of sanity. She'd remember nothing of this (not that he'd ever bring it up – or if he did, he'd only hint at the time spent in the desert, near a bomb shelter, to which she'd just laugh and shake her head, say *you're crazy*, give him one of those confused, amused glances he was so used to). He turned and kicked through the darkening stretch of sand, slamming the metal door to the shelter on his way.

Cosmo felt good. He regretted tossing away the Native American symbols. He'd defaced his own environment, this mobile extension of his youth. He shook his head; it was a moment of weakness when faced with such strange adversity. But everything would be better, he thought; he'd buried his three brothers safe into the ground's receiving womb. He was lucky, extraordinarily lucky: he was able to say he'd buried himself. He kicked the van into DRIVE and turned on the headlights. He'd need them on the dark scrub, roaring back to the main roads and racing north, for the trip was definitely over. Before sliding down the hill in reverse, he caught Sandra in his lights: rubbing her arms, tiny and green, squinting into the harshness of the glare. It was the way he'd leave her, stuck in memory as if in amber, left alone and waiting for her ghosts and rides. He honked the horn, wheeled about and headed north.

Everything – the ground, the rattling frame, the rumbling engine – felt good. He pushed PLAY on the stereo, the Amboy Dukes launching back into the first song on the CD: 'Journey to the Centre of the Mind.' After the first verse and chorus, he hummed along with the lyrics, savouring the psychedelia, the drugstore mysticism.

And then he laughed, long and happy. They were stupid lyrics. They were written during a ridiculous time to be alive – a time when bomb shelters were still serious investments. He weighed the word in his mouth as he rolled onto the nameless, north-south road. *Bomb.* How Sandra's stand-in had said it so oddly. She'd emphasized the *om* inside it. The *om* in *bomb*, kind of like the *om* in *tomb*, in *womb*, but just pronounced differently. It was dumb and profound, but he tried it out on his tongue, a low monotone hum: *ommm.*

It meant peace, he thought. It was a word that meant nothing, and nothing meant peace.

OM.

He had an idea, passing just beyond the reach of his understanding. He hit REC.

THIS IS NOT AN ENDING

Claude Brazeau: His name is Pierre Lebrun ...
911 Dispatch Operator: Does he wear glasses?
Claude Brazeau: No. He stutters.
        – 911 emergency telephone call, April 6, 1999, 2:39 p.m.

'Hey, Terry,' says Joel, a shipper. 'Ask Scabby what kind of bus it is.'
'What kind of bus is it, Pierre?' asks Terry, a mechanic.

Pierre Lebrun feels a lurching drop in his stomach, a stinging rush of blood to his ears. Although his eyes are lowered, he can still make out the blurry shape of Terry's smile: a looming, left-leaning grin. Without looking up, Pierre reaches across the central workbench of the garage and wraps his hand around a Black & Decker vise. To calm himself, he thinks.

'Yeah, Scabby, I think you know what I mean,' Terry says, taking a sip of his Timmies.

Pierre drags the vise closer. He stares hard at the wooden workbench, watching hazy, oil-stained hands stumble over tools. Someone drops a screwdriver. Someone sorts noisily through rivets and washers. A piece of brake mechanism lies cleaned and gutted on the far side of the hangar-like repair shop, awaiting the strong, dexterous fingers of its operators.

'Well, let's narrow it down,' Terry says, chuckling. 'It's not a *slinky* bus.'

Over the bright clink of metal, Pierre can still make out the faint hum of traffic from Saint Laurent Boulevard – a long stretch of commercial zones staggered in quick, corporate succession, a steady stream of cars flowing liquid in the sunlight, reflecting the glare of gravel, glass and steel girders, grass dead or dying. The long length of tarmac inching toward suburbia, to Pierre's home: a late-century sprawl of concrete power centres, big-box parking lots, fast-food highways.

'C'mon, Scabby, think. We're *waiting* here.'

Other adults – co-workers, fellow employees – smile. *This is a collective attack*, Pierre thinks. He tightens his grip on the vise, feels hot in his sweater and collared shirt despite the chill temperature of the garage. He recalls, briefly and with a child's sense of monumental injustice, the glossy brochures he received at an Ottawa-Carleton Transpo job fair ten years back. They described the company in terms of modern workplaces: places where employees are granted securities and non-negotiable rights – the right to a safe and healthy environment, say, or the right to benefits and meaningful salaries, steady raises that reflect the rising cost of living. Rights reputedly protected by the powerful Amalgamated Transit Union (ATU), Local 279. Pierre remembers these as promises, as rosy guarantees. He thinks of safe zones and essential services, places of mutual respect and adult camaraderie. He thinks of meaningful employment in a capital-city service that demands excellence from all its partners.

'It's not a *ben*dy bus, right?' Terry asks, sounding goofy.

Pierre holds still, letting his thoughts meander, self-pitying. Again, he perceives his transfer to the main garage – his fourth move in the company since 1986 – to be a tremendous mistake. Each consecutive transfer representing a *redistribution of talent*, according to the ATU. Pierre requesting these changes in position not out of ambition, an aspiration to ascend ranks of financial seniority or even respect, but for the comforts afforded by lesser interaction, more independent work. Beginning his career as a driver, operating the #16 Alta Vista, Monday to Thursday, and finding himself incapable of dealing with the demands of actual passengers: the grotesque particulars, the spitting and whinging horrors. Then the irrational transfer into customer service, assigned to handle telephone queries, yet again finding himself unable to speak, unable to contain the hiccups and stalls of a stutter that seemed to rise and fall with his quivering distress. Transferring for the second time to a position he barely understood: travelling across the illogical spiderweb of the Ottawa transit system with an already hardened and compact maintenance team to attend to malfunctioning or snow-stalled machines, towing obstinate buses back to the main garage at 1500 Saint Laurent. Never getting the proper training, being placed beneath a pugnacious high school dropout with semi-coherent real-estate ambitions and ostracized from the cohesive team from the first shift onward when he was asked simple questions and as answers gave nods, shrugs, knowing his stutter was *bad that day*, as if hungover, vindictive. As if needing to be held and cradled, soothed into silence like a tantrum-prone child. How the experience drained him, lowering the natural defences of his body to allow for infection, invasion. His ensuing illness, sapping and depressing him, and the doctor's orders to remain at home in bed during the strike of 1996. The unanticipated hostility he faced upon returning to work, having never walked the picket line with his co-workers. Picking up the name that rides him into sobs, fury: *Scabby*. Now here, in the main garage, working belts and brakes and batteries and the maladaptive components of the modern city bus.

'You drove a bus, didn't you? You can't tell me what *kind* of bus it was?'

Pierre clenches his jaw, grinds his molars. He tries to stare through the wooden workbench, the vise heating up in his hand.

'Now, now,' Joel chimes in, as if hushing a child.

Terry rips into a bark. 'Ar-ar-ar-ar-ar-ar-ar-TIC-ulate, my boy!', answered by what Pierre interprets to be a roar of hoots and guffaws echoing off the towering walls of the repair shop. He glances up in time to catch Terry leaning back in laughter, his lips curled away from his teeth.

Pierre's open palm strikes Terry's cheek, making the surprisingly loud and fleshy *clap* sound heard in countless crime dramas. Terry is caught bewildered; he drops the wrench in his hand and stares, stunned. Conversation stops, giving the antiseptic pop song chirping from the nearby radio a strange sort of significance. And before either Terry or Pierre can react – both standing speechless, unsure of what just happened – loud male voices push between them, *hey hey hey*s, Pierre still holding the vise in his right hand, fingers clenched around the metal.

*I can't really say anything today that would say he was whacko,
you know.*

— *Ozzie Morin, OC Transpo employee*

So Pierre is asked to gather his things and leave. The grinding routine
already pierced by vacancy, by the thought of a thousand empty, virginal
days. He drives home mid-afternoon to the closed-window warmth
and stillness of his mother's home. A twenty-minute drive. Birds warbling
through the glass. He watches sitcom reruns in bed, blinking occasionally.
And this is heavenly: jaw-melting, drool-inducing. The hours of the
afternoon white and empty of memory. He imagines his immediate
future and smiles, humming with the pure pleasure of captured time:
no work in the morning, no exaggeratedly gleeful DJ shrieking through
the radio at some hard-edged, pre-dawn hour, no cold steel and stink
of gas and clenched shoulders in the garage. Pierre is out of a job, fired,
and he is happy.

This is how the first afternoon ends, how evening arrives. His mother
eating in the kitchen. Three light beers nursed while watching television,
listening to the scraping of her spoon. Tinkering on a length of damaged
fence in the backyard amid the muddy reaches, reading an old issue of
Field & Stream. As if nothing could alter the course of this new, comfortable life of unemployment.

But he can't avoid his mother. He can't avoid the revelation of his
offence, dancing about the laboured conversation of *what's to be done*
now, *what's to be done about* money, *what's to happen to your* career?
Pierre *slapped* another employee. Pierre raised his hand against a co-
worker in a modern, egalitarian workplace; Pierre stressed the unthinkable
physical fact of his being in a space of camaraderie and respect. To deal
with his mother, Pierre chalks it up to a man's rights, to taking only so
much abuse, to standing up to a bully. His mother speaks this language,
can relate to it and be proud, but she cries thinking about the money,
about how Pierre's going to have to start from *scratch*. (Not that he
minds starting over; he imagines a job plugging cords into a switchboard,
pulling a lever over and over again like an automaton. Working alone
and silent in perpetual, daydreaming mediocrity.)

Of course, this isn't what happens. The ATU, Local 279, is there for him; he's informed in a letter sent the same week as his release. A man named Paul Macdonnell keeps calling him; his mother writes down the phone number, his name, scrawling *CALL BACK!* on a pad of paper with urgent underlining. And Pierre does, feeling dreamy, feeling out of control. The ATU is determined to get him his job back. The ATU won't let an employee with his particular *needs* be dismissed so summarily. Macdonnell says they have a strong case if Pierre wants to pursue it. That the committee will be making an appeal, but they'll need his help and full co-operation.

'You have my, uh, co-operation,' Pierre mumbles, still dreaming.

'You have a disability, yes?' Macdonnell asks. 'You've indicated as such in your contract. Speech impediments are just as valid as any other disability, just as deserving of sensitive treatment. Expectations between employees differ according to ability, aptitude, functionality – elements out of our hands, M. Lebrun. Your ability to articulate your needs is compromised by your condition. Other employees are required to make certain *allowances* when working with a person with your particular needs. And discomforts may arise.'

'Yes, I have a disability,' Pierre says over the phone, without a hint of stutter. His mother nods ecstatically by his side in a white bathrobe. *Oui, j'ai un handicap!*

'But having a disability is no permission for violence, M. Lebrun, of which I am sure you are aware.'

'*Oui.*'

'Nevertheless, we have a written record of your attempt to contact OC Transportation about the individual in question, Mr. Terry Harding. You filed a complaint of harassment, *oui*?'

'Not quite …'

'Well, you spoke with Chairman Loney about the situation, did you not?'

'Yes.'

'What we're trying to assemble is a case of accumulated, prolonged harassment, that your actions on the date in question were the result of exacerbations, antagonisms that should have been dealt with in a professional manner. An adult manner. You made every reasonable attempt to rectify the situation before it could escalate any further, yet the situation in the main garage was left to worsen and grow volatile without proper company intervention. Is this correct?'

'Yes, correct.'

'Well, we're confident that we have something here. Hold tight, Pierre.'

Pierre holds tight. He drives his Pontiac Sunfire across the Ottawa River and unloads a rifle into distant wisps of cloud. He strips bark off a dying tree and punches until his knuckles rip and tear. He screams once, long and as loud as he can, just to test his limits. Birds rise from the folds of the wood, scattering in air like in a movie, something dramatic and picturesque, Pierre's anger lingering above them in echo, sweating. The summer drops its petals, gets sticky like spilled Coke.

> *We're going to look for causes, but really, I don't think we're going to find a cause. This individual was just sick.*
> *– Paul Macdonnell, head of the Amalgamated Transit Union, 2000*

A boy sits at a table in a kitchen, chewing a mouthful of cereal. He is staring at the cornflakes rooster. The boy's eyes are large and unfocused. His jaw grinds slowly, like a cow's, while the cornflakes become soggy in the milk in the bowl. A drop of milk dribbles over his bottom lip, making his chin glisten.

The boy's mother walks swiftly into the kitchen, holding a thin cardboard box. She is wearing a brown corduroy skirt and a lacy blouse. She has black curly hair and tiny eyes. The boy stops chewing. The woman rummages noisily in a drawer beneath the sink.

It is a warm day in June. It is a Saturday morning in 1968. The boy notices their home address written in black ink, capital letters, on the middle of the box. The woman finds a pair of scissors in the drawer, turns back to the table and slides the sharp edge of the scissors across a line of packing tape. She pulls out a square shape, packaged in mismatched newsprint. In a picture on a section of ripped newspaper is a man in a tuxedo, standing before a giant spinning roulette table. The man appears to be laughing, crow's feet and laugh lines cut deeply as if by a putty knife, his right arm beckoning behind him.

She unwraps a vinyl record from the newspaper and slides it toward her son.

On the cover of the record, thick letters read: *YES YOU CAN! A Student's Guide to Overcoming Stuttering, Volume One.* The lettering looks yellow, as if dried by sunlight or smoke.

'You're going to listen to this,' she says. The boy looks at her, swallows. 'We'll listen to this together, on the record player.'

The boy looks back down at the record.

'Wipe your mouth,' she says. She walks to the counter and wrings out a dishcloth.

The return address on the package is *LAS VEGAS, NEVADA.* The boy wipes his mouth.

All in all, he was a pretty peaceful lad. I didn't think he was ill.

– Ozzie Morin

Things Pierre is taught to remember:

That anger is a natural human response. That anger is a normal human emotion. That he should not cower from nor ignore his anger, nor allow his anger to build up inside him without a proper outlet.

That he should cradle his anger. That he should treat his anger like a crying baby because a baby cries in response to need. A baby cries in response to discomforts and longings, physical and emotional, because crying is all it knows. Crying is a natural response buried beneath the veneer of control and maturity and masculinity, as is fury.

The room in which Pierre receives these lessons is modern and bright. He sits on faux-leather couches and chairs surrounded by waxy plants and windows that offer a view of the parking lot and road and swaying trees and sky.

That *everyone* has so-called boiling points. Points at which things tend to spill beyond reason and control. That he should watch these hot points with patience and care. The tender boundaries.

That anger does not have to be the deciding emotion of his life.

That Pierre's anger comes from easily identified traumas. That all of these factors assemble to form a portrait of a real person who has *resolvable* problems.

Pierre sits with four other people, three men and one woman, who are enrolled in Anger Management Therapy as part of various work-rehabilitation programs. His therapist is in her mid-forties. Her voice is sharp and tough, but she speaks slowly, pushes her eyes into his eyes, doesn't let him look away. She wears a necklace of translucent gems and clunky bracelets, has dependable lines on her face.

Pierre, have you ever lost a job because of your anger?

Pierre, have you ever felt alone and misunderstood?

Pierre, are co-workers and peers concerned about your anger?

Pierre, have you ever been so angry that you forgot things you did or said?

At the end of his therapeutic treatment, Pierre apologizes to Terry in a sincere manner in the company of his therapist and an ATU representative. They sit in an empty boardroom and shake hands. Terry shakes as if trying to snap Pierre's knuckles, looking him in the eye. Smiling.

Pierre is not to return to the main garage at 1500 Saint Laurent; he is to avoid the scene where his anger got the better of him.

Pierre is not given the same job. He has to explain this to his mother three times before she understands. He is instead given another job, this one more suited to his particular needs. He is scheduled to begin work as an audit clerk. Paperwork, mailing, filing, accounting, written correspondence. A low-stress environment. Cubicles and witnesses.

As Terry leaves the boardroom where the apology takes place, he turns and smiles and silently mouths a word so only Pierre can see: *Scabby*.

Pierre feels a tender boundary, a hot point, a boiling line. He thinks of Terry's smiling, receding face, of collective attacks.

Participants in Anger Management Therapy are asked to complete an end-of-session evaluation. An evaluation of their therapists, their time spent under scrutiny, the process of healing. They are asked to circle a response ranked from one to five to the statement *I found this therapy to be successful.*

The response Pierre circled: *Strongly Disagree.*

This happens in August 1997, an extremely hot and humid month in Ottawa. Pierre thinks, sees, can feel tenderness everywhere: in the laughing faces of boys, in the skin-tight skirts of girls, in his dreams of slow-motion mechanisms unfolding. As if the city were an enormous stopwatch. The air a pulsing electric storm.

Pierre, do you often feel moody or sad because of your anger?

He had a bit of a speech impediment and he was teased a little bit. It got to him because he had sensitive feelings about it. But maybe they just got him at a bad time when maybe there was other stuff going on in his life.

– Robert Manion, 1500 Saint Laurent Boulevard
garage supervisor, 1999

Mrs. Boros, Polish and severe, sits at the end of the dining room table. A twelve-year-old Pierre watches her lips move in slow, exaggerated pantomime, mouthing sentences that spike in sharp, stenographic contortions: *Pierre presently proposes a particularly preposterous pursuit; David delights in daring, duplicitous disguises.* Pierre fails, consistently, to work his way through the words without halting, chopping regular alliterative metre into staccato fragments. His mother sits at the opposite end of the table, her hands clasped on the wood, her lips a polished red line. Each time Pierre fails – which he does *every time*, choking on consonants, oblivious of words stressed and unstressed, his jaw aching, his tongue lying thick and heavy and dry – Mrs. Boros smiles weakly, taps her fingertips on the tabletop and closes her eyes. Pierre doesn't dare look at his mother.

'Is it the order of the words?' asks Mrs. Boros, her eyebrows a conjoined storm.

Pierre shrugs. He doesn't know. The stutter bubbles up and shoots skyward like bilious oil.

'You know' Mrs. Boros continues, 'it might do for us to look at the sentences out of their normal order. English has strict, rigid word order. We think in subject, verb, object. Active sentences. We think in chronological, linear terms, as everyone knows, but it's even there in our text, our written language. It's encoded. We look for stages, words providing the framework for other words, other meanings blossoming from the precise, uninflected word order of our preceding statements.'

Pierre stares at a spot above her hairline.

'Rearrange the words so that they are more elements than stages. *Presently particularly Pierre proposes pursuit preposterous. Proposes Pierre preposterous presently particularly pursuit.* It's the individual words you need to look at. Let's just look at their shape and sound.'

An hour passes in frustration, terror, Pierre praying for some sort of ending. He puts his fingers into his mouth, pulling his lips and cheeks away from his teeth, attempting to physically force his flesh into utterance. He arrives at something absurd, clownish. His face flushes; his eyes well with tears. His mother reaches across the table and slaps his face, hard, making a cartoon *clap* sound, thinking he is mocking Mrs. Boros, who sometimes holds her chin or throat to demonstrate proper positioning, clear enunciation. Pierre's mother's hand comes away wet with his tears.

Mrs. Boros says nothing, has nothing to say: unversed in the true nuances of articulatory phonetics, a mere novice in the demands of vocalism. Oblivious to psychological trauma.

This is October 1969, after school. Leaves wither and fall from the maple trees on the front lawn. A vehicle heaves and sighs somewhere in the street. The moment Mrs. Boros leaves the house, Pierre's mother puts her arms around him, begins to cry. Says *I'm sorry* over and over.

Later in the evening, in the soft yellow glow of the den, the record player percolates and crackles beneath a series of cloying and simplistic nursery rhymes. A man's low, sonorous tenor recites the lyrics, is joined in the second verse by a chorus of high-pitched children. Pierre sits cross-legged on the carpeted floor beside the player, pretending to listen to the words. He reaches into his pocket and carefully removes a folded piece of newspaper. The fibres have deteriorated; the once-rough texture has become soft and flimsy from folding. He stares at the black and white image of a man in a tuxedo, smiling, standing before a roulette table spun into a seamless blur. Pierre imagines blazing lights and the heavy scent of cigarette and cigar smoke, the taste of bourbon and water, the giant whirling wheel an ill-defined haze of red and black, colour bleeding into colour until luck and chance and expectation become a single image, a gripping fear and exhilaration without words. Six-sided dice clatter from his open palm, collide and ricochet down a pool-hall green, and come up seven. A lithe, boa'd arm slinks around his shoulders, and sunglass-wearing spectators erupt in cheers. *You've won,* they scream, as the chips are pushed toward him and the slot machines whistle and Pierre doesn't say anything at all.

There, he thinks, *you don't have to speak. A happy ending.*

The record player rolls forward in a singsong voice, no stutter. A muttering incantation, the murmur of a congregation's prayer:

See, saw, Margery Dawe,
And Jack shall have a new master.
He shall make but a penny a day
Because he can't work any faster.

He was very clever, very nice. You just don't think you'd see this in your lifetime. I thought it was a joke – everybody did.
– Grant Harrison, OC Transpo auto-body repairman, 1999

Sex no longer even remotely available, now elevated and perverted to the level of pure mystery. The kiss and taste and heat of a woman – all meaningless abstractions. Infuriatingly meaningless, when it's all been shoved so violently down his throat (at home or work, on TV, in dreams). Or, rather, almost meaningless: some vestigial memory of a physical encounter from 1988 still lingers, but barely (he was drunk, details get distorted). Pierre's conceptions of coitus, pre and post, have settled down into the sediments of personal fantasy: a pastiche amalgam of pornography, soft-core romantic flourishes, sitcom couplings, Discovery Channel documentaries, Grade 12 sex ed. Every now and then he tries to imagine what it's really like. Rubs and kisses his own skin. Feels icky. Gets off to old familiars: pictures wrenched from real-life scenarios, thrust into the hot, masturbatory lair of his imagination.

Martine Berthelot, twenty-five, audit clerk, co-worker. Co-worker and slight superior in his new environment of stress-free paperwork, clerical monotony, sedentary labour. To Pierre's co-workers, details of last year's strike are still vividly and bitterly intoned – the lack of strategy, the indifference of management, the prolonged negotiations. The scabs. But Martine is new; Martine has no memories, has no reason to sort co-workers into camps determined by political lines. She gives Pierre a moment, a space, in which to breathe. Every other room and hallway is ruled by the battle lines of politics.

'Good weekend?' she asks him this Monday morning, catching him off guard. 'Go *hunting?*' she adds, with a little quiver of a laugh (a joke) appended to the question mark. He lets out his breath and rushes to speak, telling her that yes, actually, he went across the river into Gatineau, Quebec. That he was using his Remington (a 760, 30.06 Gamemaster, a variation of the model that James Earl Ray used to murder Martin Luther King, Jr., in Memphis, 1968 – something he doesn't share) to hunt deer. He stutters brutally when he attempts the word *deer*, so much so that he eventually gives up, says *game*. She nods through it all – the d-d-d-d-ing, the massaging of his jaw muscles, his exhaustion – and he knows instantly that any attempt at furthering the conversation into the personal (the intimate?) is ruined.

She'll find him hopeless, handicapped, he thinks. She'll find his combination of speech impediment and passion for rifles murkily disturbing in that modern, womanly way. Her eyes will glaze over with disgust, a grossed-out scoff about to bubble up in her throat. He's seen it before, heard and imagined the assumptions. To these women, living with Mom into your forties equals too much time at home. Possible abuse. Hobbies turned into obsessions. They might think he has a sort of dopey, forgivable homeliness (and this is what he clings to in odd moments of hope: the appeal of the pathetic, the loner, the misunderstood), but he knows they always imagine his existence – the particulars of Pierre, the irreplaceable qualities of a singular life – as a mere caricature of a lonely man's. Entire bookshelves filled with vhs tapes on gambling tips, counting cards. An immaculately clean apartment. Hunting magazines stacked atop worn and outdated *Penthouses*. Posters of Asian schoolgirls in short skirts flaunting stick-thin white legs.

Silence again arrests the office. Pierre, now daydreaming, watches Martine work at her desk. He imagines the luxury of telling her that the

Remington's wood finish is *fine-grain American walnut stock*. He imagines telling her about the gun in a more intimate setting – his mother's living room, say, in Orléans, after dinner. He imagines speaking calmly and mellifluously, his voice a sure, confident metronome. He imagines showing her his rifle not out of eagerness or bravado but because she has begged to see it. She is awed, powerfully aroused, as he unzips a black canvas carrying case and places the surprising weight of the rifle on her lap.

'Was it fun?' she asks, bored, again cutting through the silence, her eyes down, turning to sort through incoming mail. He says yeah, sure, it was fun, before trailing off. He holds his mouth shut. He does not tell her about the white, painful look of the November sky, the light dusting of snow on the pines, about how much he enjoys the ribbing on the fore end of the rifle. How much he likes the way the professional finish catches the sunlight when the gun is cradled in his arms, his left eye shut tight, his right eye pressed against the thick glass of the scope. The way the light becomes a bead on the barrel, becomes a fist at the end of an arm.

Martine begins to lick and seal envelopes. Her fingers pinch the paper and her tongue laps and darts along the adhesive. Pierre watches her large, heavy-lidded eyes, the sway of her highlighted, glossy hair. He thinks of a mature buck he found in the hills, the way it lifted its head, snorting, as its ears turned and flattened. He thinks of the crosshairs of the scope resting over the buck's neck, the cloud of steam from its breath, the shot tearing through the stillness of the wood. All things he has studied, measured, in mixed strains of longing and affection and frustration. He watches the tiny brown freckles on Martine's chest, scattered above the line of her blouse. He thinks of the animal buckling, its legs flailing, its last attempt to stand before it shuddered and fell forward. How its hooves clawed the earth, ripping up clots of snow. He watches Martine's small breasts, the subtle press of her rib and sternum. He wants to put her earlobe in his mouth, bring his teeth together, press his nose into the crook of her neck and breathe. Trace his fingers along the lines of her mouth, wrap his hands about her jaw. He thinks of how she would smell: the milky scent of skin, light perfume, soaps and creams, making him dizzy, dazzling heat in his bladder, his crotch. Back in his mother's living room, brushing her hair over her ear, he imagines her leaning in, quickly, and licking his lips. He imagines pulling two tickets to Vegas from a jacket pocket, watching joy and desire contort her face into a painting, a film star, a saint. Then he can deliver his kiss, the kiss of dreams and childhood. He thinks of the buck's lips quivering, mouthing words, as he stood beside it, somewhat out of breath, watching the bright flow of blood stain the snow.

He whispers something in a singsong voice. No stutter.

Martine doesn't look up. She folds the envelope and throws it into a box. Walks out of the room.

Pierre resigns from OC Transpo after thirteen years of employment in January 1999. *The ending*, he thinks, relieved and shivering in a bus shelter, headed home. *Finally, the end.*

It's very curious why he selected certain individuals to kill and permitted certain people to live. He could have easily killed more people.
— Inspector Ian Davidson,
Ottawa-Carleton Regional Police, 1999

What's a kid from Ottawa know about Nevada? Only what he can imagine, dreaming of roulette wheels in early-stage childhood depression; only what he can glean from television westerns, tales of Paiute trails, fallout from nuclear test sites. In Pierre's boyhood imagination, Nevada is as cold and unpopulated as the cliffs and craters of the moon – which it may as well be, coming from a kid sheltered by the leafy suburbs of 1960s Ottawa, where even a good bike ride leads into the checkerboard slopes of the downright bucolic (this being before the population booms of later decades, before the amalgamation of the townships, before the Ottawa-Carleton Regional Transit Commission).

Expectation and reality collide violently in early 1999. Pierre approaches Vegas by day, bumper to bumper with a heaving vanguard of glistening metal. Freon whispers from the plastic dash; carbon monoxide makes the air livid. He has just left the mountainous, invigorating air of Logan Lake, British Columbia. His bid to find new work – something monotonous, solitary and quiet – has been unsuccessful. He feels that a gamble must be made; that after so many losses, the odds, finally, are in his favour. He drives through the serpentine highway systems and into the heart of the city: the strip, the wonderland pastiche of iconic cliché, pastels and the King, the homeless in flip-flops, big-chested transvestites, red leather, Siegfried and Roy. Tourists genuflect in khaki shorts and Tilley hats, snapping cameras at monstrous replicas of otherworldly culture. Pierre winds his car toward the Best Western, a gaudy porno flyer caught in his windshield wipers. He checks in at reception, rides the smooth elevator to the seventh floor and sits on the pressed sheets of his double bed. Perspiration dampens his underarms and back as he closes his eyes to the ceiling fan, the white walls.

At 2:51 a.m., fifteen hours later, Pierre returns to his room and lies back on the bed. He has lost almost $10,000. His bank account is empty and his credit card is maxed. The casino was too loud, he thinks. He has made a list of people who have offended him but doesn't need the list any longer. Something slips, quietly.

What were you expecting here? he asks himself. *You were expecting what here? Here you were what expecting? Expecting were you here what?*

Quite apart from what's alleged or otherwise with Mr. Lebrun's situation, we know we've had a very unhappy work environment for a long time.
– Al Loney, chair of Ottawa-Carleton Regional Transit Commission

One night Pierre has a nightmare. In the nightmare, Pierre drives to the main garage at 1500 Saint Laurent Boulevard with a massive plastic Walmart bag containing springs, gears, screws, bolts, nuts and caps: a pile of fasteners and disassembled metal. His mother sits in the back seat of his car. She wears a white blouse reminiscent of something from the 1960s and smokes a cigarette.

Pierre rises from the car and walks to the employee entrance, the Walmart bag slung over his shoulder. It's early in the morning, still semi-dark, and hours before employees are scheduled to arrive for work. He walks from room to room, floor to floor, looking for his locker – it isn't until he has searched the entire complex that he remembers that his locker was cleaned out after his altercation with Terry Harding, which was long ago. He shoves the Walmart bag of machine parts beneath a red tool cabinet in an empty storeroom, concealing the spot with a folded janitor's towel, and waits for employees to enter the building, for the day and his shift to begin.

As no one arrives to work, Pierre becomes worried that he has made a mistake. Perhaps today is a holiday, he thinks. His mother will be furious with him. There will be no way or route home because she will have taken the car, and no buses run on this particular holiday. To his mother, Pierre is head garage mechanic.

The garage is utterly empty; Pierre begins to feel this, sense it in the settling silence of the vacant halls, the dark offices. He feels how keenly alone he is in such an enormous structure; the size and loneliness and cold are unnerving. But he hears something fall, distantly, something noisy and metallic. He fetches a handful of screws from the Walmart bag and begins to search for the source of the noise.

The noise leads Pierre to the hangar-like repair shop. He walks onto a second-storey rampart that looks down onto the floor. Below him is an enormous metal maze, a perfect square, with walls roughly ten feet from the ground, cobbled together with fist-sized iron bolts. Clearly visible within the maze is Terry Harding, or the ghost of Terry Harding, or a person with the body and bearing of Terry Harding with a face that is not quite present. Or a present face corrupted by decay and malice. Pierre sees over and above the labyrinth, as if floating against the ceiling, gazing down on the confusion of walls and alleys, Terry's rotted body wandering and blundering through its intoxicating emptiness. Pierre knows there is no exit or entrance. It knots itself in confusion, the walls melding and tying off, forming bows and nooses. Shadows begin to echo, make noise. The maze grows to the size of a city. It is the most horrible thing Pierre has ever seen or heard, and in the dream he loses his mind completely. He hears his own breath rising suddenly in his ears. He lifts his handful of screws and bellows like an ape. He trips down a flight of stairs, rushes to the side of the maze and slams its metal edges with his fist. Terry is screaming from some distant shadow. Then Pierre runs backwards out of the main garage and into the parking lot, the maze receding in size. It's raining outside. The moon moves as if in fast-forward, slipping between clouds. The city is empty, evacuated, but incredibly loud, as if the rushing wind and weather forced its inhabitants into shelter or escape. Of course, Pierre's car is missing. His mother has driven home to attend to her errands. He has mistaken his profession and his role within the organization, within the adult environment, so he begins to walk like a fugitive toward downtown. He sits on an abandoned highway embankment, utterly alone, and begins to moan, wracked with grief. He realizes that he has passed into some sort of afterlife, a punishment for his pretending to be something he is not. That Terry's bloated absence is the ruler of this world. Pierre's sorrow turns to bitterness and anger. Everything is in flux. This is Judgment Day, Pierre thinks, waking up to a motel room in Idaho.

He should have realized that nobody is against anybody.
– Grant Harrison

Two p.m., April 6, 1999. Pierre watches the main garage through the windshield of his black Sunfire. His eyes flit across rows of vacant, corrugated bus ports, a serried stutter of yawning lots. The tarmac surrounding the garage is edged by melting banks of rigid, blackened snow: the stubborn, clinging snows of early April. Everything is dirty, wilted, daunting. If there are trees, they are black fingers, arthritic and pathetic.

The sky is wan. The sky is a piece of paper. Pierre's face is drawn tightly. There are bluish circles under his eyes. His hands are in his lap. He looks over his shoulder at the Adidas gym bag on the back seat of the car.

A #95 articulated bus heaves onto the tarmac from Saint Laurent Boulevard. The bus is empty save for a brown-skinned, squat driver, wearing an OC Transpo uniform: a faded navy sweater vest over a light blue, short-sleeve dress shirt. The parking lot is dotted with cars and trucks and minivans. The driver in the #95 crosses Pierre's line of sight, turning around the side of the garage.

It is quiet and warm inside the car. Pierre's heart thumps steadily in his chest. He pivots his waist and reaches into the back seat with his right arm, grabbing and hefting the awkward weight of the gym bag onto his lap. White, momentary spots flash in his periphery. His hands remind him of a jonesing junkie's, shaky and clumsy, in need of a fix. He brings his hands to his face, feeling along his forehead, his cold, shaking fingers an insufficient balm to the hot, dry skin of his nose and lips. He has not slept since Detroit, Michigan, two days before, in a motel that reminded him of an OC Transpo station: a cold-lighted sign-post impossibly remote from anything warm or recognizable or welcoming, his mind swarming with the entire spiderweb of half-memorized timetables, charts and graphs and circuit speeds. How it all seemed so small, so enormous – time trapped in light, wants bludgeoned by needs. And then it was perfectly graspable, as if crosshairs weaved over the image of his hurt. Standing in Detroit, staring into the halo of the VACANCY sign, thinking of a Transpo station he was once stalled at, long past regular hours. A Transpo station stranded off the shoulder of an empty highway, sometime between two and three in the morning, in the middle of winter, snowbanks knee-high against the curb, the wind so wicked the glass howled and moaned in D-minor sympathy. Cold so draining that the ache became all there was: fingers and toes curling and unfurling through a pins-and-needles torture, so much worse for its sodium vapour glow. Thirteen years of employment reduced to this image carved from ice. Thirteen years stomped to *mistake* in an instant of time no one heard or saw or could take note of, reduced finally to the pale glow of a bus stop in the middle of the night, imagined in the parking lot of a Super 8 on the outskirts of Detroit, awash in the pale neon blaze of the VACANCY sign. Transformed finally into something terminal and black.

While Pierre Lebrun stood facing the unravelling of his adult life (wordless, soundless), Martine Berthelot was sleeping in her apartment on Bank Street in downtown Ottawa. She was roused during the night by the sound of her roommate dropping a jar of moisturizer on the toilet seat. Her dreams were banal in their ordinary insensibility: a giant wasp hovering in the corner of her bedroom, a bicycle shop's floor buried in sawdust, her mother laughing. The illness that would leave her feeling deflated still only in its formative stage, having yet to move from a mere tingle in her sinuses.

By the time she opens her eyes, she's sick for real. She calls the office at 7:03 in the morning on April 6, 1999, sniffling into a dry Kleenex, eyes red, lymph nodes as swollen as ping-pong balls.

And thus she avoids the fires, the heaps of recycled paper and wood shavings salvaged from Blue Boxes and garbage bags that go up quickly, promisingly, but are doused by the efficient ceiling sprinklers before they can become more than showy piles of grey, smouldering detritus.

She avoids the PA speaker pronouncements, the frantic, shrill cries. She avoids the clusters of employees cowering beneath desks, in supply closets, whispering in huddles, doors locked.

She avoids the moment Pierre stops thinking: the sharp, sudden recoil of his lips as he finds the metal of the barrel still hot from the firing.

Pierre runs a red light at 7:04 a.m., eager to push past the boundaries of the City of Toronto, having been awake for nearly twenty-six hours.

The 401 is long and grey and heavy. Suddenly it is two o'clock. Suddenly he is pulling into the main garage. Unzipping a canvas gym bag. Staring at a moving bus. Suddenly it is Judgment Day.

He thinks of Mrs. Boros's tight smile. Thinks of a dying buck. Rearranges all the words. Tries to put together a plot line, his head in his hands, the rifle on his lap. Isn't there somewhere else to go? Some final opt-out, a safety switch, a booked ticket to Vegas?

Vegas! Pierre thinks. *This isn't the end!*

He thinks that this is not an ending.

That this is not an ending.

Clare Davidson, 52. Brian Guay, 56. David Lemay, 45. Harry Schoenmakers, 44.

FRANKIE+HILARY+ROMEO+
ABIGAIL+HELEN:
AN INTERMISSION

The key is the ability, whether innate or conditioned, to find the other side of the rote, the picayune, the meaningless, the repetitive, the pointlessly complex. To be, in a word, unborable ... If you are immune to boredom, there is literally nothing you cannot accomplish.
— from The Pale King, *David Foster Wallace*

By Frankie, I mean, of course, Francisco James Muñiz IV (1985–), son of Francisco 'Frank-a-hey-ho' Benjamin Eugene-Wallace Tyler Muñiz III (a Cuban-born restaurant owner of Puerto Rican descent), and Denise (ex-nurse of mixed Irish and Italian heritage), now divorced. The particular Frankie who, after watching his older sister Christina's sterling performance in her Knightdale, North Carolina, high school musical, decided to pursue a career in acting, and who first got his chops as Tiny Tim in a local theatre production of *A Christmas Carol*. The home-schooled Frankie who slogged through several no-budget productions (*The Sound of Music, The Wizard of Oz*, etc.) and commercials and made-for-TV movies (e.g., *To Dance with Olivia*, 1997, starring Louis [or Lou] Gossett, Jr.) until his role in the David Spade/Sophie Marceau romantic comedy *Lost & Found* (1999), which, though roundly panned by critics, raised him in the eyes of Hollywood casting agents and facilitated his first big splash at the awkward age of fourteen in the Fox sitcom *Malcolm in the Middle*, a mid-season replacement in which Frankie played the eponymous leading character with such aplomb and earnestness that he was nominated for Golden Globe Awards in 2000 and 2001, an Emmy Award in 2001, and was awarded the *Hollywood Reporter* YoungStar Award for his overall performance in the series. *Malcolm in the Middle* being the long-running comedy series detailing the antics of a middle-class family modelled after a sort of 'dysfunctional American post-nuclear' (perhaps best epitomized by *The Simpsons*), lauded and known to push specific target-audience envelope thresholds and known as the vehicle that enabled Frankie to star in several feature-film productions through the early to mid-2000s, such as *My Dog Skip* (2000), *Dr. Dolittle 2* (2001), *Big Fat Liar* (2002, matched with actress Amanda Bynes), *Agent Cody Banks* (2003, alongside actress, singer and activist Hilary Duff), *Agent Cody Banks 2: Destination London* (2004) and *Racing Stripes* (2005, voice only), as well as to make numerous cameo appearances, such as in the films *Stuck on You* (2003), *Stay Alive* (2006) and *Walk Hard: The Dewey Cox Story* (2007). The Frankie who, over the last few years, has been transitioning out of traditional Hollywood acting roles, experimenting with various producing gigs (for example, producing in 2006 the film *Choose Your Own Adventure: The Abominable Snowman*, an interactive animated feature based on the popular 'Choose Your Own Adventure' novels, for which he also provided voice-acting alongside actors William H. Macy and Lacey Chabert) and expressing a desire in print and online media to do some 'growing up' outside the limelight. The Frankie who has decided of late to pursue an exciting and rewarding career as a professional race-car driver (ever since gaining his driver's licence in 2001, Frankie has been consumed with a powerful love of driving and of cars [no doubt influenced by his father, Frank-a-hey-ho, who similarly indulges in car adoration but has publicly expressed fears regarding Frankie's safety behind the wheel] – a love which has led to the purchase of several exorbitantly expensive automobiles [a total of nine in Frankie's first year of licenced driving], such as the white 1995 Volkswagen Jetta from the film *The Fast and the Furious* [2001], a 2002 Cadillac Escalade previously owned by Penny Hardaway of the New York Knicks and a 1950s Porsche Speedster). The Frankie who, after more or less committing himself to the sport, took first prize in the 2005 Pro/Celebrity Race at the Long Beach Grand Prix and promptly signed a two-year contract with Jensen Motorsport, allowing him to race between the years 2006 and 2008 in the Formula BMW U.S.A. Championship, the Champ Car Atlantic Series (including the Las Vegas Grand Prix), the Sebring Winter National SCCA race, and drive for the PCM/USR team, finishing in the top ten in three races and completing the 2008 season in eleventh place (also bringing home the 2008 Jovy Marcelo Sportsmanship Award for his gracious and honourable conduct during the year's competitions). The particular Frankie who, in 2005, was briefly engaged to hairdresser Jamie Gandy (a woman who bears a passing resemblance to Frankie's ex-co-star Hilary Duff and whom he met on the set of the film *Stay Alive*) – an engagement that was swiftly called off due (in part) to Frankie's hectic racing and travelling schedule, which left him a grand total of only forty days at home in 2007. The Frankie who is also currently engaged to Hollywood unknown Elycia Turnbow, aka Elycia Marie (a five-foot-four vintage clothing store-owner [standing one inch shorter than Frankie] tagged by many bloggers as 'super hot') who, in early 2011, reputedly assaulted Frankie and damaged numerous expensive artworks and pieces of furniture around his mansion in Phoenix, according to a 911 dispatch call made by Frankie himself, who was reputedly embroiled in such relationship stress and drama that he was pushed to hold a pistol to his head and threaten to commit suicide. The resilient Frankie who is currently mending his relationship with Turnbow/Marie and denying any ongoing suicidal urges, and who, among other appearances and racing projects, is currently playing drums for the rather middle-of-the-road, radio-friendly rock band You Hang Up.

And by Hilary Duff, I mean, of course, Hilary Erhard Duff (1987–), daughter of Robert (Bob) Erhard Duff (owner of many successful convenience stores) and Susan Colleen (née Cobb, homemaker turned film producer and Hollywood manager), now divorced. The precise Hilary who was born in the dry September heat of Houston, Texas, and – like Francisco James Muñiz before her – was home-schooled from the third grade onward and introduced to acting via various theatre productions at age six (along with her older sister, Haylie Katherine Duff, also an actress and musician of considerable fame and two years Hilary's senior). The singular Hilary who leapt from acting school to local theatre productions (most notably in a production of *The Nutcracker Suite* in San Antonio) to a move to California with her mother and Haylie Katherine (while Bob Duff lingered in Texas) to television commercials and small roles in TV series such as *Chicago Hope* or the miniseries *True Women* (1997, uncredited) to her first leading role in the critically condemned, direct-to-video snore-fest *Casper Meets Wendy* (1998), the ill-fated sequel to 1995's *Casper*, which starred Bill Pullman and a young Christina Ricci. The Hilary who endured the loss of a role in the ill-fated NBC sitcom *Daddio*, which shook the foundations of her preteen confidence and sent her spiralling into a depression related to feelings of inadequacy and failure and terrified envy of her older sister and guilt at the beseeching of her mother to move from Texas to California, which presumably helped tear the Duff family asunder and contribute to the elder Duffs' eventual divorce – directly caused by Bob Duff's illicit affair – in 2006 (believed to be described in certain of Hilary's later songs, such as 'Gypsy Woman' and 'Stranger'). The specific Hilary who broke through to stardom as the eponymous heroine in the television series *Lizzie McGuire* (2001–2004, originally airing on the Walt Disney Channel), a children's broadcast recounting the exploits of a young girl with geeky parents and supportive, eccentric friends who on occasion morphed into a cartoon character (known as Animated Lizzie) in order to address the audience in fourth-wall-breaking digressions and asides revealing McGuire's *real* feelings, not unlike the audience-addressing function of a Greek chorus. And while *Lizzie McGuire* drew roughly 2.3 million viewers per episode, won Favorite TV Show at the Nickelodeon Kids' Choice Awards in 2002 and 2003, won Hilary the Favorite TV Star at the Nickelodeon Kids' Choice Awards Australia in 2004 and garnered numerous successful merchandise endorsements (such as *Lizzie McGuire* Happy Meal CD-ROMS, Dakin toys and plush dolls, and TOKYOPOP cine-manga spinoffs, etc.) collectively earning the Walt Disney Corporation over $100 million, it wasn't until Hilary reprised her role as Lizzie in *The Lizzie McGuire Movie* (2003) that she really 'blew up' (though some might argue persuasively that her role in *Agent Cody Banks* [2003], alongside Frankie Muñiz, was the true catapulting vehicle of her cinematic career). In line with her previous efforts, *The Lizzie McGuire Movie* was near-universally disliked by critics, who associated her promotion of Lizzie with other celebrity 'cash-in' ventures, such as Britney Spears's disastrous but image-reinforcing performance in *Crossroads* (2002). The certain Hilary whose subsequent films fared considerably worse, both financially and critically, than her earlier efforts – such films including perfect flops such as *A Cinderella Story* (2004), *Raise Your Voice* (2004), *Cheaper by the Dozen 2* (2005), *The Perfect Man* (2005) and *Material Girls* (2006), all of which earned her Razzie nominations for Worst Actress in their respective years. The Hilary who, in 2008, *declined* a major role in the CW Network's *90210* remake series because of a desire to edge away from the tween-to-teen market, similar to Frankie's stated interest in pursuing non-traditional film involvements; strangely, Duff appeared the following year on the highly successful CW television show *Gossip Girl* (2007–present), apparently prepared to embrace whatever pigeonholed 'teen' actress roles came her way, or to at least linger in the hyperactive pastels of the genre for as long as possible. The Hilary whose film career, at least since 2008, has significantly declined (both in terms of frequency of appearance and visibility of roles), with the Charlie Sheen–co-produced non-event *She Wants Me*, released in April 2012, being her most recent film credit, receiving a score of 3.7/10 on IMDb and no reviews or rankings on Rotten Tomatoes. But this is also the Hilary Duff who electrified young audiences and certain older men with her successful singing career, debuting in 2002 with a cover track on the *Lizzie McGuire* sound-track and a song written for a compilation album entitled *Disneymania*, followed by the full-length Christmas album *Santa Claus Lane*: a certi-fied-gold CD that featured duets with sister Haylie, rapper Lil' Romeo, singer Christina Milian and other mid-2000s sensations. The Hilary who, in 2003, launched *Metamorphosis*, the pretentious-sounding soph-omore album that nevertheless went on to become certified quadruple-platinum, sell out arenas across the world on its tour and boast the singles 'Come Clean' and 'So Yesterday' – songs of adolescent confusion, romantic freedom and simplistic, almost nursery-rhyme melodies that reduced tweenage girls to a kind of synthetic, fantasy-world mush. The

Hilary who followed up *Metamorphosis* in the next year with *Hilary Duff*, a collection of original tracks that was immediately followed in 2005 by *Most Wanted*, a compilation album that went platinum a month after its release, featuring the catchy and inoffensive, Good Charlotte–written single 'Wake Up,' which was supported by a music video of Duff attending parties around the world, clearly demarcating a line between her earlier, tepid child-pop and this new, more danceable, more mature sound. This was further expanded upon in her following album, *Dignity*, released in 2007, which pushed her personal image into more vixen-like territory and that expanded her musical repertoire with a more committedly dance-hall, electropop and New Wave sound (even earning mixed-to-positive reviews from major album-reviewing publications, to the surprise of just about everybody). The Hilary who, after the 2008 release of *Best of Hilary Duff*, mentioned via Twitter and her own website that she was back to recording another album, stating that she was 'going to mess around in the studio and work on some music.' The entrepreneurial Hilary who also founded the preteen-targeted clothing (and jewellery and fragrance and furniture) brand Stuff by Hilary Duff in 2004, which sold at fluorescent-lit, headachy chain stores such as Kmart, Zellers and Target before fizzling out in 2008. The Hilary who fearlessly entered the women's fragrance market in 2006 with With Love ... Hilary Duff, the perfume that boasted hints of mangosteen fruit, cocobolo wood, amber milk and musk, which was followed by Hilary's second perfume, Wrapped With Love, a fragrance sparkling with a wider array of fruits, flowers and musk-based scents, including mandarin, honeydew and white lily. The Hilary who, having witnessed the demise of Stuff by Hilary Duff, partnered with DKNY to promote Femme for DKNY Jeans, a line of women's clothing that took inspiration from trendsetting New York fashion icons (jeans ranging in price from $39 to $129), and that was supported by a series of videos called *The Chase*, filmed in various European cities and uploaded in serial fashion as a seven-part miniseries to Duff's official YouTube channel (the first video receiving 22,000 views in its first week of publication). The ever-ambitious Hilary who also co-authored (with Elise Allen) the *New York Times*–bestselling book *Elixir*, a young-adult novel that received overwhelmingly positive reviews to the surprise of absolutely no one in the world and spawned its sequel, *Devoted*, also co-authored by Elise Allen, which continued the paranormal story of Sage and Clea and the Elixir itself (for Hilary has insisted upon her love of reading, having publicly praised other recent top-selling books such as *The Hunger Games* by Suzanne Collins, *The Pact* by Jodi Picoult, *Water for Elephants* by Sara Gruen and *Eclipse* by Stephenie Meyer of *Twilight* fame). The philanthropic Hilary whose generous financial donations and personal appearances and endorsements have assisted with numerous premier charities, such as the Think Before You Speak campaign, Kids with a Cause, the Audrey Hepburn Children's Fund and more, including generous work with Hurricane Katrina relief, animal rights and LGBT organizations. The Hilary who is known to have dated Aaron Charles Carter, pop and hip-hop singer (with adolescent-friendly lyrics similar to those of early Lil' Bow Wow or Lil' Romeo) and younger brother of Nickolas Gene Carter of Backstreet Boys fame in the synth-rich, McWorld years between 2001 and 2003, before dating Joel Rueben Madden, vocalist for the pop-punk band Good Charlotte (now on hiatus), between the years 2004 and 2006 (Madden being twenty-five and Hilary being sixteen at the beginning of their relationship, to the genuine and legitimate concern of many well-meaning observers). The Hilary who, on August 14, 2010, in Santa Barbara, California, married the Edmonton-born, now-retired NHL centre iceman Mike Comrie, with whom she has now mothered her first son – Luca Cruz Comrie, born on March 20, 2012, weighing in at seven pounds, six ounces.

And by Lil' Romeo, I mean, of course, Percy Romeo Miller, Jr. (1989–), currently known by the performance name Romeo, though clearly better known as Lil' Romeo, a moniker that acknowedged his precocious age and diminutive size when he debuted as a rapper and recording artist in 2001 (and first signed to his father's music label, No Limit Records, at the age of five). The Romeo born into the world of hip hop and basketball as the eldest son of ex-rapper Sonya C and rapper, entrepreneur and mogul Percy Robert Miller, Sr., otherwise known as Master P (otherwise known as P. Miller), rapper of over a dozen albums (such as *Ghetto D* [1997], *MP Da Last Don* [1998], *Only God Can Judge Me* [1999] and *Ghetto Postage* [2000]), who reached his apex of fame in the late nineties but who steadily declined in influence, record sales and critical reception throughout the early 2000s, mirroring the declining success of his once red-hot rap music label, No Limit Records, which spawned an empire of related businesses (and for which P. Miller worked as CEO, personally earning nearly $57 million in 1998, and once estimated to be worth over $600 million) including No Limit Gear, Bout It Inc., No Limit Films, No Limit Communications and No Limit Sports Management. No Limit Records most impressively showcased as a dominant force in the rap industry in Master P's 1997 track, 'Make 'Em Say Uhh' (from the album *Ghetto D*), notable for a refrain comprised mostly of groans and a music video featuring a platinum tank, a basketball court writhing with cheerleaders and gesticulating groupies, and frequent, over-the-top slam dunks. P also being brother (and Romeo thus being nephew) to two other popular musicians: C-Murder (Corey Miller), rapper of seven albums (including the platinum-selling 1998 album *Life or Death* [No Limit Records]), ex-lover of R&B phenomenon Monica and a convicted murderer, serving a sentence of life imprisonment at the Louisiana State Penitentiary for the 2002 beating and shooting of sixteen-year-old Steve Thomas; and Silkk the Shocker (Vyshonn King Miller), rapper of five studio albums (including 1999's *Made Man* [No Limit Records]), ex-lover of and collaborator with R&B sensation Mýa, COO of the new incarnation of No Limit Records, No Limit Forever (co-operated with his nephew, Romeo), aspiring director of the documentary *Conviction by Name* (which argues for the innocence of C-Murder) and father of two children (Lil King and Jianna Miller). The Romeo who is older brother to Valentino Miller, also a rapper, and Cymphonique Miller, recently nominated for Best Female Hip-Hop Artist at the 2011 BET Awards (despite having released only one EP [2009's *I Heart You*]) and current star of the Nickelodeon sitcom *How to Rock*, based on the young-adult book *How to Rock Braces and Glasses* by Meg Haston. The Romeo who reached the No. 1 spot on Billboard 200, making him the youngest artist to ever reach such a dizzying peak, with his first single 'My Baby' (sampling the Jackson 5's lighthearted 1969 mega-hit 'I Want You Back') from his first, now certified-platinum album, *Lil' Romeo* (2001). The Romeo who followed in 2002 with the double-platinum album *Game Time*, boasting the singles '2-Way' (sampling 'It Takes Two' by Rob Base and DJ E-Z Rock, featuring lyrics by his father, Master P and his uncle Silkk The Shocker) and 'True Love' (featuring lyrics by Solange Knowles, younger and less successful sister of Beyoncé). The Romeo who released a third and final album under the moniker Lil' Romeo in 2004 called *Romeoland*, which reached certified-gold status and #70 on the Billboard 200 chart (considerably worse than his last two albums). But this is also the Romeo of the five-man rap group Rich Boyz (comprised of Valentino, aka Young V, Romeo's younger brother, and his cousins C-Los, Lil' D and Big Doug), releasing the album *Young Ballers: The Hood Been Good to Us* in 2005 (receiving no reviews) on the internet via Guttar Music (aka New No Limit), founded by Romeo and his father in 2005 after (uncle) Silkk the Shocker purchased the original No Limit Records the year before (No Limit, aka No Limit Forever, currently operated by rappers known as Black Don (CEO) and Lil' D (President). In 2006, Romeo saw the release of two new albums, both signed under the new name of 'Romeo' (dropping the 'Lil'' that pegged the rapper as a child star): *Lottery* (featuring a rumoured lyrical rebuttal in the track 'U Can't Shine Like Me' to a rumoured diss in the 2005 track 'Fresh Azimiz' by Bow Wow, formerly Lil' Bow Wow) and *God's Gift*, the soundtrack album to the 2006 direct-to-video film of the same name, directed by Master P, distributed by Guttar Music Entertainment and starring Romeo, Young V and Zachary Isaiah Williams. In 2007, the world witnessed the release of *Hip Hop History*, a poorly selling collaboration with his father from Take A Stand Records, and 2010 saw the release of *Spring Break*, an album by a new, post–Rich Boyz collective called College Boyys (involving Romeo, Valentino Miller, K Smith, Taz, Kyros and other acts) committed to writing empowering (and cleaner) lyrical messages, promoting a school-positive attitude and elevating the jerkin' (or jerk) street dance style of 2009 (transitioning into, or supported by, the Romeo-designed College Boyys clothing line, promoted by young artists such as Jaden Smith and Justin Bieber and boasting polo shirts, argyle sweaters and a generally more preppy style than what was popular among rap artists in the early 2000s and late '90s). The Romeo of the rather confusing fourth official studio album, now known as *Intelligent Hoodlum*, featuring the YouTube-released first single, 'Hug Me Forever,' that samples '(I Just) Died in Your Arms' by Cutting Crew and is scheduled for release sometime in 2012 – all of this extremely confusing to outsiders because of the erratic release, naming and recording schedule between 2008 and the present. *Intelligent Hoodlum* originally bore the name *Gumbo Station* and was supported by the single 'Get Low wit It' in 2008, which failed to reach a spot on the Billboard charts; however, songs destined for *Gumbo Station* appeared on the compilation LP *Get Low* in 2009, and the fourth album was re-announced as *The College Boy* and then (again) as *I Am No Limit* in the year 2010. This new incarnation was supported by the singles 'Tell Me a Million Times' and 'Ice Cream Man Jr.' Matters grew even more complex with the 2010 release of a new (and aptly named) mixtape, *Patience Is a Virtue*, two new EPs (called *Famous Girl* and *Monster/Practice*) and the previously mentioned *Spring Break* College Boyys album (this being the same year in which Romeo rebranded No Limit as No Limit Forever and released the singles 'You,' 'She Bad' and 'They Don't Know': three songs that failed to reach any standing on the Billboard charts). In 2011, matters were further entangled regarding the now mysterious and fabled fourth studio album with the release of the (again aptly named) EP *Don't Push Me* and the mixtape *I Am No Limit* (previously the working title of the fourth album but now released in miniature). But this is also the Romeo of erratic film roles throughout the last decade, debuting in the 2001 children's film *Max Keeble's Big Move*, distributed by Walt Disney, and appearing in the 2003 film *Honey*, starring Jessica Alba, Mekhi Phifer and numerous rap and R&B musicians (receiving devastatingly poor reviews but debuting at #2 at the U.S. box office and garnering Romeo nominations for Choice Breakout Movie Star at both the Teen Choice Awards and the Black Reel Awards in 2004). The Romeo of numerous direct-to-video releases from 2004 to 2011, such as *Still 'Bout It, Don't Be Scared, Crush on U* and *The Pig People*, the Black Reel Award–nominated and NAACP Award–winning comedy film *Jumping the Broom* (2011) and the summer 2012 dramedy *Madea's Witness Protection*, directed by, produced by, written by and starring Tyler Perry. The Romeo of frequent television roles between the years of 2001 and 2011 on such series and specials as *The Brothers Garcia, The Hughleys, Raising Dad, Proud Family,*

One on One, *Static Shock*, *All Grown Up!*, *Ned's Declassified School Survival Guide*, *Out of Jimmy's Head*, *The Defenders*, *The Bad Girls Club*, *The Cape*, *Reed Between the Lines*, *Charlie's Angels* and *Dancing with the Stars* (originally scheduled to appear on the second season but forced out due to injury before filming and replaced, appropriately, by his father, only to compete alongside Chelsie Hightower in the twelfth season and reach the top five before being eliminated), but most emphatically and enduringly on *Romeo!*, the fifty-three-episode, three-season Nickelodeon children's series (filmed in Vancouver, B.C.) starring Romeo as the main character: a young aspiring rapper and basketball player managed by his father (played by Master P), and for which Romeo won the Favorite Male Television Actor award at the 2005 Kids' Choice Awards and received nominations for a Young Artist Award, a NAMIC Vision Award and an Image Award. The Romeo who, in 2007, signed a deal with the University of Southern California as a point guard for the college's basketball team, allegedly due to Romeo's personal association with DeMar DeRozan, now playing for the Toronto Raptors, who was signed simultaneously by coach Tim Floyd at the suggestion of Percy Miller, who insinuated that the two boys were in effect a package deal. While both DeRozan and and Romeo competed in the 2008/2009 season for USC, Romeo (playing as #15) played under twenty minutes over the course of two seasons and scored only five points: all in all, a catastrophic end to his sporting career and pretty clearly an example of power begetting power and big-money nepotism. This is also the Romeo of various charity endorsements, including *Variety*'s Power of Youth project, which raises money for the Starlight Children's Foundation and L.A.'s Best and places Romeo in the company of other young stars, including Miley Cyrus, Selena Gomez, Dakota Fanning, the Jonas Brothers and Abigail Breslin. The Romeo of Loco Tonic Energy Drink endorsements (mentioning the beverage in recent songs) and of various modelling gigs, appearing in the pages of *TROIX* magazine and on the cover of *Brave Mag*. Also the Romeo of a recently released tweet claiming he was 'The youngest to ever perform at #coachella. Shut it down!' before hitting the stage at Coachella 2012 with contemporary rap act A$AP Rocky and his father to perform P's 1998 No Limit hit 'Make 'Em Say

Uhh' to thunderous applause – a family and hip-hop reunion of sorts, enforcing the continuity of the Miller family and Master P's now classic, old-school status.

And by Abigail Breslin, I mean, of course, Abigail Kathleen Breslin (1996–), born on the 14th of April in the city of New York, New York, under the third, soulful decanate of Aries during a week of exciting filmic and literary activity, including the reign of bestselling novels such as James Redfield's *The Celestine Prophecy* (1993) and Nicholas Evans's *The Horse Whisperer* (1995) and top-grossing films such as *Fear* (starring Mark Wahlberg and Reese Witherspoon) and *James and the Giant Peach*, produced by Tim Burton (April 14 also being the birthday for renowned public figures Adrien Brody, Brad Garrett, Sarah Michelle Gellar, Loretta Lynn, Pete Rose and Anthony Michael Hall). The Abigail who appeared in her first motion picture at the precocious age of five, playing Bo Hess, daughter of protagonist and widower and ex-Episcopalian priest Graham Hess (played by Mel Gibson) and sister of Morgan Hess (played by Rory Culkin) in the M. Night Shyamalan sci-fi/horror *Signs* (2002), a box-office success for Shyamalan (garnering close to $228 million in domestic sales) and his fifth directorial feature. *Signs* being the alien-themed thriller in which Abigail's character, Bo, [Warning: Spoiler] enabled the destruction of the invading interplanetary creatures by leaving numerous glasses of water scattered throughout the Hess family home, allowing her uncle Merrill (played by Joaquin Phoenix) to douse one such intruder with the harmful liquid during the film's ostensible climax (such aliens were illogically and simplistically injured and/or killed by direct contact with water, infiltrating our planet unarmoured and unprepared despite the vast amounts of water vapour, rain and fresh and salt water across the Earth), and for which she was nominated for the Phoenix Film Critics Society Award for Best Youth Actress, the Young Artist Award for Best Performance in a Feature Film: Young Actress Ten or Under, and was praised for her performance by David Ansen of *Newsweek* magazine (however, like so many before her, Abigail had appeared in television commercials before her leap to the silver screen, debuting in a Toys 'R' Us commercial at the cherubic age of three). The Abigail named after Abigail Adams (née Smith, 1744–1818), First Lady of the United States and beloved wife of John Adams (1735–1826), second President of the United States and Founding Father, and mother to John Quincy Adams (1767–1848), sixth President of the United States. The Abigail named after this celebrated and learned woman of revolutionary times by Michael Breslin, father, consultant and telecommunications technician, and manager Kim Breslin (née Blecker, daughter of Lynn and Catherine, close-knit and loving grandparents from New Jersey and abiding today in Pennsylvania), the third and final child of the family and younger sister to Ryan Breslin, born in 1985, and Spencer Breslin, born in May of 1992 and also an actor, appearing in films such as *The Cat in the Hat* (2003), *The Shaggy Dog* (2006) and *Raising Helen* (2004), in which he played Abigail's sibling and Kate Hudson's ward. The rising actress Abigail who appeared in four other films in 2004 and 2005: the family comedy *The Princess Diaries 2: Royal Engagement*, the independent film *Keane*, the family film *Chestnut: Hero of Central Park* and the made-for-TV movie *Family Plan* (for which she received zero award nominations but was noted for her acting chops by various stunned and bored reviewers), and who also appeared from 2004 to 2006 on various uninspired television shows, such as *Law & Order: SVU*, *NCIS*, *Ghost Whisperer* and *Grey's Anatomy*. The Abigail who received, as all actors must receive, a breakthrough role – hers being in the 2006 critical and box-office success *Little Miss Sunshine*, in which she played young beauty-pageant hopeful Olive Hoover and for which she received *nine* major acting awards and *nine* nominations, including an Academy (for Best Supporting Actress), a BAFTA, a SAGA and an MTV. *Little Miss Sunshine* being the Academy, AFI, BAFTA, BFCA, SAG, WDCAFC, ISA and Palm Springs Award–winning film directed by Jonathan Dayton and Valerie Faris that grossed over $100 million at the box office and that recounted the blackly humorous exploits of a darkly dysfunctional American family (the Hoovers) as they band together in a VW Microbus to crawl across the desert toward the Little Miss Sunshine youth beauty pageant (an 800-mile journey from New Mexico to California) in which Olive Hoover (Abigail Breslin) is partici-pating [Warning: Spoiler] despite her rather roly-poly body shape and quirky precociousness and sexually suggestive dance number ('Superfreak' by Rick James, arranged at the encouragement of her heroin-injecting grandfather) and despite her various family members' assumedly bleak (and thus quirkily comical) emotional travails, including failed business investments, illness and heroin addiction, failed suicide attempts and intense Friedrich Nietzsche adoration: all in all, critically heartwarming. The Abigail who rounded out 2006 with three other films – *The Ultimate Gift, The Santa Clause 3: The Escape Clause* and *Air Buddies* (voice only) – only to receive two more major award nominations for her portrayal of Zoe Armstrong in the rather predictable and surprisingly glum Catherine Zeta-Jones/Aaron Eckhart romantic comedy *No Reservations* in 2007 (her only film appearance in that year). The Abigail who would continue to appear in romantic comedies (often as the biological or adopted child of one of the romantically entangled actors) or in family films throughout 2008, including the Adam Brooks–directed Ryan Reynolds vehicle *Definitely, Maybe* and the children's films *Nim's Island* and *Kitt Kittredge: An American Girl*. The Abigail who, by 2009, once again landed a leading role in a massively successful film, *Zombieland*, a 'zombie-comedy' (a genre recently resurrected by the Edgar Wright/Simon Pegg film *Shaun of the Dead* in 2004 but with clear precedents in previous decades, such as the *Return of the Living Dead* series) that co-starred Woody Harrelson, Jesse Eisenberg and Emma Stone as survivors of a zombie apocalypse (modelled after the scenario established by George A. Romero in his groundbreaking film *Night of the Living Dead* but featuring the accelerated 'zombies' of *28 Days Later*, which portrayed the victims of a rage virus and not undead creatures) who travel across the United States in search of safe haven – a film that received mostly positive reviews from gag-hungry, irony-infused critics and that grossed over $100 million in theatres. The Abigail who stormed the world of Broadway acting as a young Helen Keller, pupil of Anne Sullivan, in William Gibson's three-act play *The Miracle Worker*, during the months of February and April of 2010 at the Circle in the Square Theatre. Although Abigail was commended for her touching and realistic portrayal of a deaf-blind person, producer David Richenthal and company were criticized by the Alliance for Inclusion in the Arts for not casting a blind or deaf actor as Helen Keller; whether this initial storm of controversy reduced the allure of the play, or whether the theatregoing public was simply uninterested in yet another rendition of *The Miracle Worker* (often rammed down the throats of high school students and theatre students alike), remains unclear; regardless, the production lasted a mere two months due to lack of ticket sales and sent Abigail back to the moneyed remove of film acting, appearing or lending voice work to films such as *Quantum Quest: A Cassini Space Odyssey* (2010, voice only), *Janie Jones* (2010), *Rango* (2011, voice only), *The Wild Bunch* (2011, voice only) and *New Year's Eve* (2011). The Abigail who will appear in yet another alien-themed sci-fi film as Valentine Wiggin, older sister to protagonist Ender Wiggin, in the November 2013, Gavin Hood–directed adaptation of Orson Scott Card's science-fiction novel *Ender's Game*, which describes a future Earth endangered by invading alien (and ant-like) creatures known as Formics and recounts the rise of brilliant child soldier Ender Wiggin, spawning eleven (and a twelfth upcoming) full-length novel sequels, a dozen short stories and close to fifty comic books. The increasingly ambitious Abigail who now also writes and performs various benefit songs and pop tracks with her rather average-looking friend Cassidy Reiff as the pop duo CABB (still without official YouTube channel, Facebook page, website or Twitter account), who plan, as all pop acts must assumedly plan, to blow up and provide relentless earworms for the Top 40 hit parade in the second decade of the twenty-first century.

And by Helen Keller, I mean, of course, Helen Adams Keller (1880–1968), the activist, lecturer, author, socialist, academic and, most famously, the deaf-blind, born beneath the sprawling English boxwoods and strangling ivy, the cloying scent of magnolia and honeysuckle, rose and smilax, that cloaked the grounds of Ivy Green, the 640 acres of land surrounding the simple, white-clapboard home of Virginia-cottage construction on North Commons Street in Tuscumbia, Alabama, built by Helen's grandfather a year after Alabama's integration with the growing Union. The daughter of Arthur and Kate Keller, granddaughter of Charles W. Adams, ex-brigadier-general for the Confederate Army, distant relation of Robert E. Lee and of hardy Massachusetts stock, with familial roots stretching back to the cultural hub of Zurich, Switzerland. The little Helen born with the powers of sight and hearing but who was tragically stricken at one year and seven months with a bellicose inflammation and congestion of unclear origin that forever deprived her of these basic sensory gateways to the exterior world. The Helen who, although already capable of using over fifty gestures and signs to communicate (however crudely) by seven years of age, was destined for a more significant education due to the reputed linguistic successes of Laura Dewey Lynn Bridgman, of New Hampshire (formerly of Hanover), who was famously known as the first deaf-blind American child to gain a considerable education in language (reading and writing English) after receiving instruction from a Dr. Samuel Gridley Howe at the Perkins School for the Blind in south Boston, which was recommended as a suitable facility for Helen's education by the scientist, engineer, inventor and influential innovator Alexander Graham Bell, who was contacted by the Keller family at the recommendation of another doctor. The young Helen who was assigned to the tutelage of Anne Sullivan Macy, originally of Feeding Hills, Massachusetts, the twenty-year-old former student of the PSB (herself being visually impaired from trachoma), who arrived at Helen's cottage at Ivy Green in March of 1887 to reside with the Keller family and to provide Helen with a rigorous introduction to the world outside the black and silent prison into which she had been so cruelly sentenced by childhood illness (the Anne Sullivan Macy who would remain Helen's close companion and confidante for the rest of her [Anne's] life). The child-Helen whose portal to the hitherto enigmatic world of shape and touch relied upon grasping that people, places and objects (nouns) bore specific and individual names – or, as Helen was shown over many arduous and combative and frustrating lessons from Anne Sullivan – that these shapes could be differentiated from one another by unique arrangements of letters, drawn upon her open palm until the life-altering and moving connection could be made: that the letters drawn upon her hand *corresponded* with the objects she touched, that they had a physical *referent* outside of their own shape and feel (Helen's first 'word' understood being *water*, or W-A-T-E-R, associating the word with the feeling of cold well water pouring over her hand – as is dramatized in the 1957 telefilm, the 1959 Gibson stage play and [famously] the 1962 film *The Miracle Worker*, among other theatrical and cinematic interpretations, including the 1919 silent film *Deliverance* [not to be confused with the 1972 Burt

Reynolds/Jon Voight film of the same name], the 1954 documentary *Helen Keller In Her Story* [winning the Academy Award for Best Documentary in 1955], the 1984 made-for-TV movie *Helen Keller: The Miracle Continues* and the 2005 Bollywood film *Black*, which won dozens upon dozens of screen awards). The Helen who, once having grasped this basic linguistic notion of sign and signified, moved with Anne Sullivan in 1888 to the Perkins School for the Blind to receive instruction, and six years later to the Wright-Humason School for the Deaf in New York, from where she travelled to the Horace Mann School for the Deaf and Hard of Hearing in Allston, Massachusetts, where she learned from Sarah Fuller, of Weston, Massachusetts, herself a disciple of the teachings of Alexander Graham Bell (a determined advocate for the education of deaf and blind people). The Helen who enrolled in the Cambridge School for Young Ladies, now known as the Cambridge School of Weston (a high school in Weston, Massachusetts), at sixteen years of age, before gaining admittance to Radcliffe College, the women's liberal arts college, one of the Seven Sisters colleges and coordinate college for Harvard University, now known as Radcliffe Institute for Advanced Study (a college education funded by the industrialist, financier and philanthropist Henry Huttleston Rogers, a leader of Standard Oil, who was introduced to Helen by American writer and public speaker Samuel Langhorne Clemens, otherwise known as Mark Twain, who was a great admirer of Helen's efforts to triumph over her disabilities and a similarly committed anti-capitalist) and from which she graduated at the age of twenty-four with a Bachelor of Arts and the profound distinction of being the first deaf-blind person to ever earn such a degree. The intrepid Helen who continued to learn to sign words and to read Braille, and through discerning the vibrations issuing from other people's mouths during conversation, burned with a great desire to speak as others did, learning to understand what others said to her by placing her fingers (her sense of touch enhanced by her lack of vision or hearing) upon their faces; and with this method, she was soon able to articulate words, speaking for the rest of her life (albeit with the understandable distortions of a deaf person), and even giving countless speeches to packed halls of eager admirers. The plucky and courageous Helen who thereafter committed her life to the causes of the underprivileged, under-represented and overexploited. The Helen who eagerly joined and promoted the cause of the SPA, or Socialist Party of America (in particular, supporting the campaigns of Eugene V. Debs, a union leader and co-founder of the Industrial Workers of the World, who ran for presidency in 1900, 1904, 1908, 1912 and 1920 [this last attempt made from within prison]). The Helen of vehement suffragist, pacifist and socialist sympathies, working tirelessly against industrial oppression and capitalist exploitation, joining the Industrial Workers of the World in response to perceived inefficiencies of the SPA and conceived as the remedy for ongoing systems of oppression and subjugation that reduced the role of women, children, people of colour and those with disabilities to slavery, lending her assistance to the co-founding of the ACLU (or American Civil Liberties Union) and the HKI (or Helen Keller International organization) – despite such political and social efforts being routinely glossed over by American interpretations of her life and work in order to downplay the connections between oppression and capitalism, socialism and Christianity, that defined and motivated the rest of her life. The literary Helen of numerous and widely translated writings – most famously the 1903 autobiography, *The Story of My Life* (not to be confused with the 1988 Jay McInerney novel *Story of My Life*), written when Helen was a mere twenty-two years old while studying for her Bachelor's degree, and the text that provided the basic source material for *The Miracle Worker* and other dramatic interpretations of her turbulent youth. *The Story of My Life* followed, in 1908, by *The World I Live In*, giving its readers insight into Helen's day-to-day struggles and observations and beginning with a description of how it feels to pet and scratch her dog, claiming that 'in touch is all love and intelligence' (Helen being a renowned lover of canines throughout her life, even introducing the Japanese Akita breed to the United States after visiting the Akita Prefecture in the Tohoku Region of northern Honshu, Japan, in the 1930s, and falling in love with an Akita known as Kamikaze-go [and younger brother Kenzan-go] given to her as a gift from the Japanese government immediately before the global turmoil of World War II began, ending Helen's trips to the Land of the Rising Sun [and soon-to-be Axis power] for some time). *The World I Live In* followed in 1913 by a collection of socialist essays dubbed *Out of the Dark*, which was eventually followed by the story of Helen's conversion to Swedenborgian Christianity, *My Religion*, in 1927 (posthumously re-released as *Light in My Darkness* in 1994). The Helen who received the highest civilian award in the United States – the Presidential Medal of Freedom – in 1964, awarded to Helen by Lyndon B. Johnson, then President, and who was inducted into the National Women's Hall of Fame. The Helen who died peacefully in her sleep – sleep being the only time when, we may presume, she could see, or hear, regardless of what those images and sounds were, or how accurate, as with Milton in the heartbreaking 'Sonnet XXIII' – on the first of June (the birthday of Marilyn Monroe, Andy Griffith and Alanis Morissette) in 1968 at 3:35 p.m. at eighty-seven years of age at home in the town of Easton, of Fairfield County, Connecticut, accompanied by Winifred Corbally, long-time companion, who sat by her side while she drifted off into that last, gentle sleep. The Helen who endures in memory as one of Gallup's Most Widely Admired People of the Twentieth Century, the visage upon the 2003 Alabama State quarter, in name as the Helen Keller Hospital of Sheffield, Alabama, and as many streets in Spain and France and Israel and Portugal, and the enduring Helen Keller Services for the Blind. The Helen depicted in the Edward Hlavka statue in the United States Capitol Visitor Center, featuring her as a child standing beside the famed well of her youth where the linguistic connection was first made, the statue adorned with a plaque bearing her famous quotation, 'The best and most beautiful things in the world cannot be seen or even touched, they must be felt with the heart': a pedestrian-enough sentiment (and one no doubt copied and reinterpreted on countless greeting cards, fridge magnets, shared images on Facebook, picture frames, coffee mugs and dog sweaters) that, through its nauseating iterations and mass-produced expression, generally slides beneath the radar of conscious acknowledgement, becoming a part of the sentimental mush of capitalist apologetics and opiating reassurances, of the surface glut of meaningless information absorbed in each blink and breath; but we must remember that such mass production has denuded the profundity of such a quotation. This is the Helen Keller who could not see or hear; all aesthetic beauty – the face of a lifelong friend, the glory of a desert sunset, Handel's 'Lascia ch'io pianga,' Michelangelo's *Pietà*, the laughter of children – was denied her, utterly. The Helen who simply cannot have known whether the most beautiful things in the world could not be seen: she had to trust to the only beauty she could interpret and experience – which is an interior beauty, in its quiet surges of emotion and proud breakthroughs of intellect and moments of religious yearning, of faith. And part of our pity for Helen, the Helen who inspires in all mature observers a deep sadness as easily as she inspires awe and respect, stems from this quotation – do we *trust* her claim that the beauty of the *inside* can defeat the entire world without? And can we confront our sadness in reflecting on what our own hearts feel, or are incapable of feeling? Simply, is there anything inside us equal to or worthy of the beauty of the world? We trust that Helen's black and silent interior world is beautiful, tough, determined, disciplined and divine – the place that inspires all our admiration, adoration and even fear – more beautiful than, perhaps, a baroque aria or the roofs of Florence at dusk or the blue teardrop of the Earth from a satellite's photograph or the first cries of our newborn daughters and sons – perhaps. But this is also the Helen who is now a black space, circumscribed by the square parentheses of birth and death, ashes interred in the Washington National Cathedral in the darkness of the mausoleum next to lifelong friend and teacher Anne Sullivan, and all interior flowers lost to our imagination, passing into dust, leaving us to search our own stomachs for something to trade or offer to match the world in its variety and savagery – a world rising all the more indifferent to us in her absence.

WIDE AND BLUE AND EMPTY

June slips into her refurbished office room at 10:49 p.m., full mug of decaf steaming in her hand, and logs in to ICQ Messenger. Finding Chris offline, she minimizes the ICQ Messenger window (heart sinking slightly, but only just – their ICQ date is set for 11:00) and begins a game of e-solitaire, promising herself she won't wait for more than fifteen minutes before logging off and heading to bed.

It is silent on the second floor of June's 2,000-square-foot, semi-detached, four-bedroom home – a property of nine-foot ceilings and deep-set cold cellar, two-car garage and oak floors, gourmet kitchen and walk-in pantry – as she waits for her son, Christopher, living across the province in a tiny apartment in Ottawa, to log in to ICQ and to chat with her. June mouths the word warily – *chat* – feeling a delicious tingle of anticipation. Having bought the internet only three months prior, June still approaches the web as a wild and newfangled landscape, still tinged with the risks of danger and provocation. Every time she logs on she feels bold and daring, strangely and surreally modern. She feels especially sophisticated considering that she, fifty-four years old and feeling absolutely ancient, could actually be in a *chat room*, and that soon her son might join her and write her text messages *in real time*, his written phrases appearing in a cute PC window with its accompanying *Uh-oh!* sound bite. It wasn't exactly how she envisioned the future, but it was certainly exciting.

Now at 11:33 p.m., June stares into the ghostly illumination of the monitor, her hands bleached and spectral as she sips a second mug of coffee and her eyes leap from card to card, from hearts to clubs to kings, feeling strained and irradiated by the garish forest green of the card table, the bright light in the dark room. She minimizes the window mid-game and restores ICQ: Chris's name still *offline*, written in the red italics of ex-communication. June *tsks*, lifting the mug of coffee with her left hand while using her right to battle with the mouse that she bought (*stupidly*, she thinks) from a local Dollar Saver. Due to some malfunction in the mouse's ball, she is forced to repeatedly brush her wrist across her mouse pad (featuring a reproduction of van Gogh's *Starry Night*). She takes extra care with every left-handed sip, worried that she might dribble hot coffee across the keyboard: frying circuits, spoiling controls, corrupting mystery.

She tenses. Somewhere close – on her pie-shaped lot, perhaps, or near the cedar hedges of her yard – an animal begins to yelp. A raccoon, she guesses, listening to its high-pitched cries pierce the deep quiet of the Forest Hill night. She holds still, waiting for it to stop. When it doesn't, she closes the ICQ window, opens e-solitaire and resumes her game.

After Chris's most recent and rather disastrous visit home, June dared only a kind of *laissez-faire* motherhood – a most careful dabbling with 'his life' that was 'not hers' to order and correct. She continued writing him weekly email checkups and sending him occasional Hallmark cards with folded fifty-dollar cheques, yet now more conscious of the threat of smothering and more carefully aware of the freedom and flush of adolescence (case in point: Chris's frequent LiveJournal.com entries, blissfully unaware of propriety or decorum, detailing some debauched embrace in *what* untold alley of Ottawa on *what* untold substance ...). It's been a silent and suffering discipline not to call him at least biweekly to see if he's okay or eating well or getting enough sleep (those bags under his eyes, that stupid eyeliner and nail polish – who was he kidding?). Not that it seems to matter: his number keeps changing, or the number he gives her turns out to be a 'cellphone,' perennially low on batteries or forgotten in another pair of pants. In any case, Chris prefers longhand letters sent via Canada Post – 'we should actually *write* each other, Mom,' he said – which, according to June, communicates absolutely nothing of the moment (the way emails can at least transmit a sense of the living, breathing present). All denied for Chris's absurd love for the romantic, turning even a simple *hello, how are you?* into a Victorian chore.

And yet, despite her excitement over chatting, 'her pro-chat stance,' in Chris's terms, June is still somewhat leery of the internet. She has long ago mastered data entry and keyboards, word-processing and spreadsheets and presentations, but there is still something otherworldly and anarchic about the net. It's as if its hidden engineers – its gods of coding and HTML, silicon and microchips – are secret barons of porn and chaos, inimical to June or to anything she might stand for. As if at any moment she might stumble upon a scene of gore or obscenity, or arouse the attention of a mainframe-destroying virus. She knows such thoughts are inane, but still: there's no good government, no caring parents, online; it's the dominion of a million brilliant and hateful children. But her little sessions of sipping coffee and playing e-solitaire and staring hopefully at the ICQ window demand at least the semblance of *surfing*, of browsing the bizarre and daunting passages of the web. To do otherwise would be to allow the connection and opportunity to go to waste.

So tonight, as she has done for the past several nights, she researches a new recipe (for catfish), scans reviews for new movies now playing in theatres (*Billy Elliot, Dr. T and the Women*), hunts for directions to a new factory outlet (Fabricland) and refreshes her email inbox once every few minutes, to see if her friends from Vancouver or the office have sent her a joke or tame piece of political satire or warm-hearted meditation on post-divorce dating (always with a jab at Marcus, her ex) or advanced age, as if these subjects could be warmly received (age being especially *un*pleasant, and in no way amusing, though June always emails these friends and co-workers back to express appreciation for the joke or maxim. No, decidedly *not* pleasant, and *not* funny, and especially not helped by that *godawful* raccoon, now crying in what sounds to June like unrefined agony.

At 11:39 p.m., Chris's name is still red, offline. Forty minutes late. She minimizes the window and hits the RESET GAME option on the e-solitaire screen. The raccoon, or cat, or skunk, or demon, continues its violent protest against dying, alone and cold and likely in tremendous pain. June unconsciously covers her ears, bites her lip. *Fuck off*, she thinks, without anger, and with a swelling of pity. *Please.*

She is back to a somewhat stable routine, if a bit stultifying; the nights of wine and crying, hating herself and each of the last twenty-six years of her married life (great, self-pitying bouts of hatred, enormously silly yet undeniably grave) have abated, receded, as more time separates her from the moment of Marcus's sudden departure, with Chris across the province and increasingly withdrawn into his new world of friends and classes. With her hands on the keyboard, she looks to see if the room can be tidied, but it's never messy – not *messy-messy*, in any case, only a tad disorderly; and besides, she rarely sits in the office, it being the square room of masculine efficiency she subtly feels like she is violating (though Marcus has been gone now for five months, it still feels like his room – where he did his work, where he retreated). She stares at the black, flaw-less oak of the desk. She stares at the forbidding shadow of the closet, the metal shelf, the sticker of Minnie Mouse that Marcus once stuck to the side of the monitor (his old nickname for her). She stares at her hands, pale and ghostly in the ghoulish light of the screen. She turns over the mouse and peers into the plastic casing surrounding the ball, trying to see what roll of lint is causing the jam, but finds nothing, the problem lodged too deeply within the mouse's arcane inner workings to mend. She realizes that she hates the mouse, but she is afraid as always that she might buy a replacement that doesn't 'hook up' or correspond to the specific systems installed and she'll end up looking *stupid*, again. She imagines, in a moment of frustration, that maybe the reason Chris hardly ever appears online is that she has done something foolish to her ICQ configuration, something that limits their time together or blocks her ID or whatever. The thought of this – that the silence so obstinate and relentless between them has potentially been her fault, her own technological ineptitude – makes her feel even more frustrated, so much so that she craves a cigarette – a Camel cigarette, the brand she smoked a lifetime ago – and she wants to smoke it in the office and watch the smoke wreath through her fingers before the pale light of the screen. But she hasn't smoked in twenty years – some thoughts are simply *crazy*.

Halfway through another game of solitaire, an unwell 11:45 on the monitor and the animal croaking wetly beyond the window, June drifts back to Chris's LiveJournal page and scans his most recent update. At the end of his last visit home, Chris left for the Greyhound station in haste, leaving his username and password scrawled on a slip of paper and leaving himself logged in to his account on June's desktop – thus unintentionally giving June access to all of his posts, even those tagged as 'private' or 'friends only' (needless to say, June was not one of Chris's LiveJournal 'friends'). June felt somewhat unethical about reading them, but then again, she rationalized, *he* left himself logged in on *her* computer, and *he* was the one who'd (once again) left her waiting for another forty-five minutes on ICQ. This whole LiveJournal crap was even more bothersome for the hypocrisy of it all: why go on and on about longhand letters when you keep a daily web diary, and one barred from your own mother? June read, and greedily, feeling entitled to know.

His most recent entry described his plans for earlier tonight: he was heading to his friend Gloria's apartment around seven to watch a taped copy of this week's *Buffy the Vampire Slayer*. June had never met Gloria, though by scanning previous entries she gleaned that she was in Chris's journalism program. In fact, June had yet to meet many of Chris's new friends from Ottawa, and certainly no one from this new group described online – Chris, Gloria, a homosexual (!) couple named Ian and Blake, and another boy named Corm (sometimes described by Chris, in what surely must be some inside jest, as 'cute'). Chris referred to the five of them as 'the Scooby Gang,' which immediately sounded too twee and dainty for Chris, who'd spent his high school career in the dungeon-warmth of his basement bedroom with sci-fi and fantasy books and movies and comics, and gawking, greasy-haired role-players. Referencing *Scooby-Doo* was definitely weird for Chris; she felt it must be in some relation to *Buffy* (in June's estimation, a show so silly and ironic that its actors and writers must be laughing at their audience). Chris's new friends are definitely ironic, and artsy (all arts majors, or artists, or writers), and queer, and aggressively sexual and drunk and nonchalant about drinking and drugs and partying, and all of this comes out through the cheeky, affected style that Chris uses to compose his journal entries.

Lots of *Oh, hello there*s to start entries, or *ta ta*s to sign off. Black slang that would hardly suit the bookish boy from two years before: things were *pimpin'* or *wack* or *da bomb* – then shifting bizarrely into an uppity sort of British vocabulary – Chris was *chuffed* to see his friends, *knackered* when tired or *daft* to have missed a class. It was peculiar in general for Chris to even maintain such a self-exposing, extroverted platform – this is not the kid who left for Ottawa, not the nerdy, morose boy who hardly ever talked about girls and whose sense of humour was more darkly absurd than irreverent and 'saucy.' By now, *Buffy* should have been long over; he should be home. The most likely situation is that Chris has forgotten about their ICQ date, or selfishly prioritized his friends over his promise to his mother, but June begins to conjure that third, more distressing option: perhaps he is hurt, or in some kind of trouble. He isn't used to living on his own, after all. She stews, clicking the glowing solitaire cards in time with one of the raccoon's more hiccup-like wails.

If she ever catches Chris online *without* a pre-ordained meeting time – if something in the arrangement of planet and zodiac actually arranges to have her sitting in these rare, late-night moments at the *same time* as him – half the time she can tell he's absorbed in work because his typed responses are slow, staggered, similar to the way he spoke when he was fourteen, in bass monosyllables, as he stared down at his plate at dinner and his father ate noisily and heartily beside him. When he is so obviously distracted she waits for each of his responses with what feels like divine patience, eventually giving up on any opportunity for meaningful conversation with an ominous ache somewhere in her gut, and tells him that she loves him and that she (lying) *really needs to go*, which, ironically (an irony not lost on June), elicits his only quick response (*see ya!*) during their entire stilted conversation. Sometimes she gets angry, thinking that if he were doing something so important or distracting, he shouldn't have signed on in the first place. Or thinking, *Jesus, who does he think I am, some girl chatting with her friends in the dark? There's no one else here, he knows he's the only name on my list.*

But those odd instances of real conversation keep June coming back, hoping for that feeling of privilege and elation, the happy noise her fingers make on the keyboard that means the computer is really being used and enjoyed. She can simply sit and type, careful to never minimize their dialogue box between responses to avoid accidentally closing it. She won't, under any circumstances whatsoever, leave the room – even if her bladder fills in protest or the phone rings, someone calling without thinking that after a long, purposeless day at work she *might* not want to speak with anyone at all. She's done enough talking in the last five months, enough 2 a.m. phone calls with wracking sobs and avowals, to never again waste another minute. She can't leave the room. If she stops typing for the brief length of time required to pee or to tell her sister she'll call her back, he might get distracted, or he'll exit the conversation with only a brief *love ya mom, gotta go,* and she'll be unable to tell him once again to be careful or that she loves him, or, worse still (things could always be worse, worse), he might simply leave, and she'll be forced to message *Hello? You there? Where are you?* until she can't wait any longer, has to log off.

She stares at a LiveJournal entry, a nightscape photograph of Chris standing amid boys wearing bowling shirts (definitely ironic, she thinks) and khaki pants. Another boy rests his jaw on Chris's shoulder, a thin arm draped across his shoulders. Chris's dyed-black hair falls over his eyes and beer sloshes from a bottle, frothing over his black-painted nails. *This* is the person typing out the affected journal entries, the new voice he's taken up to introduce himself to the public: so different from what June knows is his *real* voice, which now and then comes ringing through the words on ICQ. This makes June most happy – and in full awareness of how it sounds, how wretched and pathetic she is to be feeling this way – that a chat window, a stupid *uh-oh* sound bite, and her son's broken grammar can lift her up from the solidness of the room, its square corners, its darkness. It makes her feel that life is indeed long and still holds an element of excitement, that they'll have many more years together, aging gracefully into better and more loving communication, that this separation and ongoing dispute is only a short, temporary adjustment. This makes her forget her office, the insipid interns waiting on her decisions, the work that is increasingly monotonous and cruel and completely uninteresting. It makes her forget her hands, wrinkled and pale and fat. It makes her think of a time when Marcus was younger, when he loved her, when his small habits were cute and sweet and not yet robotic and false (*my Minnie*, he used to say). June craves those moments of real conversation with such an intensity that if she could – if a legitimate exchange was guaranteed at least once a night – she would spend every evening like this, waiting in the dark, playing e-solitaire over and over, drinking decaf and surfing the web.

At 12:01, she finds herself growing restless. The animal – louder now, as if crawling toward the garage – makes a sound that June imagines to be a satanic effort to swallow its own tongue. She stands and makes sure the window is closed – it is. She sits back down, frowning through the screams. She realizes that a concession must be made – that she can't sit before the monitor all night, let alone another hour. She waits another sixty seconds, watching his name, imagining Chris in danger somewhere, stumbling through the city. Then she drags the cursor across the screen, signs out from the Messenger window and shuts down the computer. The screen drains of colour, as if cooling down, losing its heated definition. Then it slips to black. June has to feel her way toward the door.

She brushes her teeth in the yellow light of the bathroom, washes the makeup from her face, rubs a swath of white skin cream beneath her eyes. She undresses drowsily and slips into her flannel nightgown (the air having turned cold, spiced with the crisp smell of dried leaf, autumn rot). In the days and weeks leading up to the divorce, Marcus might have still been watching television in the basement, or maybe working with his papers spread across the dining room mahogany. She would know if he were in bed, reading. She'd know by the way he'd cough and clear his throat in his slow, shaky rattle. If he were in bed before her she would climb in beside him and roll to face the closet and the door. He might ask a few prodding questions, and she'd answer impatiently – unless, of course, she'd made contact with Chris and was able to tell him some detail about their son that would make him really listen. Tonight, with Marcus downtown in a twenty-floor condominium tower, she lifts the sheets and rests her head on the pillow, too tired to read, to think. She turns off the lamp on the night table on her side of the bed. She closes her eyes, imagining the pattern of Marcus's breath, the turn of a page.

Even with her ear buried in the pillow, June can still make out the ragged gasps of the animal. She decides it must be a raccoon – it has that squealing pitch, that almost-human scream, grating sporadically against the wave-like roar of her heartbeat, the tempting weight of sleep. She closes her eyes and tries to relax every muscle, until her body feels as thick and heavy as the nightgown around her. But her thoughts turn, vividly, to a memory, 1985, maybe '86 or '87: the way she used to put Chris to bed in similar flannel pyjamas, only patterned with He-Man or *Star Wars* characters, his specific companions in sleep. And just when her door was shut and the night seemed to close in for good, he'd rush back into their room, jumping crazily on their bed in wild, smiling transgression. She imagines him jumping, throwing his stuffed animals. He'd owned a stuffed raccoon, too. Or no – was it a fox? A bear? Something small and grey and furry, his arms around it constantly, there as protector and friend at night. Suddenly it was very important to know what it was, to tell the difference.

The raccoon manages to scream, wetly, every few seconds. The noise is too irregular, she thinks, too full of surprise, variation in pitch, to sleep through; and she was never a deep sleeper. But the noise also seems too ridiculously cruel to bear, so bottomless and wretched – some strange caricature of suffering. There again, the wailing. How long will she have to wait and listen? Marcus would have no trouble snoring through this, she thinks resentfully, but she sees herself writhing, at the end of her wits, until the hours begin to slide away in gradual terror and morning takes on a malevolent light.

At 12:25 she sits up and turns on the lamp. She slips into a pair of slippers and walks out of her bedroom, descending the curving flight of hardwood stairs. She reaches the quiet gleam of her stainless-steel kitchen and gazes over the indistinct furniture of her living room, caught in white curtains of moonlight. She can hear the animal's cries coming from somewhere near her hedges – the place where she grew tall, healthy tulips during last year's summer (a summer literally in another century, she thinks, the twentieth century, the last). She drifts to the cupboard, finds her flashlight and tests it in the murk of the foyer: on off, on off, casting mean shadows upon the door.

What the hell are you doing? The question comes breathless and sharp. *Are you going outside?* She imagines standing on the porch, the surrounding horror-movie glow of porch lights, the sharp white stones of the driveway beneath her slippered feet, the flashlight before her to ward off whatever it is – something dangerous, rabid, a skunk? *Then what, June? Are you going to call somebody, some animal rescue centre, to come stitch it up?* Not likely – with those noises, and for this long, it's obviously too far gone to save. Or she can speed up its suffering, end its misery. By bashing in its skull with a shovel, a rock? June knows that there is no chance she'd be able to. She can bury it, she thinks, when it's all over. At least she can give it that, but it's only the glimmer of consolation. What June really feels is relief: relief in her inability to make such a decision, confront something so elemental, and the guilty relief that she can stay inside and try to sleep.

She shivers, feeling tired, precarious. She can hear the mountains of dry leaves swirling in the wind, roaring up the drive with the sound of rakes scraping concrete. She imagines the animal, the blood on the soil. And she feels sure, all at once, that Chris's stuffed animal wasn't a raccoon. That it was probably a wolf – nothing so defenceless, so pathetically vulnerable as the dying mammal outside. Something savage and noble to protect Chris from monsters and nightmares, but only if he went back to sleep, if he stopped jumping on their bed. It wasn't bad behaviour or willfulness or rebellion – he did it only to postpone the moment of separation, the lonely privacy of dreams. It's been lodged in memory for over fifteen years, but it isn't something she's ever brought up. One memory that she knows is private, classified, something *just for her* – liable to be banished if ever shared with Marcus or even brought to words.

It was part of the long, rich record of June's secret life. Just as waiting, as she has done tonight – and as she has done for many, many nights – has become a long thread in the tapestry of her memory. She remembers living in a cramped ninth-floor apartment during her third year of university in Vancouver. She shared the two-bedroom with another girl: someone who spread herself across the city, in clubs from school and on dates with boys. June studied while she partied; she felt there was always something to shore up, something to save. And on many nights, June would sit alone on their balcony watching the night rain lance the city into steam and puddle, blurring the lights from downtown into vivid smears of blue and yellow, while she smoked and thought and waited, and an enormous, indescribable ache churned inside her, equal parts lonely and exquisitely sweet. Her roommate would return home in a great convulsion of dropped bags and cigarettes and conversation, cackling over what disasters or triumphs occurred among the night birds, and the exquisite core would diminish and harden and fuse to what June knew was her real life: the secret, most precious part of her, and forever private.

The best nights of my life have been spent alone, waiting, she thinks. *And keeping the pleasure and hurt of the waiting, the loneliness, to myself.* She thinks of Chris's storming of the bedroom, the jumping and throwing. Secret things.

'I'm going to give you a gift, Chris,' she mutters, and climbs the curving stairs, shuffles into the office and again boots up the computer. She waits through the screen's deliberate awakening, impatient to see the cursor move at her command. Once it's on, she opens her internet browser and heads to her email account. And she begins to compose a message: typing out the memory she has of Chris leaping on the bed and throwing the stuffed animals, taking her time to make sure it's just the facts, without embellishment, without undue sentiment. It takes her about ten minutes of thinking, typing, allowing the animal's death throes to fade to background noise while she works. When she is almost finished, she takes a moment to give herself some distance from the email, drifting almost automatically to the ICQ window, to the e-solitaire screen, to LiveJournal.com.

While Chris's name is still offline on ICQ, he has made another entry in his journal. The date and time (12:47 a.m.) and line breaks and general change in shape to his page slap June to attention. *So he's home,* she thinks. *Safe.* Relief drops her shoulders, makes her sigh in exhaustion. At least he's home, out of the cold. Inching closer to the screen, June rubs her neck and reads:

i wager i have made one of the biggest mistakes of the year. Thirsty Boy Thursdays, The Lookout (of course; need i say more?). all i can say is that things were said to, or attempted with, corm. even typing his name now makes me feel sick and stupid. it was just the rush of the music and the encouraging words and the drink (of course). and now back home early and the rest of them still there. the colour of the lights. gin!

fuck you, gin!

i figure i'm past the point of cliché, past the point of pity. it was easier to say what needed to be said back in august, accepting who i am, than i could ever imagine. but maybe it was too easy, too accepting, too PREDICTABLE. much love to the Scooby Gang, for sure, but where's the challenge?

if there was someone to talk to who knew this and could be a life coach or something. ridiculous. but there's no one since mr. a. moved to b.c. and i lost contact with r.

i feel like I'm lacking prayer or devotion or something.

being young is like that, we remind ourselves; sliding down to the future. there will never be another dawn I don't hate, another dawn i don't worship. learning and forgiving. every moment a rush. these days like flowers exploding! blooming explosions, the bloom and speed and sun coming up. heat! like in kerouac with the 'yes' chant on the road. morning's gonna be ugly, like a horror show, but I see it red and white and yellow and holy and rising up over the shitty hospital at the end of nelson street and I DON'T CARE who knows ...

true, it's horribly cliché ... being young ...

goodnight xo

June sits quietly for a moment. She scrolls down the page, somewhat disgusted: a wretch or a knot inside her, twisting. The cries of the animal return to their full-frontal tenor, demanding attention. She closes the LiveJournal page, signs out of ICQ and saves her unedited email to Chris in the Drafts folder of her Hotmail account. *Not tonight*, she thinks. *I'll leave this here.* It was easier to save it, to leave it alone.

She stands and walks to the window. The rising and falling of the circular winds push the raccoon's cries into a place firmly beyond her reach, into a place of unknowing. Her sense of powerlessness wells like tears. But rising now to meet it – her inability to stop the pain or the crying, her failure to be of comfort – comes a resolve to wait it out, to be vigilant. To be awake, and to bear witness. Though she is tired – tired now in great bone weariness – she has her imagination, and her will to wait, and the company of the dying thing, and the deep gulf of night, even with its wind and cold, and she knows the animal has her quiet, purposeful attention, however distant.

She thinks briefly of her morning, of the coming light, of work: a three-pointed star of pain and weakness. But she closes her eyes and presses her forehead against the glass, and with Chris – Chris with his drunken horizon, his youthful, pathetic flowers, his coming dawn – imagines her own clear space, her own clean air.

And suddenly and with great clarity she imagines skies that are wide, and blue, and empty.

THE LAND OF PLENTY

Date: February 9, 2005
To: Szychszczecin, Gary <gary.szychszczecin@subway.ca>
From: LNC <l.c.royale@sympatico.net>
Subject: Re: Advertising Arrangement

Dear Gary,

I've been considering your offer. It's a deal, man. You'll be helping me more than you can fathom. Sincere thanks to you (and your father) for thinking of me in my time of need.

So how about we jump right in. How's this, for instance:

If I decide to buy the small veggie subs (and by small, I mean the modest six-inchers), and I politely refuse those thin bricks of processed cheese (American cheese, they're called in happy commercials) or even the smallest dollops of mayonnaise or oil (called 'sub sauce' by those in the know) or other fatty and high-caloric sauces (Chipotle Southwest, say, or Sweet Onion, light of my life), and I have this assembled and rolled in Nine-Grain Bread with its roughish, earthy exterior and thin particles of flax seeds, then I can begin a new life – not necessarily a longer or more worthy one (for who can foresee the stupidities and vagaries of time: public transit dragging, falling ice, penis tumours, high-profile legal betrayals), or even a life remembered by a generational fetish group, or one preserved in pigeon-shit-splattered iron and bronze or in the pages of rotting, useless books that stand with jutting chins before the last fire or storm wipes away their synthetic inks, but a life that is now and then touched by beauty, and goodness, and occasional mercy, because SUBWAY, you obviously know the secret – that life is shit.

I know this isn't what you're expecting. But I think it would be a refreshing change of tone. You don't need to coddle people into eating your sandwiches. Plus, you know, it will keep up appearances – I have a reputation to maintain.

Forgive me if I sound defeated. Obviously things have changed: the thought of only $150,000 in savings stretched across another decade (but who knows – I may live for only another year) has necessitated some changes to my lifestyle. I have taken to using public transport – a Money-saving venture, surely, but one that maintains a sense of realism: there is no chance of transcendence on the subway, is there? Can you imagine me pressed into the common dark of the Metro, the local routes, the shuttles of the STM? Amid the armpit webs, the sneeze radiuses, the slow dawns of groping recognition? It's a weird scene. It's got me jumbled.

I forgot ugliness was *ugly*, Gary. Last night I hobbled from the subway to your SUBWAY dodging the usual spurs: black ice, passing Bixis, hurried elbows, my jaw chafing on my coat's cashmere caresses (reminding me to savour what's left of these luxuries), and wincing at the scream the buses make in their hot and endless suffering whilst ferrying the *shapes*. You know the type – shapes with eyes and noses and ears in the way, blocking my shuffle up the kneeling (*condescending*) bus steps, enduring the squeak and shoulder pain of bags and garments under the grey lid of the concrete sky that poets and pop stars call beautiful, and fording the rivers of filthy slush and cold that make the shapes miserable – all in search of your SUBWAY or some filthy route underground.

A study in ugliness: just last night I was treated to a withered mass weeping at the back of the bus, plastic bags slung under her parka'd arms, her Polish, razor-slit eyes as black as mass graves or as the charcoal sketches of a mother intertwined with lifeless children, hideously and unchangeably dead, mouthing words like *oh g-d I missed my stop oh no oh g-d no please no I missed my stop oh g-d no*. And the rage simmered and boiled beneath the parkas and bags of other shapes because of her pathetic blubbering and illogical outpouring of ancient emotions. I trembled here, worried I might encounter a sighting, a fan – someone for whom I would beautify, or reflect, or *make lyrical*, this dark bouquet of humanity. No one noticed or saw me – lucky. So I left her in the swirl and scream of another transfer while the concrete sky sucked tears from my eyes and the yellow light of your SUBWAY loomed on Mont Royal, beckoning me home.

I'll stop there – no more rants from me. It's just the thought of this, until the aching end. None of the comforts of old age, eh? No nest egg like your father's, no last summer idylls; simply dole lines, coupons ... But back to the task at hand: how about we end that first riff with this:

Believe me, brothers and sisters. I'll be dropping in to buy the six-inch veggie subs because if I choose the healthier options, I will lose weight and become healthy physically, and we all know mental health is a by-product of physical health.

Good? Let me know. It's great to be on board. And pass on my hellos to Dad.

Sincerely,
L. Cohen

Date: February 12, 2005
To: Szychszczecin, Gary <gary.szychszczecin@subway.ca>
From: LNC <l.c.royale@sympatico.net>
Subject: Re: Advertising Arrangement

Dear Gary,

We know things, man. Even with your PR, your corporate sponsors. Even with your cautious resistance to what you *know* is cutting edge. As pigs, we understand that existence is ignoble, hobbled by gooey mouth sores, pained erections, bladder infections, metal knees. Take your dad's body, now as bent as mine, but once so fresh-smelling, so strong. I have hooked my thumb and forefinger around the shriekingly white roll of flesh that now wraps my middle, given it a vigorous and horrified wiggle in my mirror's black reflection. Asked myself, *what is this shit?* and received no answer, save for the slow crunch of tires on midnight snow, my pulse's agonized march through these seventy-year-old veins. When did I become so *doughy*, so weakened by sloth's slackened jaw, gluttony's whimper and suck? It's enough closing my legs, averting my eyes, fighting the urge to pinch and punch. It's *enough*, Gary, without the raw remembrance of Money.

Money, Money. That sweet departed bitch.

Which is, I should say again, so generous of you to promise. And yes, sure, I don't have to say 'life is shit.' It's implied, anyway, with or without the curse. We're here about Money, after all, and not some sense of artistic integrity. Let me give you a lesson, if I may. Money is a proper noun; it should never be left so commonly lower-case (as SUBWAY, magisterial, is always written in all-caps). I used to imagine Money in a different way, as you might easily recall (I gave *back* awards, remember? Can you imagine me refusing the Governor General? Your father can, in any case). But that was a different time, a separate peace. I am now living post-Money, acutely aware of its absence, writing gospels and testaments to its return.

If only you could remember back, Gary. Your dad must have told you stories. There was Money when I was a child, when we were children, vague but comforting, padding the walls of the Belmont Victorian, the Westmount streets, falling through the leaves in the parks and ravines, painting the creeks with a golden foil. There was Money in the clothing business my father left behind when he died, Money in the Canadian Jewish Congress, Money in the gold watch that felt cumbersome and heavy in my prepubescent hand. And there was Money, of course, in McGill University, where polished heads (your dad and I among them) debated and sweated; Money in Columbia, in New York (the lonely skylines, the Manhattan imperium of the fifties) where I learned to fear the Law. All of existence seemed to conspire to keep Money and me as one thing. I was given Money's golden key, and all happiness lay before me as a ripening vineyard, the spice box of the earth.

And so blessed, I said Money didn't matter. I aspired to Money's rogue antithesis: art and song. Leaving school, I worked in factories, posing as a prole. A mentor published my first, most precocious poems; a growing Canadian house published a second round. I dipped into the Money from my father's inheritance, living without labour, and fled to Hydra, where Money preserved my stasis between the blinding white buildings, the cobalt sea. I lived against a wooden desk, a tiny window and four clean walls, bare of ornament. Women, sensing this rejection of convention yet the safety net of old, untapped, unceasing Money, unpeeled and parted in oiled assemblies. The bronze limbs basting in the light of Parc La Fontaine. The chestnut skin scampering from Greece's furious sun for siestas, for rest of wine-weary heads. It was the sexual revolution. It was the end of Money's dominion. I didn't need to talk about Money. I would talk about senses, morals, sins and music. I would *indulge*.

Today, I think back to those days of pleasure with a psychological, if not scientific, interest. If the brain can release the chemicals that make us happiest, who are we to stand and refuse? To instead weather, golem-like and insane, the groin-jabs of life's cruel, steel-toed boots? Money was created for pleasure, or at least freedom from pain; which amounts, squarely, to power: those in power *dole out*, rather than *endure*, the pain that marks this human passage. And what pleasures could I have afforded, what pains avoided, without the gilded walls of my Moneyed youth?

Each vinyl record a revolving golden coin, spinning out its riches, roaring out its privilege through the radio's cough. I worked in factories because it seemed noble, only to flee to Warhol's Factory in the Big Apple. It was the place to be; Nico and Joni and Judy all liked me. I could pluck a tune, give a poor performance a kind of ugly grace by putting my poems to song. So I slithered to Nashville, the Isle of Wight and Montreux, picking across the broken jaw of Europe, where bronzed imps played peekaboo among its shattered teeth. I arranged beautiful, strong-throated women to coo and cry over my once-nasally voice, now ground down into the dust of ten thousand cigarettes, a crushed urn of espresso. And after the love affairs, the Spector nonsense, the children, I turned gloomy, sad. Another lesson for you: time moves so quickly. All privilege makes us tired – tired of maintaining the illusion that we live for art's sake. I became the fedora-wearing prophet of pessimism. Mocked by people who'd never read a poem, watched my movies, heard entire songs. I retreated like an exile to a mountain to pray, telling myself that $400,000 a year for the rest of my years was a modest budget. Let my millions grow in investments, in bonds, accumulating for Adam and Lorca and their children.

What a sorry tale of Money.

Your boys made my complimentary sub this evening, Gary. I watched them weave it together, the hands of eunuchs, little sculptors in training. I ate it at home, spying out the window at the night's ice, but I was warm, hunched over the dribbling bun so recently raised from your ovens. And with each bite, a line was scored ever deeper into the broken earth. As on Baldy, when I offered prayers to nothingness and stripped my bloated soul of Money's sinful chains (another Moneyed privilege I was only too happy to indulge), my resolution stands. We can work this out, man. People will love my endorsements. They'll be charmed, baffled, in love with the irony. So how about this (a longer ad, maybe, or a serial web thing; imagine throat singing as background):

> Brothers and sisters, if I stick to the veggie subs, stripped of their sweet processed cheeses and oily condiments, the artery-jamming steaks and fatty chicken strips (the temptations of *egg mayo*, for starters), and I complement such discriminating, self-denying eating with regular cardiovascular exercise (such as organized jiggling or repetitive squatting, heart-rending, puke-inducing), and I avoid the chocolate chip and peanut butter cookies rising tumescent and spheroid to imbue the restaurant air with the doping scents of *home life* and *childhood*, standing as half-true, half-mythic residuals of something that once was, once breathed; and yes, I avoid the Doritos and Lays salty-crisp products that line the self-serve rack near the soda fountains of bubbly Coca-Cola products and their safer, wiser, diet alternatives, such as

Coke Zero and Diet Coke, then I may lift myself from the muck of the quotidian, the venial, the curse of the white flabby roll around my middle. The curse of the *pud*, my friends – Cheetos-fuelled, beer-braced, blind and albino.

For what can SUBWAY suggest for a shape drowning in a vale of tears? For a shape tiptoeing over the cracked concrete, eyes averted like a beaten horse in a burning city, nosing nutrient-deficient roots, riderless skin stretched over starved ribs? Eating the suicidal microwave dinners, the gift-wrapped meals reserved for local masturbators and the criminally insane? It suggests something incongruously fresh, my friends – making it new, renovated, redone. It means getting clean, bathing in baptismal soda water that wipes away the sins of your personal dirt, dislodging each vile image stored in your overheated brain's pixie-filled spank bank. Let us commend their practice, brothers and sisters; let us rub each sub topping [and here I'll rub my fingers and thumb in the universal sign for dough, dollars, Money] between our minds' fingers like prayer beads of some dismantled religion …

Watch the way they cut the bread, toss the open loaves into the ovens. Watch with delight as they coax the ingredients into *being*. Take the cheese slices, for example; watch them take advantage of their natural isosceles design by tessellating the triangles to provide maximum sandwich coverage – something so often overlooked by common sandwich artists. Take the tomatoes, say, those exacting slices without excess seeds or bloody innards – simply the most appetizing shades of supple crimson, recalling barrack row upon barrack row of hothouse hydroponics, rich and water-bloated earth, a hazy humid flush. Sun-dappled, pliant to thumb, to piercing nail. Cuts of green peppers bursting with cell-trapped moisture, irregular design of bell-blossom and tapered tip, sitting St. Patrick's Day green on their soft beds of shredded iceberg lettuce, green-white and holiday-pale, adding fibre and refreshing addition to any encompassing bite. Cucumber discs slung onto the rising assemblage, their slick towers of vitamin A and B and antioxidants tumbling over the edge of the bread in bounty and gladness, in cucumber and pickle *too-muchness*, in supper-table providence. And it's all for you and me, paying customers, the receivers, and I am for this small suggestive millisecond happy, not because of a vaunting ambition or achievement or because I can in any way avoid the void, the shit-filled abyss we skirt in the groaning commute through our meagrely allotted months and decades, rubbing against skin for warmth and avoiding violent shapes, collapsing our way out of time, but for the reassurance and small comfort of daily improvement, of sticking to a goal, of ironing out a weakness in the flesh because that's all I am and have: this, this *pud*, brothers and sisters (here I will point to my stomach), the dross of which SUBWAY is helping me burn away through study and discipline and through the salty, meat-replacing consistency of green and black olives – the marbles and jewels of the sub, nestled between tomato and green pepper, in rocky clusters or lone, noble outposts, onyx and emerald rolling in excess onto the cutting board, forgotten by a plastic-gloved swipe into the attendant trash bags. And yes, let us take jalapeños and banana peppers, those vibrant reds and screaming yellows, spice to light the tongue with end-of-days passion, with a deep burn that cries *plucketh me not!*

You can take an excerpt from that. Rearrange it. Change or add. It doesn't matter. But just think – you could have a sensation, and overnight. That shit would go, as some might say, *viral*.

Let me know what's working, what isn't. Many thanks again for the voucher for unlimited subs in lieu of my first official cheque. It's allowed me to get into character, so to speak.

Sincerely,
L. Cohen

Date: February 20, 2005
To: Szychszczecin, Gary <gary.szychszczecin@subway.ca>
From: LNC <l.c.royale@sympatico.net>
Subject: Re: Advertising Arrangement

Dear Gary,

Before I make the following comments, I want to remind you that each and every time I limp through your doorway (for another freebie, granted), I feel blessed. Really – this isn't the character speaking. There have been so many betrayals, so many assassinations of character. They are trying to take my entire retirement – both Greenberg and Lynch now, as if entangled, venomous – as if to remind me to never trust a snake.

Last night the slush froze over and fresh snow fell. The SUBWAY sign shone through trillions of snowflakes, dazzling crystals, and for a beat I was moved, feeling the light millipedal dance of flakes on my face, waiting beneath that warm glow of neon before the scent of fresh bread and melting cheese again sharpened my focus, turning my thoughts to the task we have before us and of the generosity you have shown me. So I'm not complaining, is all. I care about what we have, the agreement we've forged. I care about you, too, though I've been a bastard to your father so many times over so many years. I give thanks to have a friend as generous, as forgiving, in the wake of Kelley's low betrayal – someone whom I thought was closer than a friend.

Nevertheless, I feel that *in order* to be your man – to send this thing viral, to blow it up – I have to *believe* in what I'm saying, if only for a second. The ancient cliché: a nugget of golden truth beneath every mountainous lie. I can *imagine* your labour as noble, can *picture* your fare as edible, even delicious, and I can definitely *attest* to its value, as Money and as a brand. I've never really seen SUBWAY as what it could be. I've never imagined its highest ideal, its striving for consumer happiness, for a kind of perfection – and knowing its (your) prouder aspirations, the Money returned to the happy pocket, I can now begin to see its real deformities, deformities like burnt, wrinkled flesh, requiring a smoothing, cooling hand.

Let me explain. Last night, while expecting the kind faces of your usual eunuchs to emerge from behind the ovens and welcome me as confidant, I was greeted by a new understudy: the short and soft shape bearing the name tag *Dwayne*. Dwayne did not make eye contact with the patrons in line before me; whether this is indifference to your customers or reverence for the toppings and tools, I cannot determine. But when I arrived to take my turn and redeem my voucher, Dwayne's reddish eyes locked with mine. Between us passed a current of palpable disgust: my frustration at the long line, missing a more familiar employee – perhaps only by mere moments – and what can only be described as a radiating terror from him (this was clearly not the recognition of a fan). As soon as eye contact was made, his gaze zapped toward the cutting board. I could barely hear his dully coughed *How can I help you*, uttered as if to the ignorant tomatoes.

It was obvious that Dwayne, understudy shape, did not relish my arrival, but I nevertheless proceeded to order my six-inch veggie sub (getting, once again, into character, and taking advantage of your generous gifts).

'Uh,' Dwayne gurgled, 'no more Nine-Grain or Whole Wheat …'

Predictable, yet frustrating – you see, this shouldn't happen at what (I've been told) is a flagship restaurant. I closed my mammalian eyes, rubbed taut fingers against my temples. 'Very well,' I croaked. 'I will take the … the Honey Oat.'

This request served to whip Dwayne into a tremor of activity, whacking open the oven door and coarsely grabbing a log of bread. Before I could choke out the words *Slow down!* he had gutted the loaf with all the delicacy of a marauder's broadsword swipe. The bread was cruelly butchered: an uneven sawing down its middle leaving an asymmetrical mess that meant certain sandwich collapse in my clawing hands (which had, of their own accord, inched up the sides of my face to intertwine in anxiety over my brow).

As soon as the bread hit the board, Dwayne's plasticky fingers went rifling through the stacks of triangular cheese. 'No!' I cried, mouth hanging open and pathetic. The shape *assumed* that I wanted cheese! More depressingly, he *assumed* I wanted *mozzarella* cheese, and not Swiss or cheddar! He dropped the slice back onto its pile at a canted angle.

The radio crackled with white noise and pop (was it? oh g-d, it was – a cover of 'Hallelujah') as my heart thundered in my chest.

'Ve– … Veggies?' came the shape's next halting question. I licked my lips, exhaled. Perhaps not all was lost.

'Everything,' I said, with sub-standard confidence, and was treated to the most frantic, careless and antagonizing sub assembly I have ever witnessed. Oozy tomatoes were tossed with something akin to hatred; lettuce was piled as if Dwayne were yanking and discarding clumps of pubic hair from a shower drain; olives rolled about the board like gasping, severed heads in an evil Chinese dynasty. I squealed loudly: something high-pitched, whiny, cat-like (and what would Roshi think of my display?). And while Dwayne massaged and beat my poor sub, I stared at his downturned face, studying his features: his thin hair without net or visor, left to fall over his pimply, oily forehead; face dusted with the barbed facial hair of a tarantula's rump; and lower lip (oh Gary, such lips!) hanging red and pendulous (as if bee-stung, albeit without such attractive, feminine connotations) over his frenzied work, a thick welt of flesh that hung preposterous and awful, immediately recalling nothing short of *glans* – yes, obscene penile glans – but glans afire with sunstroke or a burning herpes (and here I recall old Layton). My palm clamped over my mouth as dry heaves seized my stomach. He began yanking at the condiment tray. 'Just mustard!' I squeaked from behind my fingers, and was *certainly* given mustard: an over-opulent belch of the stuff that drenched the bread and veggies and paper itself. And before I could stop him from proceeding, Dwayne squeezed the mess together and wrapped it hurriedly to-go, jamming it into a plastic bag *assuming* that I would be dining at home or away. I could see moisture and mustard seeping out the ends of the wrapped roll. I would most definitely encounter cata-strophic sandwich collapse. I would have to reassemble, get my fingertips stained and greasy, get mustard on my pants.

'Five dollars,' the shape whispered (the voice now a scuttling sow bug in some derelict laundromat), gesturing toward the electronic cost display. I handed him my voucher, my forever-coupon explaining that this would be *on the house*, which he took from me with another shudder. And before I could hook my fingers around the bag's carry hole, he held out a thin, glossy brochure that I stuffed into the pocket of my hay-smelling cashmere coat as I limped out the door, feet scuttling along the mud-puddly linoleum, in need of a mop.

Just to let you know, Gary, how things are. After all, you are the manager, an executive, and responsible for so much. I know you have to be out of the shop for countless important meetings, but it's hard to really *relish* the experience of being your spokesman if you've got people like *Dwayne* on your front line. Really. I want to embody this company without reservation, to enter into a financial situation – something I've always discredited as beneath my interests – with all my renewed respect for Money's dominion. Let us forge ahead without these stupid mistakes wrecking our endorsements.

Sincerely,
L. Cohen

Date: February 23, 2005
To: Szychszczecin, Gary <gary.szychszczecin@subway.ca>
From: LNC <l.c.royale@sympatico.net>
Subject: Re: Advertising Arrangement

Gary,

Let us be honest. Today is … hideous. It's something I think you can understand, or at least you did. I haven't had a drink or a line in months, but I woke up to a hangover: a wincing, raking heat behind my eyes, an inability to move (the Torah says we move in g-d, so I understood this to be a form of Gehenna). Is this an after-effect of daily subs? Am I being poisoned, slowly, into solidity? Anjani seems to think so: she claims I smell like mustards and oils, despite our baths and salts and incense. Like *mayonnaise*, despite my denials. She left last week for Israel, claiming to need a different air. How I must disgust her: sour in my poverty, my post-Moneyed geriatrics.

But I climbed from bed, missing her olive warmth, her whispers, slurping cool water to dull the heat of my headache. Bored, and with the blank day before me, I read your recent email.

Gary. Are we being serious?

So unexpected, it sent me out-of-doors. I needed to clear my head of your change of plans – your 'announcement.' And do I have to describe the scenes I witnessed, sniffed, rubbed up against along le Plateau's grey February? Or do you still understand the basic plight, the fundamental diseases, of who we're dealing with here? I'm not entirely sure if you do, Gary. Let me remind you of your clientele.

The shapes had donned their dour commuting masks, and all at once there arose the hive-mind crackle of *suicide* and *last-ditch gambles* and vast religious brocades, precious things, precious missed sleep in each eye and yawning mouth dragging the dull metallic air into *daymare*. Hurt and angry shapes listened to their static earphone music so loudly that their artificial beats competed for control of the stale busmosphere, mirroring the centre of the insane universe and its endless pan-piping. A tiny shape screamed in tickle and radiator discomfort. A beaten, spider-grey shape gurgled, *Don't trust anybody*, again and again against the nape of my sensitive neck until I was aquiver with her delirium and demons.

All of this to give that email some distance. Hurtful, too, that the glossy brochure that *Dwayne* slipped me already trumpeted the same wrongful turn (and oh, how I wish I hadn't searched my pocket, rifling about for loose change or a crumpled bus transfer). I will not lie, saying that I kept my composure, seeing that the plans were already in effect and without a word of consultation. Performing a series of breathing exercises, I rode the bus past my usual stop, the seats around me swiftly vacated. I puffed, I wheezed. I needed to know more – I needed to know the grubby, corporate details, beyond what your email offered – and suffering from Anjani's absence, my own sad rooms, I rode to the public library to think.

Reaching that stone ruin, I scuttled through its pretentious double doorway. Crossing the grey sensor gateway, I endured the revolting recognition on the wrinkled face of the shape behind the desk when I asked to use a computer system, to log on. Around me, your clientele assembled: peanut-faced shapes drooling in detention corners, lost in headphone skull fog, or muttering to themselves in prisons of personal hiccups and rhythms. A clown shape wore mismatched patches of leather and denim, a flat hat and scarlet political pins. Someone screamed, warbled, *tabarnac*. A child shape fell down a flight of stairs. It smelled like a burning circus. I clutched my parka'd torso in the germy, grotty men's room, getting it together, as a small horde of autograph seekers hiked up their collective courage to ask me for a scrawl (*these* people, Gary – we're not dealing with angels).

So let's confront the matter head on, and forgive me my distempers and preambles. There's so much to deal with these days – days that should be spent in sun, in the thralls of epic, old-age naps. It wasn't long before I found what you and the brochure so gaily celebrated. SUBWAY CAFÉ, 'an upscale upgrade to your local sandwich joint,' or so you declared. SUBWAY CAFÉ, 'a cross between a coffee shop and a sandwich shop.' 'SUBWAY CAFÉ, SUBWAY's yuppie, toolish stepbrother,' or so an observer wrote in a snide column online.

Say this isn't so, Gary. Say that you wouldn't stoop to *assuming* your regulars – the steady clientele who consume your subs, who respect the value of the exchange, if not the taste of the meat – require some sort of status upgrade, some sort of urbanite ego boost. That this class-based elevation necessitates a trade-in of your tried-and-true Formica and sturdy faux wood and shadow-destroying lighting. (For isn't SUBWAY's nighttime glow our best protest against the inevitable dark?). I cannot believe that the stolid drip coffee you've served for the last many years is now no longer good enough for your jaded shapes, whose cancerous and entitled tongues require a more piquant or citrusy or aromatic or 'full' or 'bold' flavour (or whatever the voguish adjectives may be, lisped from the menus of unnameable chains that pretend to deliver 'culture,' that barren slut)? What new forms of halitosis to be breathed onto my neck, what mirroring of this morning's spider-grey mumbler? Why promise a hideous spread of overpriced, milk-watered lattes and mochas and macchiatos and americanos and cappuccinos, artificial candy water picked by tired migrants? An array of imported teas with their precious attempts to situate the sipper in some kind of Eastern paradise, branding their lucre with insulting names such as Zen, or Lotus, or Awake, or simply Calm? How insulting. What will become of my hard-backed, unbreakable seating, the kind that subtly encourages boorish shapes to eat their subs quickly and *leave*? Replaced by cushioned stools and chairs, mid-century modern, leather surfaces. You promise fake bricks, the illusion of an unfinished wall. You provide pictures of bookshelves – bookshelves! – as if any of your regular shapes wish to browse the hollow spines of literature (for what else could you offer them – science? Physics? History? *Art*?). Oh, Gary: a fireplace? Wi-Fi internet access? I imagine a nest of adolescent shapes plugged into plastic computers, filaments dangling from enormous ears, sipping the 'best' coffee the ruins of Seattle have to offer. Hours of this crowding, this congregating. You throw your jewels before swine, Gary, if you move ahead with such a venture. You lose the heart of the restaurant by courting the café, the fetishists who pretend to philosophy while scrawling in their chain-store journals and notebooks, casting guilty eyes at other lonely monads picking away at work or their useless educations in the liberal arts.

And above all, you lose the *irony* of my role as celebrity endorser. I am in a particularly specialized position here, pimping the subs. Don't you think there've been enough cash-ins on my coffee-house mystique? I take this as a real blow, a real insult to my integrity – and perhaps a larger and more emotionally charged blow than someone else might feel – but you *know* I'm sensitive these days, man. You should read what Kelley's been saying about me. Hateful stuff. And this is after almost seventeen years of business, correspondence, even love. You know about our little 'thing.' She's even claiming I arranged a SWAT team to raid her home in Cali, arrest her in her bikini and take her to an asylum (only half-true, after all). Thank g-d I'm strong, that I've got that molten core. Otherwise, I'd be a wreck.

I need time to think, Gary. We should talk about this. I'm too sensitive at the moment to decide whether we should continue building our campaign. We were on to something great (even with Dwayne involved) ...

Sincerely,
L. Cohen

Date: February 25, 2005
To: Szychszczecin, Gary <gary.szychszczecin@subway.ca>
From: LNC <l.c.royale@sympatico.net>
Subject: Re: Advertising Arrangement

Dear Gary,

I've been accused of conspiracy, defamation, extortion. I've been accused of blowing it on extravagances – as if I've been living like Michael Jackson, for g-d's sake. I'm vulnerable from both sides – with Kelley on my left, and Neal Greenberg on my right – and now it seems I'm running out of friends. The Money's all gone, they're saying ... *gone*. Anjani hasn't returned my calls to her hotel room. Sharon's similarly indisposed, in New York for backing vocal tracks. All the profits from the albums, the tours, the appearances: gone. As if *I've* been the one to mount a conspiracy or break the law ...

So, for the purposes of maintaining our ties, the friendship between our families, please allow me to retract that last letter. The stresses, Gary, have been almost too much for one old man to bear. I wrote out of passion when a cooler head should have slowed my hand. Maybe it's all the mustard: thinking on veggies and toppings. Please forgive me, friend.

So I'd be happy to advertise anything you want. If you need a song, or an appearance, I'm yours. Let me warm my joints by the crackling fires of SUBWAY CAFÉ. Let's raise a toast to the fine coffees and herbal beverages that warm the mouths and bellies of your literate, romantic clientele. By all means, let's throw on a little jazz, read a snatch of poetry and stare at the moon.

Yours, in humility, and in good faith.
L. Cohen

Date: March 9, 2005
To: Szychszczecin, Gary <gary.szychszczecin@subway.ca>
From: LNC <l.c.royale@sympatico.net>
Subject: Re: Advertising Arrangement

Dear Gary,

My apologies for not returning your emails and calls sooner. I've been extremely busy over the past few days and weeks attending to legal matters in California (as well as a nasty cold – I feel a bit devastated, to tell you the truth: as if pulled apart, frazzled, despite my new tan).

Instead of stringing you along any further – more than I already have, to my discredit, and remorse – I'll simply come out with it: I am going to have to decline any continued participation in an endorsement deal with your restaurants. Believe me – it has nothing to do with you, or with the direction you've taken the SUBWAY franchise, or these new plans to open the café line. I've decided to pursue other Money-making ventures, is all. I hope you can forgive me for wasting your time. And please let your father know that this is, of course, nothing personal.

Now equipped with a tighter, more competent legal staff, I've made some important choices regarding my career and financial options. Last year I made the ridiculous (but understandable) decision not to promote *Dear Heather*, but that was before all of this legal nonsense. I haven't made a public appearance in, what, twelve, thirteen years? And yet there are websites and fan clubs and message boards devoted to tracing my movements, for fans to follow me around and stake out my home. People are rabid for my anti-Money messages from the last forty years (people who eat at SUBWAY and people who do not – it really doesn't matter, in the end).

So, first, we're putting out a new album. I am still sapped for songs, but Anjani's been sitting on a store of great tracks – we're going to get them into shape, record and release them as soon as possible. Co-written, of course, by me. Anjani's returned from her trip, no doubt appeased by my decision to seek better counsel and to put my shoulder to the wheel. The record will be out (we hope) sometime in 2006, if you're at all interested. Should sell enough copies to help us start climbing out of this pit.

Second, we're getting the band back together! I'm not sure when, or exactly how, but I've decided to lighten up and put aside my reluctance to tour. If all goes according to plan, we should be able to book a world tour by 2008. Can you imagine how fast tickets will fly? You'd be surprised at how eager some of these fans are, how rabid, from Dublin to Toronto to Dubai.

Third, I'm back to the scribbling. A way to deal with the nightmares of our post-Moneyed world. No exaggeration, Gary. Poetry saves, despite what I've said to you about art's inability to relieve the grinding pressures, the terrors of poverty and old age. I'm even drawing pictures. Pictures! I sent around some feelers and I've already got a bite from a publisher – one of the first to publish my work, back when things were happy and young. You should see a collection by next year. I've already got a title: *Book of Longing*, a testament to my time of crisis, to when the world turned against me, and all I had was hope. You and your dad will surely be thanked in the acknowledgements.

I'm also in the process of filing a civil suit. Don't worry – I won't bore you with the details, won't jeopardize our relationship by involving you in its intricacies or confidentialities. But rest assured, Gary, that I *will* see some measure of justice, if only to sleep happily at night knowing my suffering has been considered and heard. Word has begun to leak; *Maclean's* is asking about the story. I think I may go public, blow it wide open, before Kelley or Greenberg can start besmirching my name.

Which brings me back to us. Once again, thank you for your kindness, your generosity, your fealty. Know that I am resolved to pay your franchise back for every *gratis* sub that I ate while thinking all my money had vanished – and it was many, many subs, over many days. My garbage bins are still overflowing with white, green and yellow paper! I started to feel a bit strange last week – a bit insane, to be honest. I'm happy to be back to my regular soups, my dicing, my local grocers. It felt as if my brain were overheating – I was even dreaming of stabbing Dwayne, of reaching across the counter and grabbing one of those green-handled knives ... how absurd ...

Not to insinuate that your product is unhealthy, or foul-tasting, or soul-destroying. Far from it – it kept me afloat when everything in my life began to lose meaning. It was a kind of loneliness, Gary, but you were there to give me solace, to provide a comfort in my confessions. I saw strange things while thinking of subs. The world seemed composed of a cruel geometry. I woke in the late mornings to the dim notion that everything – the clock, the table, the heaps – were arranged by some unseen hand. That everything around me was *put there*, so to speak; even the shapes crawling toward senility (or another sub) seemed part of the palette. Yet whoever or whatever assembled it all was obviously insane, or painting while asleep. I felt – and please don't take this the wrong way – often trapped in a slasher film, its plot beating an illogical metronome. The pulse of trees cried for more weeping, a weird mandate for blood. It was a daze, and I marched through the city convinced of its falsehood and intemperance. A geometric mess.

No wonder I wrote of public transit, and shapes, and toppings. No wonder. Though terrible, I realize now that I will miss this time. A time when you and your father seemed my only true comrades. I can safely say, and without exaggeration, after so much falsehood and exaggeration, that I love you, young brother, as no other. And I will miss the bizarre picture of me in a SUBWAY polo, visor pulled low over my eyes, squirting more mustard onto Nine-Grain bread.

I hope you find who and what you're looking for, Gary. And I wish you all the Money in the world.

Yours, always,
L. Cohen

LAST WORDS

The doctor points to an X-ray of my lungs, circles an area near my trachea. The office air goes queer – pressurized, headachy – as she opens her mouth to speak. *Tumours*, she says, delicately, as if invoking the name means invitation. *Here and here and here*, tapping the photograph, signalling the first signs of a cancer that may spread from my lungs to my throat and to my brain. *Or not*, she adds, careful; *we can't predict the process of the disease.* So, they might otherwise head south, passing through my capillaries to leech into my stomach, my liver, my pancreas. They may shrink, or they may just stay put, grow to the size of ripe plums in my chest.

Who knows? Once you've got a weed, I'm thinking, the whole lawn is lost. I've spent enough time gardening, knees and hands stained with soil, to know how the whole grisly show operates. One arrogant yellow bloom pokes its tufty head out of so much healthy green, and then there's a legion. But these weeds aren't happy yellow dandelions, won't fade to spidery white filaments that blow to bits at the end of summer. And I can't simply rise and retire, put away my tools and abandon the manicured fight. No, the next few months will be shadowy, elusive, spiked with the brooding talk of tumours: morbid entanglements of *humour* and *tomb*.

The doctor has a beautiful smile, I think. All laugh lines and condolences. Like my wife, Katherine, seemed when she was most happy: as if in some other universe, her knees pressed into the supple earth, dappled sunlight falling through her straw hat as she looked up to me with a squirming worm on her spade. The doctor's hand rests comfortably over mine, her wedding ring cold and hard against my knuckle; her eyes say *I'm sorry*. We make another appointment, give a tentative *yes* to chemotherapy, to waiting lists, to making an informed decision.

I leave the clinic and walk to my car. I buckle my seat belt, slide the key into the ignition, and watch the skies clear and the sun finally peer through the clouds: two weeks of rain and fog and now this radiant white light, this delicious, stirring warmth. Yes, I have cancer, stage four, terminal. Before the summer is over I'll be dead. I've been living with the pain and the sleep-wracking coughs and the fatigue for many months – bottling it, explaining it away – but now there is no more room for postponement, for avoidances, for *maybe it's something else*. I have not smoked a cigarette in fifteen years, but twenty years of smoking have finally caught up. Strange now, to think of cigarettes, relics of an older, brighter world ...

The next week passes in what I assume is a sort of numbed disbelief. I'm informed of treatments, my chances with chemotherapy, and I inquire attentively and uselessly into an encyclopedic parade of drugs and cura- tives and chemicals, acting as if understanding or knowing the names of my treatments will make them any easier to endure. We talk about irra- diating and breaking apart the black cells. We talk about the chance of returning, after a long period of baldness and weakness, vomiting and agony and clinical hell, to a regular and functional lifestyle. We talk about support groups and therapists, organizations to help assuage what some patients describe as an unbearable sense of loss – lost opportunities, lost potential. I find myself online for hours and hours, spending a bright and breezy Sunday morning on this, the last June 1st of my life, toying with alternative avenues, holistic or naturopathic healers outside the realm of traditional medicine, and retching in the wastebasket beneath the desk.

I don't *feel* tremendously worse. I have classes to teach, a semester to finish. Life goes on as if nothing were different – it's just charged with a kind of tremble, quieting me, leaving me withdrawn and dizzy. I carpool to my high school in the early morning, roam through the linoleum staff room, place my bagged lunch in the fridge and shoot the shit with younger colleagues. *Get that cough checked out*, they say, laughing. *Sounds terrible. Sounds like death.* The words recited in the clinic – *tumour, chemo, cancer* – are not mentioned, though they're there, beading like drops of black dew on my tongue, wanting to share the news, to say the *names*. I drink weak coffee and read the *Star*, and then it's off to teach uninterested teenagers their mandatory English classes, reciting this week's exam review for *Macbeth* or *The Lord of the Flies* or another book that makes them drift, bored, to their cellphones. I wonder what they think of me, of my remarkable slenderness, my steel-grey hair, the thick glasses I'm forced to wear and the droning bass of my voice. The rattling cough that forces me to pause and wince every few minutes. Then I drive home, a pile of marking in my briefcase, and after downing what food I can stomach I sit in my living room, my Grade 10s' unmarked essays awaiting my important, ridiculous decision.

The house has never felt so quiet. It might seem a natural effect, this blanketing silence, given that I live in the southern, shaded recesses of suburban Burlington, Ontario. Yet years ago – decades maybe, now that I think of it – it seemed there were dozens and dozens of kids in the neighbourhood. Halloween was a bustling carnival, and street hockey was more common than traffic. Screams and hoots would linger long past sundown in warmer months. But now all those kids have moved away. It's a borough of retirees, of morning strolls, of indoor dinners and closed curtains. I've known this kind of silence for almost ten years (ever since Katherine passed, leaving the house to its settling weight), but it hits me now, the resounding emptiness. The soundproofed consistency of my mortgaged walls.

After dinner and marking, I sit and close my eyes and allow the silence to take over. It's so heavy, a stuffing that clogs the halls, prevents passage. I turn off the fans and take the batteries from ticking clocks, ensure appliances are unplugged. Then I sit, eyes closed, listening. Sweet, full and endless. I lose hours and hours. *Last hours.*

Another few weeks. Another round of painful appointments, a depressing prognosis. There's blood in my mouth, bright against the tissue that blots my lips, as ominous as the clots wiped away by Hemingway's ruined bullfighter. My arms are pricked to pieces, sore and achy, and I'm losing weight. One late June afternoon, exams almost over, I drive to a convenience store down the street from the clinic. I need bread for sandwiches, cream for my coffee. While putting my bag and carton on the counter, I ask for a pack of Player's Light, king-sized. The request slips from my lips before I know what I'm doing – as if I were dreaming, or insane. As if the secret smoker inside me had been merely biding his time, waiting for his chance to pounce. A small pack means twenty cigarettes. I buy a Bic lighter and leave, feeling like I've gotten away with something. Back in my car I rip open the plastic, tap down the tobacco and light up.

And here it is, after so long – the first catch in the throat, the instant head rush and buzz, the total-body pleasure so complete I have to pull over to avoid a collision. I watch the smoke twist and cavort, in love with itself. It's ecstatic. I let myself cry for the first time since the diagnosis, and the tears are strangely heavy, making soft *pat-pat-pat* noises as they land on my seat belt. The sunlight in the smoke. The burning shaft between my fingers. Chest pain, earthy and immediate, and severe. I pull onto my street with the cigarette in my mouth, and there, in my driveway, sucking the butt down to the ash and soot of the filter, greedy, I reaffirm my commitments.

I'm not a young man. There's no real tragedy in my death; at sixty, one must have no illusions of sprightly vigour, of blossoming talent. Nor can one maintain hopes for a romantic end, the hard-and-fast burnout, all that sentimental sap. I'm realistic: I had imagined my remaining years as a grinding decline. Next year would be my last as a teacher. I looked forward to retirement, to the time devoted to books or travel, a map of Florence tucked away in my desk drawer. I figured I'd have another decade before enduring the true indignities of old age, the weakening moan of muscles and joints. I imagined the routine of the old-age home, the feeding tubes, the slide into death that would come, if I was lucky, like a sigh in my sleep. Sweet-hearted nurses, charmed by my politeness, the pictures of Katherine around my bed, would come to hold my hand and stroke me gently on my bald head while they watched my chest rise and fall and finally come to rest. That was the death I expected, even hoped for. One long, laboured rattle, and then –

Aside from my dashed expectations of a later, slower end, the thought of losing fifteen years of solid reading comes as a profound disappointment. Up until the cancer, I read compulsively, savagely, each book dog-eared and broken on my shelves: another addition to my accumulated frustration. It's the books, the reading, I'll miss, if I miss anything at all. Thank God for the cigarettes, I remind myself. They're the best way to distract me from all that missed potential: the covers never broached, the words never read.

For I have returned to cigarettes, it seems, in earnest – returned like a prodigal boy, so long lost to the horizon, crawling upon my knees toward that stiff pillar of a father. I smoke while I perform my end-of-days inventory: something to soothe the pain of recollecting, sorting and filing. I have so many books. Thousands upon thousands, on towering shelves, in messy piles, sealed in boxes and stored in heaps in the crawl space. I've planned garage sales and trips to the second-hand shops to get rid of the titles I'll never read, but some selfish hand reaches out to stop me whenever it seems I've gathered the guts. There is no *me* without books; they're everything I remember from childhood, from maturity, from facing down the doom and loss of these last few years as a *widower*, that other wretched word (ah, so close to *window* – like one cruelly shut, one letter short of escape). All that's happened to me has been coloured, permanently, by my reading. And even here, facing the pages of my rambling library, I realize that cigarettes were there in the beginning, too, enhancing and souring and murdering in decades-long plumes of pain and bliss.

I was nine years old the first time I put a cigarette in my mouth. It was the same week I'd read my first adult novel, a Gothic romance of ghosts and ancient debts. *The Italian*, or *The Castle of Otranto* – something I probably couldn't follow. I was in the park across from my parents' home near Toronto's Christie Pits. An older kid's discarded, half-finished smoke landed on a blade of grass of few feet from where I sat and read. After he was out of sight, I stooped, retrieved the cigarette and sucked at the burning ember in a sad worship of whatever it was I thought the kid possessed. I coughed, and spit, and wobbled home to wash the taste from my mouth, careful to avoid my hard-smoking parents who obviously wanted me to wait at least a few years before I took up the habit. And yes, I felt shame; I felt filthy, detestable, but there was still a buried impulse on my tongue telling me that it was an agreeable sensation. A taboo had been transgressed. It has forever been the same feeling, only diluted by time and repetition. This is why I buy cigarettes today like some men buy pornography: demure, nervous, terribly excited.

For years, I'd smoke the previously enjoyed: the still-burning butts from off the street. Or my friends and I would steal half-killed Marlboros from our parents' ashtrays, meeting beside monkey bars and slides to get nauseated and green. High school meant drinking, of course, so we'd drive through our sleeping Toronto neighbourhoods, Little Korea and Portugal and Italy, suddenly free, a bottle of rye passed around a borrowed car. At the University of Toronto, Trinity College, we smoked over endless drinks, tapping our ashes into tart trays in lecture halls, or we shared a smoke with our professors in their offices. I smoked incessantly, budgeting my scant savings to pay for another pack of Lucky Strikes. My fingers and teeth were stained yellow, my clothes and bedding and books all tarnished by the scent. As soon as I was old enough, I flocked to college bars, gulping down pints of beer and filling ashtrays with my addiction. No night was too dark, no disappointment too acute, when I knew I had the comfortable weight of a full pack against my thigh. I read somewhere that having a full supply of smokes was like knowing you had a loaded gun resting heavy and murderous near your heart. They were like that, sort of: a defence mechanism, an escape route from the socially awkward, a solution to all threats of boredom or that last rumination or heartache at 3 a.m. But they were more tender, too; I came to think that their smell, lingering on my fingers despite all fragrant scrubbing, was my own. I was in love with smoking and told my other twenty-something friends so in no uncertain terms. Everything would be all right, I said, only half-joking, if cigarettes and I could keep up our delirious affair. Nothing could pull us apart; I could tolerate no intervention, no love triangle between tobacco and myself.

Reading was the only occupation that kept pace with every deadly, mashed-out butt (and only barely). Two addictions growing in almost perfect tandem. On one of the last days of high school, ubiquitous cigarette kissing my hand, I sat in the park where I first inhaled nicotine and groped through the collected works of Robert Frost, falling recklessly, destructively in love with poetry. I say this with full sincerity; I felt the stirrings of true commitment, of a lifelong heartache. The bees and the flowers and the long grass, knowing New Hampshire and Vermont and every willow and buttercup and bumblebee, old roads and snowflakes, summer dust and oozing sap. I decided that I would write, or try to write, to make poems with the same wry cunning, a wit and emotive power leaping from heart and mind to pen. After I consumed Frost in his entirety, my days of exploration began. I read *The Divine Comedy* while leafing through E. E. Cummings. I read Sidney and Milton and Shelley, piecing together my own aesthetics, my own defence of poetry. I felt alone and religious and desperately sad. Prose came like a great and sobering blow, a grounding, a shot from Hemingway's rifle and an orgasm from Leopold Bloom (how I lined them up, my modern heroes: Joyce and Fitzgerald and Faulkner and Woolf, bullets in a revolver, cigarettes in a little tin). Language spread its warm, absurd rays over all my adolescent thoughts, and I felt the way we all long to feel: moody, lonely, lovesick and explosive with the prospects of tomorrow.

Now, in these early days of summer and terminal cancer, I find myself sorting through box upon box of those first, earliest volumes, each first page marked by my juvenile signature. Sitting and coughing in my dry crawl space, the hanging bulb a white glow above me, this seems like the best and easiest place to start scanning through my life's lingering effects (only easy because I'm pawing through *my* things, I realize: journals and diaries and albums of life before Katherine, a love affair so tremendous that thinking about her means breaking another bottle in my stomach). I clutch a cigarette in my teeth and tear through taped-up cardboard, looking for my boyhood stuff: the smell of spilled wax, of decaying paper, of old ink and rubber and the hint of grease, all bringing flashes of some irretrievable year when things were almost certainly sweeter. The house rests above me, as silent and still as all these slow-ticking days, and I find so much here, such richness, and it's all about me.

I find a box filled with notebooks and loose-leaf pages. These were my first drafts, my first attempts at writing. At twenty I was willing to plunge my entire life into a pursuit I could barely define. I wrote terrible, terrible stuff, but mountains of it, and it's all here: novels and novellas and spools of poetry, notebooks spilling over with my left-handed scrawl. Where could I not travel with words? I thought. Why not remake everything unsightly, everything blasted by greed or hate or stupidity, with the power and flash of language? I wanted poetry and prose to expand consciousness, to redraw the boundaries of self and subject. I wanted art to be ethics, to replace the remnants of my religion as the real indicator of virtue, of the divine. I saw myself in terms of escape: disentangled from politics, from dogma, from the nets of family. I saw full potential, burgeoning wisdom, and little else.

When you first start smoking, it's all romance and kindness, the sustaining fuel of a new affair. But years pass, and after countless packs the tar and ash take their toll: wheezing on short flights of stairs, the dry persistent hack that betrays a smoker like a scarlet *S*. I scan through these first fledgling notebooks, stained with my unbelievable aspirations, and see only the rush of new love, drunk on possibility, on the strange canyons and crannies of a newly discovered body. Everything was experiment, everything the happy failure writing and art (they say) is supposed to be. But writing and I soon felt the strain of our extended cohabitation. While I was wheezing up stairs and nicking like a maniac, I was also panting with the effort of pushing my art into more complex acts of love. I was embarrassed by my flailing, intimidated by writers who could woo me with a single sentence, and so I dug into the writing life as one settles into a long and unsatisfying relationship.

I'm not sure what happened. I rented an inexpensive apartment (my stupid romantic garret); I got a day job doing manual labour, hefting bags of bread and buns from delivery trucks, dusted with flour and meal, returning home to my cramped quarters to begin tapping away at my typewriter. I did all the things I thought were necessary: going to readings, buying the small magazines, following the small-press publishers, discovering the stranger voices I never got in school. All I can say is that I grew afraid – afraid of rejection, perhaps, for all my late-night, malformed births, stained with spilled ash and coffee. Afraid of being discovered as a fraud, an imposter; that all my passion was just the disguise of a middling thinker, born of middle-class parents, fraternizing with the same group of art-oblivious men I'd known since high school. What would the real writers think of me? Rejection letters, returning my long-winded stories and avant-garde poems, merely reinforced the general theme: that I wasn't destined or invincible or immortal, or even notable.

So I came up with a surefire backup plan: teaching. Something to pay the bills, I thought, while I wrote my masterpieces, not knowing how difficult and trying, how absolutely soul-fatiguing such a profession can be. I was twenty-seven by the time I'd trudged through teacher's college, still delivering crusty buns and croissants, occasionally writing and finding a tiny publisher in some distant corner of the country. I was lucky enough to find a job in Burlington when I did, luckier still to find the woman there who would be my wife. Katherine was put in my path by a squad of prescient angels, I'm sure; she was the only person who could at least temporarily alleviate my need to write, who could transport me to a place where writing didn't matter. And so the scribbling urge went on the backburner for a few summery years, filled with Katherine's tender laugh and her own bag of addictive loves. We gardened and took long beachside walks, drove to the States and went camping. We talked about books like readers, not writers: in awe of our betters, jealousy and bitterness all but evaporating in her easy company.

I moved in with Katherine, trying for a baby in two years, only to find us unable to conceive. It was a blow, the news that we had about a 1 percent chance, shaking our little suburban shrine to its stone basement (our shrine to each other, to the future). Miraculously, we were enough for each other – the two of us, complete, compact. We would keep trying for ten years, crossing our fingers for that 1 percent, but if nothing materialized, it was enough to be who we were. And I thought I was better than my stern writer models who warned me never to marry, or have kids. In these days I was careful to smoke only in the mornings and at night, keeping my distance from Katherine, who said the smell gave her headaches, could spoil our chances of becoming parents. And while at night, smoking with abandon (the way lovers must devour each other in adultery, in shadowy motels, emerging into post-coital sunlight in glorious filth), I tried to get back into the swing of writing, tried to pump out a novel-length project every couple of years. By sacrificing sleep, I managed about an hour or two a day, spent hunched over an electric typewriter, watching headlights out the windows and the minute hand stalk by. After midnight or one, I would climb the stairs and collapse into bed, Katherine softly mumbling beside me (heartbreaking nonsense, as if these were last words, oracular messages, mist and divination), my hands still twitching with the thud and click of the keys. And I'd think, lying there after so much exertion and so little result, that I wouldn't have even tried if it weren't for the smokes, or, more distressingly, that maybe the writing was only a pathetic *excuse* to smoke. There was something evil and organic in the way the two passions were linked. Every puff reminded me that I should be at work, erasing and failing. And whenever I wrote, I needed at least a full pack by my side. I began to doubt that I could compose a single, measly sentence without dragging toxins through my lungs.

After Katherine's increasing exasperation over my cravings (and the fear, all too legitimate, that I was killing myself), I felt a swelling sense of shame over my cigarette breaks, over the way my tweed jackets smelled like chalk and stale butts. The commercials were hitting the radio and TV in full force. Smoking was now, almost overnight, unbelievably gauche. As the years passed, I began to toss away each failed manuscript with thoughts of the soothing forgiveness and the guilty release of cigarettes. Every time I climbed the sad steps of our home, huffing and puffing like I was exhausted, I would vow to quit smoking. Only now do I realize that I was vowing to quit writing – to quit and abandon an entire life.

So one day I simply screwed up the nerve. Quitting both the smokes and the scribbling seemed long overdue. After a half-dozen botched attempts, false starts, it seemed done. I felt healthy. I felt energized. I wore the patch and chewed gum, played with an elastic band in my pocket. I also threw tantrums, lost my temper, held my throbbing skull in my hands while thundering headaches forced me to cancel classes or pull over on the freeway. I overate and gained weight, had to avoid all social situations involving alcohol or bars. But I was no longer a failure in the make, a man bereft of respect or achievement. I was now a teacher, a son, a husband, a reader and nothing more. I didn't *need* to be anything more. My entire empty being no longer screamed that no matter what I was doing, I should be somewhere else, working over the ripple and taunt of words. I was free: free from both a burdensome addiction and a destructive ambition. Which was worse, I couldn't tell.

Understandably, my wife was delighted. We were happier than we'd been in years: spending summers travelling through Europe on our childless budget, cultivating a modest flower garden in our backyard, giggling away each squabble before any real hurt could sink in. But Katherine soon developed a tumour much like my own: inoperable, malignant. I kept shaking my head after the diagnosis, muttering *this is crazy, this is crazy*, astounded by how fast the cancer arrived and blew our lives to hell. I'd been careful to smoke outside or away from her; though the doctors pointed to bad genetics, it didn't soothe the guilt. She deteriorated quickly, becoming ever more skeletal and gaunt, a hollowed-out version of someone I knew, could smell, could match in the slow rhythms of sleep. This was the woman whose tears could push out any sliver of anger or upset from me, turn me into a worried mess as I sought to make amends. This was the woman who awoke from bad dreams clutching for me, whom I comforted and held in the dark while she fell back to sleep. Death – this is really happening, happening to us, happening to us *now* – came with a vicious and staggering speed, ripping out the remnants of her grace and beauty and leaving her a bleating, frightened animal in the pastel wards of St. Joseph's Hospital. I held her hand and tried to tie up what was left of my life. I would go on, I supposed. I would walk down the path that was opening for me: teacher, retiree, reader, *widower*.

If we had a daughter, like we daydreamed and fantasized we would, even past the point when we knew it was impossible, we would have named her Hilda. If Hilda was alive today – say twenty, twenty-five, thirty, let's say living and studying abroad – she would very soon be alone in the world, bereft of both her parents, shuffling home to bury her father.

I wonder what I would say to her now. But it's a stupid train of thought, and I don't linger on it for long.

I light another smoke.

At the bottom of a box, creased and folded and coated in dust, I find the last piece I tried to write. I give it a once-over, notice how the words rush and tumble across the page, clumsy and discomfitted. I stumble where I should find footing. But there's a certain admirable flow here, too, and I wonder how much skill might remain after fifteen years of negligence.

I take a long haul and grind a butt against the floor. I sit with my back against the wall in my little underworld and start reading through this last, nameless work. I remember it now – another novel, another meandering narrative tacked on to my ever-expanding chain of abortions. I haven't thought of this – the actual piece – in fifteen years. It seems I was following in the example of a book dear to me – *Zeno's Conscience* (*La coscienza di Zeno*), self-published in the early 1920s by the Italian Italo Svevo. It tells the story of Zeno Cosini, a man forced by his psychiatrist to keep a memoir to help him break the habit of cigarette smoking. It is a book full of lies, full of trivialities, full of familial traumas, much like mine – a domestic and mundane autobiography. It was also roundly rejected by Italian publishers, who forced Svevo to find support abroad (a similar fate no doubt would have awaited my little book, should I have ever completed it). I remember its extended descriptions of Zeno's first encounters with smokes, his inevitable addiction, the mental tricks he attempts to help quit (trying to quit on dates of special significance, for example, or giving some cigarettes the honorary title of 'last cigarette' – a trick I've cherished and despised, watching that so-called 'last' smoke, *'ultima sigaretta,'* reappear in my hand with each firm attempt to be done). I realize, now, how much we share, Zeno and I: men very much in love with their wives, both of us with an unfortunate obsession with tobacco, occupied completely by the relentless enormity of the past. As I flip through the pages, I reach a sentence that trails off, unfinished. I can't recall how it's supposed to end. Much of it is senseless, garbled, but of all things, I take this ratty pile of papers out of the crawl space, emerging up and into the ruins of my life.

It's gorgeous weather, limpid blue breezes and streaks of white contrails stitching the sky. I endured the last of the semester's exams by being unusually taciturn. Co-workers said farewell for the summer, heading toward their cottages and home improvements and months of babysitting. I lingered in my classroom, Room 225, like I do at the end of every year, relishing the silence, soaking up the nostalgia, the constant sad recycling of generations of students with their renewed boredom and lust and frustration. This time it was the last, my final linger, and it was sad, sadder than I could bear – I rushed back to my car, ashamed of myself, and terrified of the summer ahead.

Now treatment awaits me, the first session scheduled for the day after tomorrow. Is it worth it, what's coming, that chemical wretchedness, being wrenched into something broken and weird? Or is there better work to occupy me, if things are so absolute, so dire, and no one to miss my departure? There are no answers, just the house's strict rule of silence. In response, I decide to forget the doctors, at least for now, and start to make my own noise. I clear off my work desk, manuscript in hand. I dust off the old typewriter, stack up my paper and ink and spare ribbon. I'll try to finish the last piece, even as the streets blossom into heat and lightness, retreating to a darkened office to finish a work destined for my eyes only. To turn it, like *Zeno's Conscience*, into some sort of desperate autobiography. I think of Italo Svevo, of another century, another world.

For the first few days, I'm just getting used to the keys. I'm making countless mistakes, losing my place on the page and struggling with the machine. And it becomes blatantly clear that what I'm writing is merely inventory, lists to later arrange into sense and story. Dazzling prose and intriguing narrative are too difficult to effect; I have no patience for plot or imaginary characters, with rising actions and satisfying climaxes. I've simply started listing things I wish I could keep with me, moments I would hold on to beyond the mystery of dying. I'm dwelling on pure memory (how great and vast that country is!), describing those holy moments in my life that reek of smoke and ambition.

But no. As soon as I hit a rhythm, my will seems to buckle and collapse. The pain flowers in my chest and throat and tears close my eyes. It's exhausting. The writing and smoking demand more time than

I've got left. I want a space to be alone in. I have the constant fear that well-intentioned doctors (or friends, or colleagues, organizing a barbecue or night of poker) will invade my home (and now and then, I think I hear steps – footfalls, creaking floorboards, as if the cancer were haunting the walls, stalking me). It takes me a day to decide what to do. I feel dizzy and uncoordinated. I have to decide what's truly important. This work, this cataloguing, who is it for? Why write again, after so many years, something I won't be able to finish? I've been away from writing for too long. It's useless to start again.

What I want is Life, but a different one from the sort available this summer, my last. I want Death, but the best sort of Death, without false hope or additional pain. What I really want is neither life nor death, strictly speaking. What I want are cigarettes. Beautiful, endless smokes. To smoke one after another, an ongoing chain from now until oblivion. Here at the end of Life, the beginning of Death, sometimes it takes being pushed to the end of the heart to realize what you truly love.

I drive back to the store, a coughing and shaky creep, and purchase several cartons. I have Peter Jackson, duMaurier, Marlboro, Export A, Player's, Belmont Milds. The clerk gives me a sad and baffled look, but I just smile. Back in my living room I arrange these in alphabetical sequence, lining up the multicoloured boxes and dipping my fingers into their tightly packed contents. I have made up my mind.

I move a mattress, some blankets and an adequate supply of food and water into the garage. I have a bedpan that I'm able to squeeze out a horizontal opening near the ground. A single bulb hangs from the ceiling. If I didn't have light, I wouldn't be able to see the smoke, and that would nearly defeat the purpose. I've left my books neglected in my study, shelf upon shelf of classics forever abandoned to dust or to the Goodwill. All those passages, the ongoing conversation of literature, what I'd return to again and again for challenge and comfort and inspiration. A conversation that's finally and strangely over. The last manuscript, that stupid narrative of smoking and transcendence, of Italo Svevo's smoky, neurotic bullshit, rests abandoned on my desk. I wonder what people will think upon ransacking my home. Will they read the pages for clues? Will it frustrate them to find nothing of value? No note or explanation? It doesn't matter. No one knows of my retreat into the garage and I expect no sympathy from those who may come looking (colleagues? neighbours? wandering ghosts?). I have thrown out all the phone numbers of clinics, doctors and specialists. Without treatment I will die very fast, but here I can smoke and leave the house untainted by the smell and the stain.

I take a roll of duct tape and begin sealing the cracks around the door that leads to my house, carefully smoothing the black adhesive along the floor and the walls. Since I don't want to asphyxiate immediately, I leave the hole near the floor alone. If I stand in a certain spot near the opening, I can feel the slightest breeze whisper in from the outside world. Otherwise I feel nothing, except for the pain in my chest, and the smoke.

I pull off my wedding ring and place it under my pillow. I want to feel smoke all over my body, want it to love and caress my indentations and hollows, my hairs and folds. I want it to tickle, to lick, to burn. I take off my clothes, fold them neatly at the foot of my bed. Smoking is good for me.

I feel as though I were still reeling from my first kiss, giddy with the news that love could visit and forgive my awkwardness. Cigarettes! *Cigarettes!* I pull out a handful from a carton, let them fall through my fingers. What are they? Just thin rolls of paper binding crushed plants, mingled with preservatives to maintain the freshness and bind the substance, though I suspect there are other elements at work (as every new love is more than lips and eyes and hair, a bag of guts). I pull the chain and feeble yellow light illuminates the concrete floor. Shadowy boxes, a tool bench, a bicycle, a lawn mower. Rakes stand menacingly, a short row of gleaming teeth. Beyond the shadows and the gloom, the sound of traffic flows through the crack in the wall, a muffled hush that becomes a blanket in the dark.

I strike a match, watch the tiny flame surge and recede, flicker in the stillness of the garage. I lift the match to the tip of my cigarette, puffing while the flame licks and ignites the paper and leaves. The stream of smoke curls and dances, surrounds my fingers and trails around my arm. As the fire traces the cigarette, the smoke changes, becomes belligerent in its variation and delight. I watch it turn and shudder and I feel humble, in awe. I remember a one-night stand I had with a woman in Montreal – how we blew Marlboro smoke toward the hotel ceiling after sex, both of us marvelling at the beauty. I remember the first time my childhood friend could manage the nostril exhale in the dusky twilight of Christie Pits – how I burned with envy and awe at his mastery of the craft. I feel a great honour to be able to hold such beauty and chaos within my body. I feel like a mother, holding the swell of her womb. I blow out the drag and feel a loss, a loneliness. I grind the cigarette out on the ground, mashing the ashes and smearing the sooty tar. Within a month the cigarette will be on the path to decomposition, returning to the earth. I feel proud to follow, burnt and scattered.

Pipes, like writing in general, are illusions of immortality. One preserves and polishes a pipe, buys cleaners, keeps the thing itself in a small velvet bag. As meticulous and fussy as any careful editor, or publisher, wanting words preserved in glorious binding. As ridiculous as an urn, engraved with a dead name, when the body should be mingled with tulips and bluebells, the soil in which it dug. One doesn't share a pipe, like one would a democratic cigarette – much like a fresh idea in the world of fiction, held and guarded jealously, protected by laws of copyright and possession. A pipe is an extension of the self, and will often outlive its owner, as does any book pushed into publication past the death of its author. But a cigarette! Ah, a cigarette is a life unto itself, a life burning before you, a constant reminder of mortality, like poems written on clouds and forgotten the moment they're uttered.

In high school I wrote sonnets to cigarettes. I was the lover, the Petrarchan courtier, and my object of affection, my Laura or Beatrice, was the slim, ivory shaft that perched between my fingers. I experimented with sound poetry, tried to say *smoke* with as much meaning as the word would allow. I think I developed a dementia and stopped breathing oxygen.

While I consider the cigarette, the urge to write fades, no doubt jealous of my preferential treatment. I dwell on the almost certain failure of any attempt at art in order to truly banish it, and leave me to my love. Be gone, fiction. *Leave me alone*, I whisper; damn the weighing and balancing of every crippling word, the sound and rhythm of lines. Damn the point at which writing becomes work, when reading and rereading become a monotonous chime of frustration, a litany of error. Damn the doubt and the inadequacy, the time away from loved ones, the time away from sun and experience, from dancing. And damn all the ghoulish figures of the past, the dead writers who sparkled with greatness and made all my broken riffing seem silly and imitative and lame.

I dream of exhaust, a belching pipe, an iron-grey sky and a procession of souls. Sighs, short and infrequent, and a bell to toll the hours. I'm following someone, someone receding from view, swallowed by the press of bodies. When I wake up it is often night, and the sound of footfalls returns: what I know now to be pure hallucination, fantasy. Someone walking very close to the door between the house and the garage, pausing at the boundary between oxygen and smoke, sanity and its opposite. The steps recede as waking sense returns, and I close my eyes, trying to imagine the years I will miss.

Time has passed. My supplies are still plentiful. My chest hurts each time I take a breath. I am coughing up great clumps of dark blood and I believe I am starting to die.

I miss those conversations with Katherine. I want to tell her I love her, tell her I never meant to hurt her with my smoking, tell her goodbye. I want to meet with old friends, visit the park where I first smoked. I want to stride down the street in the spring, a student, with a cigarette clutched between my fingers, electric guitars wailing from patio bars around me and the forgiving wind rippling my hair. I want to pore over photos of my wife, our life together, smell the blue blouse I've kept in our closet, read the first letters we wrote. Life is so full, so long, but our crooked little cells are all we know. I want books, but I know I wouldn't be able to concentrate; I would fidget in anticipation of my death. The only thing I can do is wait, and smoke.

Before long there is a soft knocking on the garage door. I lie perfectly still. This was inevitable, surely, but I want to keep quiet. The knocking lasts only a few seconds, but it leaves me shivering, afraid. Someone wants me; someone knows of my escape into the garage. I am dreaming, maybe, but I have the sure sense that although the knocker wants me to return to the world, I know that he (or she) belongs to the land of the dead.

This goes on for days – every now and then the soft knocking, the echo, the tentative blows. The bulb burns out, leaving me in perfect darkness. I have to wrench my body around to stare at the tiny crack to the outdoors to see if it is day or night. The process of watching becomes too difficult, and I give myself up to blackness, to my eyes' widening sense of shadow and smoke, adjusting to the constant night. Those knocking inquiries, my terrified shivers. The sludge of time, unchanging dark, and now a man standing in the corner of the garage for a second – I see him outlined by match-strike. A lightning flash of evil. I hear him smoking. I moan now, petrified. Some nights later (or minutes, or worlds) he's standing above me, darker than the black around him, watching me. He lights a smoke and it's Italo Svevo, bald, moustached, dead, smiling from a photograph. I scream in pain and push my face into the mattress. He's speaking in a shadow whisper, in a language that makes no sense.

To drown out his pleas – and they're pleas, I'm certain, nonsense or untranslated or maybe perfectly clear if I listen closely enough – I sing softly to myself. Eventually I jam a cigarette in each ear, burying my head under the pillow.

I know what he wants, then, in the sudden bite of a dream. He wants me to finish the book. He says only I can write the last chapter, the last sentence, the last words. He's kept my desk for me, clear of clutter or distraction, with a new electric typewriter, a notepad, a pen and a fresh pack of Persian cigarettes. He's scrapped all my pages of inventory; it's time to get back to the story, he says. He promises that my wife is not gone but merely sleeping upstairs, her lips parted, her skin oily and warm, a tiny life growing inside her. That this could be the night I finish my life's work, the work I've been dreaming of since my first smoke. How good it will be to finish, he teases. To write the last words. To give up and let the work live. To walk up the stairs of our home and slip into bed, into an embrace, knowing the struggle to be over and done. *I'm so happy that you've quit*, my wife says, whispering across the pillow before we fall to sleep.

I consider it. I moan on the mattress, reaching for a handhold, trying to stand. Maybe I should. Maybe this was a mistake; maybe struggling and failing was the point. Maybe the end is nearer and easier than I could ever imagine. All it will take, he suggests, is that I try.

The pain surges. I lie on my side, refusing to rise, curled like something wilted, wet. Remembering.

One night, one day, one moment, Italo begins to fade. He limps around the garage. He is waiting for me to emerge and finish the work so that he can go on living. Italo cries pitifully, no longer fearsome but pathetic. Death is not a strange land. Death is when the garage door opens and I return to life. I call out, asking if I can smoke in heaven, and try to laugh, thinking that's all Heaven is. I catch a whiff of smoke and start thinking I'm going somewhere else, but there is no fire, no waiting pit for the damned.

Then all of a sudden he's quiet. No sound of Italo, no presence, just the dirt and grime and darkness of the garage.

A minute. An hour. A day.

And I lie still, rigid, straining to hear.

'... the sentence itself is a man-made object, not the one we wanted of
course, but still a construction of man, a structure to be treasured for
its weakness, as opposed to the strength of stones'
                   – from 'The Sentence,' Donald Barthelme

With regard to my appeal of the sentence: yes, I am well aware of our 'relationship' being, in plain language, non-existent; and yes, I can admit to accusations of infatuation and obsession, even though such allegations have been framed in a largely provocative and erroneous manner, laden with dangerous, predatorial connotations, suggesting that I possess some sort of skewed psychosexual mania (or worse, the likelihood of *pedophilic* desires); and yes, I admit to such accusations in full awareness and acknowledgment of the grave fact that we are indeed 'unacquainted' (in a rather delimiting interpretation of the word, I must note), despite my numerous letters and telephone calls and emails to her agency, Cunningham Escott Slevin Doherty (CESD), and to her publicist, the inestimable Meghan Prophet, and to her music label (Hollywood Records) and to the Disney Corporation (to wit I have not yet received any written or oral response but soldier on in the hope of expressing my deepest gratitude and my sincerest congratulations on her innumerable successes and innovations, even though [thinking rationally] I knew these efforts might be futile due to her immense responsibilities and extremely busy schedule, regarding which I could testify at length if only brevity were not a factor, if only you weren't already so weary with listening), so for the sake of such direly required and oft-requested succinctness, I shall plead with the court on this day that my interest in Ms. Cyrus is purely scholarly, and in good will, and that I have been cruelly maligned by certain lawyers, Cyrus family representatives and members of the immediate and amalgamated Cyrus family at large (read: William Ray, Leticia, Brandi, Trace, Christopher, Braison and little Noah, though he could not form the terrible accusations but is known to live, in a childish sort of way, 'in fear' of my return), as a 'delinquent,' 'stalker' and 'predator,' and, though the precise words were not spoken, as some sort of 'sexual deviant' – for I insist that my sexual preferences abide by the straight American medium (even, one might say, particularly *puritan*, given my noted reluctance to engage in auto-erotic acts of any kind after the recorded period in Tennessee), that my study of Ms. Cyrus's life and work and charitable contributions has indeed been both consuming and 'enflaming' but only in the strictest intellectual sense, for surely I would not bother to know the petty details of her birth and education, her conceptual circumstances and humble origins, if not for strictly intellectual fulfillment, for surely if these were outré masturbatory phantasms I could have simply downloaded some leaked cellular photograph, leered at an innocuous patch of film in grisly slow motion (made *obscene* by such slow motion), and had my *way* with myself, so to speak, forgetting the details of Ms. Cyrus's birth: that she was born on November 23, 1992, the same day that the last deadly tornado was seen in northeastern North Carolina as part of that cold, late-season outbreak that affected much of the southeastern part of the United States, ranging from Houston, Texas, to portions of the Gulf Coast states, from the Ohio Valley to the Carolinas – a deadly maelstrom of end-of-days leanings that narrowly skirted the edges of southern Tennessee in late November as if fated, destined, preternaturally aware of Miley Cyrus's imminent arrival into the world, allowing Leticia 'Tish' Cyrus (née Finley), most worthy mother and vessel, to deliver through the harrowing pains of labour in peace, granting her that small but significant respite from worry or fret over natural disasters,

Oz-ferrying cyclones, flying cows or cold-cellar emergency deliveries, in that place and time so very different from my own (notwithstanding all possible action on my behalf to violate the sequential workings of the world, bound by laws of immutable, inhuman physics), as I was (as the court has duly recorded) 'beginning a new life on the west coast in full accordance with the law away from the forbidden person[s] and property,' leading to my recorded confessions of anguish and pained sobbing over my missed opportunity to cradle Leticia's hand, kiss her wrist (strong, slim, adroit) or wipe the beads of sweat from her forehead (lined, now, by another three symmetrical creases since that long-gone November day, or since our initial encounters in high school, where she ruled the narrow halls with a sort of haughty, southern authority, now bearing the lines of motherly latitude that I have often watched, slightly sheepish at my fear of their integrity, timid of their magisterial power over my daily musings and nightly terrors, in photograph and in glossy tabloid over state-appointed distance, obeying the court's order to stay away and sow 'wilder' oats), missing my chance to watch the wailing, mewling Miley emerge from the womb and into the light; and these are issues that have, as stated, embroiled me in irresolvable frustration, leaving me to feebly imagine that I was there to witness, oh lucky witness, her headfirst slide into the charged, electric air of that great city (*my* city, *my* air), home of the Grand Ole Opry at the legendary Ryman Auditorium, the 'Mother Church of Country Music' where I watched my first rhinestone-studded cowboy band, its state home to the Country Music Hall of Fame and the Belcourt Theatre, canonized television shows like *Hee Haw* and *Pop! Goes the Country*, and, of course, legendary country singer William Ray Cyrus and Leticia Finley, who married secretly in Nashville on December 28, 1992 – obviously over a month after Miley was born, a fact telling of the nature of their marital commitment, revelatory of their appropriate interpretation of the sanctity of marriage, portent of William Ray's understanding of paternal obligations, for the young family lived on a 500-acre farm in Thompson's Station, a bucolic Elysium, just a short drive outside of Nashville where the grass *is* really green and the willow trees *do* catch the sunlight red and yellow and dappled and holy and all things make music and imbue the simplest sentiments, the most casual words, with the soul-buoying charge of choir-based anthems: words such as *Destiny Hope Cyrus*, written in indelible ink on a Tennessee birth certificate, now stored in a locked drawer in a sprawling mansion in Los Angeles forever removed from my fond gaze, spelling out its secret message to anyone perceptive enough to read it: *Destiny* the inevitable fulfillment of a family's dream, *Hope* the means by which the dream would be achieved, and *Destiny* and *Hope* thus together representing a portentously *American* knot of dreams – knotted and entwined like the veins and tendons mapping Miley's country-rough hands beneath the Tennessee star-scape; Destiny being, of course, the softer sister of Fate (fate implying the cruel predetermination of Calvinist dogma, the Oedipal tear at the incestuous iris, the natural fall of dying leaves blown from cold autumnal branches: souls of the dead eager to line circles of a just and appropriate Hell); softer still in its insistence and encouragement of active participation on behalf of the subject, saying *life is what you make it*, saying *reach for the stars*, saying Destiny is my vague green light beyond the storm, always in the becoming, the manifesting, our boats borne ceaselessly back on waves of Hope – and so, charged by the harmony of the farmstead, the serendipity of the marriage and the ineluctable bond between her parents, I declare that *Destiny Hope Cyrus* is answered hope, the answered hope of a modern America: a nation of willing, striving and gaining, of proud immigrants running millions of blunt needles through department-store linens, raking through the sodden shit of dog parks, scrubbing bleach against porcelain urinals stained in the daily rub of living, or driving up and down the apocalyptic California coast between blurring redwoods and whitecaps trying to dream their way back into the homeland nectar of the south; and who amongst them, these proud brown-bodied working people, these people sentenced to punishments beyond the scope of their crimes, who amongst them would not gain or profit from the weight of such a name, a name so pregnant with purpose, a name like a tiny pilot light of great expectations, ensuring that *destiny* and *hope* were forever entangled and inextricable in Miley's memory, forever a part of who she is, was and will become, her past, present and future, bound in one time, one memory (*two* memories, if you count mine, which cannot forget), without even mentioning her public moniker,

Miley, merely one of many milestones on a winding highway of public support and love from William Ray, who comments, in interview after smiling interview, that '[Miley] was always smiling, she was always letting you know she was happy – such a happy, smiling, laughing baby' (and who can't help but smile, who can't help but picture the tiny limbs and giggling, cherubic face of the dancing, playing child, innocent of all woe and sadness, loving with a sort of unrestrained golden-retriever sincerity that crushes the heart and makes one moan and beg for William to get to the point and relate how they called her Smiley, smiling himself as he says this, saying 'Smiley' was her nickname around the house, but she had problems with the word – it just didn't come out right, 'cause of the lisp and all – so she could only say 'Miley, right, and so this name sort of stuck – and though this may sound silly (the remnant of an affectionate nickname adorably debased by a toddler's lisp), it tied *Destiny Hope* in a sort of electric, unspoken current to Ms. Cyrus's first creative distortion, her first calculated move toward self-actualization and identification, her first mumbled gesture of *authenticity*: somehow more American than *Destiny* or *Hope*; somehow *more* attuned to the shifting, sliding ideals of the end of the century, as if such a small baby could already ascertain that the ideal of personal authenticity was inexorably obliterating any ethical or moral insistence on the True, or the Good, or the Just, ascertained like one of Pound's cultural antennae – invisible lightning rods of anticipatory wisdom who walk among us – our artists, our visionaries, our prophets, those who speak for and to us (*us*, of course, being the gibbering, howling masses who have not the radar for such subtle vibrations of change, present company included); and again, to make myself perfectly clear, this praise is made not to exclude William Ray from this conversation of prophets (and please cogitate on the careful and fair way in which I speak of him, considering the accusations at hand), not to ignore his own contributions to culture by becoming the successful singer-songwriter and actor he is, recently promoting songs like 'Runway Lights' and 'Nineteen' on his twelfth and latest and ravishingly patriotic studio album *I'm American* despite how many of his peers failed along the way, dragged down by drugs or misplaced ideation or a destructive desire for fame or wealth or the adoration of an asinine fan, or, most commonly, through a simple lack of natural talent, or talent squandered through a lack of repetitive labour and the sacrifice of all other comforts, through *work*, through an intense study of the history of pop music, which in truth is littered with these marginal, forgotten, tragic fossils, who burnt up too fast, or too soon, or who never had a break, who now play (if they play at all) in obscure cover bands or in the shadowed corner of a university or college bar, crying into their pints of lager, memory mingled with false projections from a foggy, denuded prime in which William Ray was always the better man, the better musician, the more successful singer-songwriter who never crashed and burned, who found God and Family, who made wise investments with his millions and fathered a child who would eventually eclipse his own tremendous fame – even though, let us not forget, he penned a cultural zeitgeist, lyrics and melody so indelible upon the contemporary psyche that I don't have to repeat the refrain; you're probably humming along now, remembering where you were when that all-too-human heart tore across America and made line-dancing a feverish act of rebellion – not to again insinuate in any way that Miley's home life was dissolute or depraved, but rather evidence of her household's musical surroundings – Miley's first intimations of childhood being performative and lyrical, surrounded by the tenor twang of William Ray's incredible ear for the melodious hook, of Leticia's graceful additions at harmony, their first hound dog, Butch, baying and barking in the late haze of marshmallow campfires, the chaos of bullfrog and cricket chirping a chorus through the rural, moonlit nights, the sweet smell of cornbread and fried chicken and ribs wafting heavy from the truck-stop restaurant on the blacktop that bisects the highway (close, you might note, to my one-time residence, so very close to Thompson's Station), the large matronly server humming to her young, acne-ridden employees, *don't cheat 'em on the sauce, give 'em what you'd want yo'self*, and all the guitar towns dotting the roads and highways of Tennessee dripping with gospel and country, blues and bluegrass: American music, miserable grace of working pain and lost love, salvation always out of reach, Faulknerian abnegations of time coruscating the worker's cheek, *oh Jesus oh Jesus give me rest, it been so long, such a long time now Jesus*, and John Steinbeck a million miles west singing about the plucked guitar and the keening fiddle and the mournful, forlorn harmonica, a reminder to forget divisions of skin colour and class because according to the dream we all labour in the fields in the morning with the promise of the sun and then descend willing or not into the sorrowful vicissitudes of night (and how cruel the nights are on the west coast, how sea-blown and breezy, saline and flat), with Guthrie a dying dream in the Grand Canyon and Dylan a wisp of a ghost on the road and Miley's musical inheritance thus mingled with AM Gold and Casey Kasem, porch-lit jam sessions with William Ray's drier friends who didn't end up snorting *everything* on mid-nineties bar tops and who still enjoyed the night air and the way a guitar met a voice, the way the first and third fingers of William's left hand could spread confidently across the fretboard of his trusty and worn acoustic, his right hand balled to a fist around a pick, a two-year-old Miley sitting at his feet playing with the reflected light of beer bottles and tuning pegs and the amber halo of a single bulb where perhaps her first high-pitched song was sung, the first formative springboard, perhaps, leading to her choir practice and solo work at the Thompson's Station's Baptist Church, her acting debut at age nine, her later acting classes at Armstrong Acting Studio in the wintry grey depressions of Toronto, Canada, her minor stumbling roles on William Ray's incredible television series known as *Doc* (2001–2004) and the Oscar-nominated, Columbia Pictures blockbuster *Big Fish* (2003), and all her persistence in pursuing the Disney character who would change our lives – convincing through dogged insistence those hard-hearted corporate executives and casting agents (who have treated me with august indifference or open hostility, it should again be noted) that she was the one, the true pubescent morning star, the future flagship of the company, the deal-maker of their top-secret series later named *Hannah Montana* to be released in early 2006 about a young girl bearing the unfortunate burden of being an immensely popular singer and entertainer with legions of fans and incredible wealth (though wealth tied intelligently to her wise and mature father, played in the sweetest of turns by Miley's own father, William Ray, who was auditioned at Miley's behest only after she was granted the role) but also determined to live a normal teenaged existence with typical experiences (like studying for exams in tiny denim short shorts, flirting with young male specimens with contemptible hair and gossiping with her loyal friends over the pink telephone), and to try to balance these two divergent and utterly conflicting lifestyles, and, most importantly, keep her pop-star celebrity identity secret and safe so as not to endanger her normal adolescent existence – a show that connected with millions of young children not because of its intricate and unique plot lines or biting dialogue, but because of Miley, that zestful whirlwind of ambition and national pride and bodily health, who was characterized by Disney Channel president Gary Marsh as possessing a 'natural ebullience,' and the 'everyday relatability of Hilary Duff and the stage presence of Shania Twain,' and I could go on in praise, the breath is full and moving, but these heads are nodding and shaking, and time has evaporated and made your faces turn sour, brought forth more beads of sweat to spread beneath your arms, has made your asses uncomfortable, and time is playing its game on me, and though brevity is the soul of wit I cannot in any eventuality be discerning, and so for Miley this means everything there is to know about her, every footprint and signature of that rare and robust and developing flower, the great surging abundance of a singular person *in defiance* of information reduced to partial rounds, the unfair impatience of quarters and divisions, of only the bottom line, of making some information the best information when there is no end to it, no end to its fullness, its baffling richness and generosity, no end to each storied detail, to what I can say before I'm dragged perhaps kicking and biting from the premises, leaving the sentence to remain on account of a half-strangled, half-finished appeal, dismissed and aborted in the eyes of the law like so many twisted, discarded, abandoned children, the children of my life and my land, though I in no way have ever acknowledged or agreed to a *single word* of my sentence – a sentence that from the standpoint of reason *cannot* make sense (not that any substitution can make it sensible, *sentences do not make sentences make sense*, I was taught; it's our punishment and a just one, living in a sad and decadent place that can wilfully and systematically ignore that incorruptible beauty, that brief parting of clouds in a low and grey unrolling regiment, a girl who will never breathe or grow or cry those big crystal tears again in quite the same fashion, so here I am to receive them, *proud* to receive those tears and that recorded laughter, receive those one-in-a-million emotions, be witness to this once-in-a-lifetime unfolding rose the way all tween and teenaged girls are momentary parting petals leaving us lonely and rocking to the radio's ambient whispers, knowing ourselves to be uncomfortable and sad and obscene, shaking in the hours of our starving nights, waiting for our sentence, hoping against formidable despair for the return of our shared horizon, the note and pitch met perfectly, all the jumbled naïveté and fragility of youth transfigured into sense and communion by one song, one note that forgives and heals the guilty chaos of our days, making sense of our loneliness, our perjured feelings, our sickness and our poverty, how we shall never be beautiful, how our heads will run over with unbearable secrets and how we are sentenced to this, serving us right – when the song should end, be cut down, finished, and the singer not go on singing).

LONELY PLANET

I

Ryan can't remember his dreams. It's been this way for two and a half years. He used to have so many beautiful, exciting nights – charging with elephants across marshmallow fields, fucking childhood friends in the stands of enormous monster-truck rallies, even dipping into libido-charging bouts of lucidity, wherein he could suddenly fly, melt time, be happy. Now, though, there's nothing – not even the faintest, most ephemeral glimmer. But Ryan's done his reading on nighttime emissions. He knows perfectly well that if you sleep, you dream; knows that he is no exception. And thus he figures these curious memory gaps can mean only one thing: that some seriously malevolent shit must be running amok in his subconscious.

Ryan guesses that if he *could* remember his dreams, he would call them nightmares. He feels he has good reason: despite the gaping dissolves in his memory, each morning is marked by a sense of dread so acute that he whimpers. He whimpers before he opens his eyes, before he is aware of himself as a being, distinct from his sticky mattress, the rattle of his ceiling fan. Whimpers as the sensation of waking life, consciousness, *Ryanness*, materializes in the slow, plodding minutes of awareness.

After two and a half years, Ryan's sense of dread has reached a rather excruciating pitch. So much so that the word *nightmare* no longer seems sufficient, summoning images and associations that have little to do with his everyday (i.e., California, fluffers, money shots, regret). Ryan reasons his dreams must trump nightmares – that his dreams must be visions of some definitive personal hell (a place without west-coast sunshine, perhaps – a place without gratification of a manic, eternal itch). So he's considered getting help, professional and otherwise – seeking out a psychologist, a psychoanalyst, a psychiatrist. He's pondered reading Jack Altman's *1,001 Dreams*, Graham Masterson's *1,001 Erotic Dreams Interpreted*, paying for a professional Tarot reading and repeatedly changing his diet, eliminating salts and sugars and empty carbohydrates. He's considered raw-food diets, protein diets, regular hydrotherapy and weekly enemas. He's even toyed with wearing runes and power stones, having his apartment smudged by a metaphysician wielding a pungent, metaphysical joint.

And yet Ryan's not entirely sure he wants to remember. All these potential aids in recollection have yet to leave the planning stage – a spiritual healer's cell number scribbled beside his dusty desktop, a chat with a New Agey webcam girl about the various pros and cons of home enema kits. Directly confronting his dreaming unconscious is for now – as it has been for what seems like eons – simply too harrowing an endeavour.

This summer afternoon, Ryan lies prone on a bare, queen-sized mattress, kitty-corner to the open door of his bedroom. Black cotton sheets lie tangled in a mass on the floor, musty with the dry residue of sweat, semen and spilled beer. His eyes open and shut, fluttering rapidly, as he realizes that he is again whimpering, high-pitched and puppy-like, as if in response to something impossibly obscene. So he stops. After a few blind and grasping minutes, he sits up.

He rubs his temples, raking his fingers through a blond crewcut and massaging his shoulders, kneading the sore, suntanned muscles of his chest and back. He sends his hands over his stomach, protruding ponderously over the elastic of his boxer briefs (another sore point for Ryan, who sometimes feels as if this whole lack-of-dreams issue is somehow related to his weight, the weakening of once-turgid muscles, the flabbiness of his thighs). He reaches between his legs and squeezes his penis, finding it tremendously and painfully erect.

Hot summer sunlight – filtered through L.A. smog, but still honeyed, golden – streaks through thin gaps in his blinds, casting rivets of white glare on a thirty-inch television set against the opposite wall. Ryan catches sight of his upper body and face reflected in the screen. Though he is foggy with the residue of sleep, he feels there is something odd in his reflection, some dreamy quality, a trick of the light. Something he can't place.

His Nokia ring tone – an obnoxious, chirping arpeggio – sounds from across the room. He pushes himself off the bed and stumbles over a sea of belt buckles and balled socks, T-shirts, seashell necklaces, mesh-backed baseball hats and wraparound sunglasses. The phone rings five times before he can fish it from the pocket of a crumpled pair of jeans. He flips it open and presses the plastic to his ear.

'I'm not going to tell you it's half-past.' Don Debris's voice is sore and metallic, a busted bedspring. 'I'm not going to tell you, but, you know. Now you know.'

Ryan slumps back down on the mattress.

'Just to let you know why I'm calling. And – I'm not sure why you deserve this telephone call. Just letting you know I'm no longer your personal wake-up service. Night before a shoot, stay at a Holiday Inn or a Super 8. Buy a new alarm clock.'

Ryan swallows, staring at his milky reflection in the television screen.

'Buy a rooster.'

Ryan's reflected skin is white and smooth, imperfections and blemishes and chestnut-tanned skin softened to a bleached consistency. His nose is a smear of shadow, his eyes black concavities. In the television, his neck appears perilously stick-thin, insubstantial. And there's something else, too – a weird shade or a smudge, hovering a few feet to his right.

'This is your life, Ry-Ry,' Don says, with something like a sigh.

'This is straight-up threesome, right? Two chicks, I'm assuming,' Ryan says, squinting.

'Two chicks.'

A tremor ripples throughout the room: a car stereo blasting Caribbean music somewhere near Ryan's block, the bass despairingly loud.

He puts down the phone. Stares hard at his reflection.

Thinks, *there's somebody here beside me.*

He holds his breath, his muscles tense, and turns to look, his heart thumping with the passing bass. Certain he's going to find a ghost, a spectre. Something white, and transparent, and dead.

'Hello?' Don's voice is tinny and small in his lap. 'You there?'

11

'So you may have heard this already,' says Michael Seidenberg, sound operator, short and over-tanned. 'Stop me if you have. I'm serious. So, this is like two weeks ago. We were shooting a scene with two brunette chicks, one meathead-looking guy with long blond hair. Calls himself Shawn Helmsley, you know this guy?'

Ryan leans against a divider and nods. He glances at a heap of garbage bags piled against the west wall of the warehouse: eight green bags bursting with crumbly muffin stubs, coleslaw, oily paraffin paper and teeth-marked ends of lunch meat. He tries to read the slogan written on the side of the bags but can only make out half the phrase: *Dust to Dust*, written in a cartoon-like, jubilant cursive.

Ryan and Michael stand in a makeshift dressing room beside a complimentary snack table offering a platter of tuna, egg salad and pale ham sandwiches, a stack of plastic plates and cups and utensils, and two-litre bottles of Snapple Lemon Iced Tea. Walls are composed of mismatched cubicle dividers and office panels, mixing taupe with slate grey, tan with cerulean. The floor is concrete and dusty, marked with dark shoe scuffs and mounds of ancient gum.

Ryan rubs his eyes, still feeling the disorienting buzz from the bowl of pot he smoked thirty minutes back. Once the THC kicked in, he found it easier to cope with entering the warehouse, thought less worriedly about sucking in his gut or throwing back his shoulders, stopped dwelling on whatever it was in his bedroom reflection that made him uneasy, made goose flesh rise in salute along his upper arms and back.

'So Helmsley's standing in this bathtub,' Michael continues, his black, six-inch goatee wiggling with each syllable. 'The shower's on and he's getting head from the two chicks. They're choking on this thing – really, stop me if you've heard this already, it's making the rounds.'

Ryan turns his head, watching crew members and technicians scurry around the set: a circular wooden platform, three feet high and twenty feet in diameter, covered by a base of mossy carpeting. A spongy, asparagus-toned blanket lies on top of the carpet, itself partly concealed by a collection of frilly jade pillows. Various potted plants – all rather exotic-looking, by Ryan's estimation – line the far curve of the base, their serrated fronds and leaves packed in a dense semicircle. *Kinda like a swamp*, he guesses.

'So it's nearing the end of the shoot. We give the cue for Helmsley to come, so he starts groaning and shit. But when he lifts his left leg to get some leverage, he slips and absolutely *bails*. On his way down he smacks his head against the faucet, and *bang*, motherfucker's out cold.'

With the loud *crackle* of high voltage, quartz-halogen bulbs suddenly bathe the carpeted base with blinding expositional lighting. The surrounding floor and background of the set are immediately lost in shadow. Ryan blinks, squinting. And what materializes before him is a moonlit jungle clearing beneath cloud-covered, canopied night, without street lamp or tail light – a lack of illumination that seems subtly sinister and secretive, enlarging the dimensions of the warehouse so as to feel immense, continental. He picks up a sandwich from the platter and begins taking distracted nibbles from a piece of ham.

'But here's the thing,' Michael says, his voice assuming a confidential tone. 'Everyone assumes he's still conscious. Nobody knows how he did it, but Helmsley keeps moaning like nothing happened. And get this – *he's still got wood!*'

Despite the loud bustle of crew members lugging equipment (including two set assistants carrying an enormous plastic femur), Ryan listens to the playful echoes rebounding upon the room's darker corners – echoes producing an indistinct, subterranean effect. Without really knowing why, he finds such noises extraordinarily unpleasant; the word *spooky* comes to mind. Turning away from Michael and the platter, he catches sight of David Yost, fifty-one-year-old production manager and almost entirely obsolete, switching on a smoke machine. The squat device begins to billow rich and greasy smoke, giving the interior set the gaseous murkiness of a marsh. Ryan turns back to Michael, wiping sweat from his forehead. The air in the warehouse is exceedingly humid. *Almost tropical*, he thinks.

'So the chicks keep on sucking and jerking, yadda yadda, and Helmsley comes with this huge groan. The girls finish the scene, we yell *cut*, but then we all realize what's happened – that Helmsley's fucking bleeding from the back of his skull. That he's out of commission. Get it? That he's been unconscious since he fell. Isn't that some crazy shit?'

Michael throws his head back and laughs, wrapping up a length of electrical cable. Still giggling, he glances toward the interior set. Ryan slowly follows his gaze to Don Debris, sitting in his telescopic director's chair, hands folded in his lap, surrounded by tendrils of fog. They make eye contact. Don gives a firm nod and Michael turns back to Ryan.

'I think Don wants to see you,' he says.

Ryan licks his lips.

'Break a leg, buddy,' he says, striding away with short, piston-like paces. Ryan wonders, was there a note of mockery, of sarcasm, in Michael's tone? He frowns, thinking. And what was that nod with Don all about? Remembering not to snack between meals, he drops the remains of his sandwich on the floor.

'You're beautiful,' Don says, walking toward Ryan. They hug, Don's hand slapping between Ryan's massive shoulder blades. He kisses Ryan's cheek, all aggressive camaraderie. Ryan stares, dazed (*you're beautiful* – was that some sort of joke?), into Don's face – a well-worn outcropping of cheekbone and jawline, curled, atavistic brow, ample forehead and dark chocolate eyes. Skin tone the average russet of L.A. and fine black hair kept short and side-parted. Staring into Don's eyes, Ryan is once again reminded of the way Don can stare at distant objects for vast periods of time, exhibiting a watchful, primitive patience, a wariness of horizons. It made him recall a Neanderthal dummy he'd seen in a museum with his dad as a child; the waxy brow, the gaze, the hair – it was all so terrifying.

As a result, Ryan often finds himself sympathizing with the many B-girls who routinely assume that Don is a stunt cock or a gofer. Upon discovering that he is their director, they immediately act simple-minded and shy in his presence: fully committed to the role of bimbo, airhead or nihilist. After several months of working with Debris, they end up calling him Daddy, sitting in his lap and giggling whenever he tickles or bites their necks.

Ryan used to think this was cute – even funny. But that was back when the whole enterprise was still some novel dream – when Ryan was still riding a late-nineties wave of high hopes and heady anticipation, days of Californian sunbathing and careless mornings under the beneficent rays of the internet industry boom. A time when Ryan was just overcoming his first few weeks of excruciating shyness and deference, when his dad, dead then for over a decade, wasn't frowning over his decisions, or lack thereof. Back when Don was still *the* Don Debris – a man known for his unerringly accurate sense of what was good for business, despite his peculiar facial features (which, in the late nineties, merely made him more intriguing). At a hale twenty-three, with boyish looks and a flawless physique, Ryan had just completed the film that would usher in all the glowing industry attention: the Adult Video Network Award nomination for Best New Stud, the flurry of media interviews, the coveted invitation to Vegas for the '98 awards ceremony. And with it all came Don: leaving him raspy messages on his answering machine, slipping him his glossy business card, talking over late-night drinks and lines of coke of Ryan's earning potential, his own line of DVDs, his contracts and his successes. A time when things could still be cute, or funny; when girls could sit in Don's lap and Ryan would still laugh, not comprehending when one particular reporter said she found the scene 'quietly heartbreaking.'

'When are we filming?' Ryan asks, still frowning, his eyes itchy and irritated, indifferent to whether Don can smell the pot on his T-shirt, oozing out of his pores and warm on his breath.

'Whenever you're ready,' Don says.

Don grips Ryan's barbed-wire-tattooed arms, and they take each other in: Don all happy bravado, Ryan still buzzing from the brass pipe he stores in his glove compartment, feeling anxious.

Don opens his mouth, revealing a row of even white teeth.

Then it happens. The sound. With relief, Ryan assumes he's just dreaming; it would account for the smudge on the TV screen in his apartment. Maybe this means he's never missed a dream at all; maybe the weight of two and a half years is just another one of the dream's more troublesome figments. He's about to wake up! But the sound rises and rips through the blur of pot, and Ryan grinds his teeth, clenches his fists. He knows, then, that it's more or less real: a roar emanating from an unseen section of interior – a roar that can only come from something huge and vicious and prehistoric – the bone-trembling scream of blood and hunger and rage.

Cubicle dividers shake slightly. Something metallic rattles and then comes to a trebly stop. Laughter and applause rise thick and cynical.

And Ryan's feeling of dread deepens with a cold depression in his chest.

'We doing some caveman shit?' he asks slowly.

Don smiles. 'Let's talk.'

I I I

Don and Ryan sit across from one another on plastic folding chairs near the west exit of the warehouse. Don sips from a plastic cup of iced tea and rubs a leather loafer against a fossilized hunk of gum beneath his chair. Ryan's hands are in his lap, his expression purposely stony. David Yost stands near the entryway to the cubicle, absently pulling on his miniature ponytail. Half a dozen bulky garbage bags (*Dust to Dust*) lie at his feet, their ends sealed with green twist ties.

A faint, repetitive roaring comes statically from the interior set, muffled by digital imperfections, echo and distance. The sound clip is a recording of the Tyrannosaurus rex's first sustained roar during the second major scare scene of *Jurassic Park*. Throughout the afternoon, the film is recalled fondly by several crew members, who separately and enthusiastically compliment David on his choice of sound bite. David is congratulated with particular warmth by Bianca Jane (BJ) Stephenson, one of Ryan's scheduled co-stars, who mentions (in her squeaky, school-girl voice) that she was a 'dinosaur nut' in elementary school, impressing those interested (not Ryan) with her ability to name even obscure hadrosaurs, such as Parasaurolophus or Velafrons, with an offhanded, precocious and undeniably cute air (also relating, to those patient enough to listen, that Michael Crichton's *Jurassic Park* was the first real adult novel she read, in the fourth grade, finding it thrilling and even, at times, moving, calling it her 'first').

'Yeah,' Ryan says. 'I'm upset.'

Don pumps his head up and down, cracks his knuckles. 'It's nothing,' he says.

'No, it's not nothing,' Ryan says. He rubs his palms over his face, scrunching the loose flesh of his cheeks, rubbing moisture from his eyes. 'It's definitely not nothing.'

'It's gonna be two hours' work,' Don says. 'Three, tops.'

'But a remake?' Ryan asks.

'Vivid remade *Debbie Does Dallas*. They knew it was a classic.' Don glances quickly at David. 'It'll sell itself. Updates the themes. Chicks look different. It's for a modern audience. People lap that shit up.'

'We're not talking about the same thing.' There – did he catch Don and David share a look? Were they laughing at him? *This is all because of my body, my gut,* he thinks. *They'll want to cover it up, make me wear a stupid T-shirt or something ...*

'Sure we are. The internet's the future. We could do all sorts of internet remakes and make a lot of money. Hard-edged fringe shit, even.'

Ryan screws his face into a mask of concentration. 'Listen, I'm kinda, um, dealing with something ... right now ...' He trails off, faced with the uncomfortable realization that he's never told another person about the dread or the whimpering, that he's never told anyone about the dreamless nights. But then again, what did Don or David really know about him? Even if he did want to unburden, who would care?

'Okay, Ryan, yeah, we're here for you, man, and we've all got problems, and we're all going through something or other but –'

Ryan stops listening. He finds himself thinking back to the night of the 1998 AVNAS. The way he got drunk and stoned after the ceremony, alone and lonely, staring into the spinning ceiling fan of his Ramada suite, listening to the dull throb of his extremities dancing in the warm embrace of booze and pot. It would be his first and last invitation to the awards, his last trip across Nevada. He fell asleep dreaming of enormous flood-lights, sweat trickling from tight, tanned skin, the burn of cocaine dripping down his throat, his dad's lifelike face hovering in his irradiated memory. And when he awoke, there was no dread, no whimpering, just the begin-ning of a burnout that would one day lead him here, to this warehouse in L.A., staring at Don sip a cup of iced tea and beg him to jump through one more pointless hoop. The dreamless nights and the ensuing dread would come later, after the kink and fringe features of the 2000s, the sixth installments in dead series, the drugs and pills and the collapse of his body. His *body* – what they were staring at, mocking, now saying it wasn't good enough to headline features or even *appear* onscreen –

'I can't believe you aren't pumped for this,' Don says. 'This is the easiest gig you've ever had, and you know it.'

'You should have told me.'

'You never asked.'

Ryan sighs.

David holds his palms out to Ryan in a pleading gesture. 'Really, man, you're *totally* gonna get into this. I mean, the set alone – we checked out the botany books, read up on all the terms, you know, like, *gymnosperm, angiosperm,* all that science shit from the late Cretaceous. We got fig leaves, sycamore maples, big-ass magnolia petals – I mean, this shit is totally fucking accurate.' David drops his hands.

'Show him the suit,' Don says, smiling.

David squats and tears into a garbage bag. Ryan shuts his eyes.

'This is really something, man,' David says. 'I mean, top-of-the-line. Close, anyway.'

Ryan doesn't look.

'The plants, the fog, the detail in the gloves and around the mouth. You've got individual scales all over the surface. It's full body. It'll feel like a second skin, and it's lightweight. You're not gonna be able to see too well, but you've got great manoeuvrability.'

'Get a load of this, Ryan,' David says. Ryan opens his eyes.

David holds a thirteen-inch rubber penis, about two and a half inches thick. The head is a rich shade of green. Two scaly, grapefruit-sized testicles hang beneath the shaft, also green. David squeezes the left ball, his tongue lying heavy on his bottom lip. A spurt of foamy purple liquid explodes from the tip, sailing in a heavy arch, landing with a satisfying *splat* on the concrete.

I V

Ryan stares at his reflection. He stands in the tiny washroom of the warehouse, his gloved hands clutching the wet edge of a porcelain sink, his face pressed against a circular mirror to compensate for the room's feeble glow. The lingering scent of shit prickles his nostrils. He spits down the drain.

Ryan's bowels feel enflamed, as if his intestinal lining were coated in a thick layer of Tabasco sauce. His recent evacuations have been passionate and prolonged, repeatedly tricking him into composure before blowing him down with another cruel gurgle of tightening muscles. Each time Ryan feels as though he has nothing left to give, he rises from the cheek-warmed seat and again attempts to don the zippered T. rex costume, one foot at a time, making room for the buoyant tail in the tiny stall, before unzipping it all again and collapsing back onto the bowl.

He inspects the ripple of the scales, the rigid bones of the spine. The costume is a combination of an old black-and-white 1950s *terrible lizard* and of Godzilla, including rigid spinal protuberances coloured a myrtle green, punctuated by speckled flourishes of garish canary. The fingers taper into black, elongated nails. The tail is stubby and soft. Individual scales link together in a poor emulation of medieval armour. And between his legs hangs the strap-on cock-and-ball mechanism, butting impassively against the porcelain. *Second skin my ass*, he thinks.

Ryan automatically compares the artificial member to his own penis. When erect, the tendons beneath the flesh of his real shaft stand like hardened, rocky muscles, veins rising in a tangled relief map. Ryan owns a large, meaty penis – an appendage that was once called pretty, and regularly toasted by directors. *What a cock*, Don would say, sweating through another frenzied cocaine crisis of the early 2000s. *What a beautiful monster.* Ten years after his first film, Ryan now has to suck in his stomach to see the full length of his dick. And all it takes is the sucking in of flesh, the curious glance down, and suddenly his eyes begin to fill with fiery tears that enlarge his sense of dread to a gibbering sadness.

Ryan focuses on his reflection. He rubs a scaly nail along his jawline. The glove is wet from the sink, causing him to shudder. He thinks, helplessly, of his mornings, waking from paralysis and oblivion and the dull anesthesia of hangover. In the haze of awakening, he imagines his penis as a tube of white, waterlogged flesh, caressed on churning waves that are insane and immense. He squeezes his new green shaft and sighs, attempting to divert the course of his thoughts, only to find himself missing those early days when his penis was celebrated as some sort of surefire investment.

Surefire. Investments. All hopes amounting to money, that constant waking dream. He'd once thought of his debut in the industry (only those outside the industry called it porn) in the same way he considered his dick: as entirely unique. But soon the shots became more belaboured, the disappointments more acute, even as he stopped thinking about what his dad would have thought, if he'd lived. He watched the same story unfold, year after year, for almost every new stud: the beginning weeks of insufferable excitement, the flabbergasted expressions pasted on the faces of the newly paid, realizing how much they received for what seemed like so little work. How the too-mature girls and the cocaine and the West Hollywood parties spun the boyish faces of the young men into haggard and sallow veterans, all sneer and superiority, still smiling despite the lack of surprise or novelty, despite the fortieth or fiftieth anal scene, the litres of come.

Every new actor's debut scene reminded Ryan of his own first shoot: the buzz of cameras and intolerably bright lights and boom mics and weirdly creepy directors, the way the noise and pressure could instanta-neously impede the natural flow of blood, causing limitless chaos and anxiety as mutters of *wood trouble* or *no wood!* reduced the chance of recapturing an erection to a grim impossibility. Ryan prides himself on his consistency in the erectile department, never once losing his compo-sure, never once requiring the emasculating assistance of a stunt cock to cover his mandatory money shot. But there are times when it's close –

when the sexual act is so far removed from anything approaching arousing that he has to focus very hard, forget his name, regress to something so basic and primitive that after ejaculating he is unable to remember what carried him over the precipice of orgasm, what shadowy ancestral nudge tuned out the lights and the flicker of cameras and filled his ears with the pounding, implacable rush of blood. Whatever it is, Ryan thinks, it makes for great cinema – scary, though, to think that the secret, buried nudge will one day be gone for good.

And what if it has, finally? What if no one wants to see it, at least not from him? Ryan swallows. It's all so easy today, what with the handheld cams and the three-person teams. Studs no longer having to pass through the fire of a full film crew, a tight schedule, a director catapulted to insanity by hard drugs. Hell, they aren't even *called* studs anymore – instead lumped together with the girls under the insulting label of 'talent.' Closing his eyes, he tries to shove these thoughts away, into some dark cranny of his psyche. He tries to remember his last dream – the last dream before the onset of the dread, the forgetting, whatever it might have been. *It doesn't matter*, he tells himself – any dream, even a nightmare, would mean happier times. He imagines it grandly capitalized: The Last Dream. But instead of The Last Dream, he finds himself remembering something entirely different.

It was a late-night Discovery Channel documentary he'd seen while lying in bed, too wired from pills and coke to sleep. It was about dinosaurs. Normally such programming wouldn't hold his interest, but for some reason this was different – it was fascinating and engaging, almost beautiful. The names, the hunting patterns, the mating rituals, even the meteor that would wipe them out: watching had been … well, pleasurable. The faint memory of the evening holds a warm, rosy aura, brings a slow smile to Ryan's lips. That was weeks before the whimpering began, he recalls; he had been taking some time off work, slowing down his pace, trying to get back in shape with some basic cardio and circuit training. It was a good time, even if it wasn't perfect, and at least he was dreaming *normally*, despite the odd nightmare.

Still grasping his new green penis and staring into the bathroom mirror, Ryan begins to feel the faintest glimmer of relief. That today, of all days, there'll at least be no need to perform. That the suit will be a stand-in, eliminating the need to actually work. All he'll have to do, he realizes cautiously, is thrust and mimic, allow the suit to work its low-budget magic. Simply recall those beautiful creatures on the television, imitate how they moved and mated, and focus on why they were so lovely. Why those *days* were so lovely – days before the nights went black and dread turned him into a puppyish mess.

He lets go of the plastic shaft and tries on the headpiece. A red forked tongue lolls between two bottom fangs. The eyes are huge yellow orbs with black, cat-like pupils, set high on either side of the cylindrical head. Once on, it almost entirely obstructs his field of peripheral vision. He's able to stare straight ahead through the meshed mouth, between rows of stubby plastic teeth that are supposed to look razor-sharp and fearsome.

A fist thumps against the door.

'We good?' Don asks. There's a hint of exasperation in his voice.

'Yes,' Ryan says, pulling off the mask.

Silence.

'We start shooting as soon as you're finished. The girls are ready.'

Ryan dabs the sweat from his forehead with a ball of toilet paper. He is determined now to make things work, buoyed by the hope that he won't need to perform, that it will all be over soon. *Things will be fine*, he thinks. *Just focus on the Discovery Channel*. He picks up the mask, fumbles to unlock the door with his gloved hand and steps out.

Ryan's route to the set takes him between cubicle dividers and around snack tables. He is careful not to knock over plates of sandwiches with his bobbing tail or dangling penis, wary of low-lying glasses or potted plants. He passes from shadow into light, fluorescents giving way to halogen. He is forced to walk slightly bowlegged, to take short, cautious steps. At one point he almost trips into a divider. Crew members make way, scurrying before him like scattering woodland creatures. He reaches the murky surrounds of the jungle clearing. The fog machine hiccups and coughs, obscuring the set with vapour.

He steps out of the shadows and onto the raised platform. Then, between laughs and sudden yelps, scattered claps begin to trickle forth. Within seconds, the applause rises in a wave-like roar, a tidal wave of joining palms – the sound like rushing water from within Ryan's mask. He blinks in the glare of the bulbs. In shadow-obliterating light, supported by giant green pillows, BJ and Chelsea Starr sit and kneel, respectively, by his feet, staring up and smiling and languidly bringing their hands together. Shading his eyes with the flat of his hand, Ryan spots Don and David standing side by side, out in the murk, looking pleased. Men drop their mics or cords to join in the whooping applause.

Ryan grins with the left side of his mouth. He drops the T. rex head on the platform and rakes his fingers through his hair.

One more hoop, he thinks.

V

Chelsea Starr is a twenty-nine-year-old brunette with an ambling scar running lip to ear. The scar has prevented her from pursuing any non-industry modelling or acting, so she claims, but it has granted her a kind of grungy, debased allure in the world of adult entertainment. She wears a leopard-print bra top and wrap skirt with thread tassels. An identically patterned armband is wrapped loosely around her left bicep. Gigantic, bone-white 'sabre-tooth' earrings dangle from her lobes. BJ Stephenson, early twenties and blond, who has only ever worked one non-industry job (at a Dairy Queen in Sacramento, for three months) wears a one-piece, polyester-furred cavegirl outfit, bought (with Chelsea's two-piece) at a Hollywood Halloween costume outlet by David Yost, who insinuated that his two girls needed the outfits for a school play.

As the scene begins, Chelsea and BJ fight over a fake bone. They act like Neanderthals. They grunt, shout and groan – no recognizable words, all animal savagery. Chelsea pulls BJ's hair. They wrestle around the fronds and pillows until BJ is on top of Chelsea, straddling her, pinning her arms. Then, rather than delivering a *coup de grâce*, BJ bends to plant a kiss on Chelsea's lips. From here, it's up to the girls: during a cut, Don suggests some breast fondling, nipple licking, heavy petting, but really, it's their scene to improvise. BJ agrees to one of Chelsea's ideas and spits in her mouth.

While the newly turned cave-lesbians explore each other's bodies, several cutaways reveal a strange and foreboding shape in the mist. Sound effects accentuate the tension: the sound of a heavy, pounding tread (also ripped off from *Jurassic Park*) punctuates the rhythmic track looped throughout the entire scene (the closest anyone could get to 'caveman music,' downloaded from a YouTube clip of a *Planet of the Apes* sequel). The girls pretend not to notice Ryan's approach – they're lost in the throes of atavistic lust. Cutaways and footfalls become more frequent. Soon, Ryan's cylindrical mask can be seen peering through a dense thicket of reeds, watching the duo writhe on the green pillows as if magnetized. Suddenly, the carnosaur bursts into the clearing, roars stiffly and slams its clawed foot onto BJ's chest, pinning her to the ground. Chelsea beats at Ryan with the controversial bone, but to no avail; he merely swats her aside and again roars in triumph.

Ryan then abruptly penetrates BJ's mouth with the dangling penis. It looks as bizarre as it sounds; everyone laughs at how unexpected the move is. Her eyes bulge and she tries to scream. It seems obvious that this isn't enjoyable. But desire also seems to mount in her bloodshot, slightly glazed eyes (a side effect of the so-called super-weed she smoked before the shoot). Without warning, she grabs the base of the fake member and begins to suck in earnest, stroking and fondling. She rubs and kneads between her legs with her free hand, moaning and gurgling into the giant extension. Ryan is told to growl in appreciation. They ask him to *cluck*, to *coo*.

Chelsea comes to with a crazed look. Ryan and the girls then exchange a number of strained positions. Ryan's apparatus is repeatedly swathed with lube between takes. The girls complain with livid streaks of profanity about its unbelievable length and width while splitting a joint of hydroponic B.C. weed. Ryan gives them a thorough screwing, from behind and from above. He is told to finger them and to be rough. Because of his headgear, he sometimes thrusts multiple times before finding easy passage into an orifice. BJ and Chelsea exchange positions, licking each other between the legs while Ryan plows the alternatingly vacant vagina. At the end of it all, Ryan pretends to orgasm, which means Chelsea squeezes the left ball, spraying both of the girls with a massive blast of purple semen. They lick it off each other's breasts and spit it into each other's mouths, complaining afterward of a bitter, acidic taste. David Yost assures them that the goo is non-toxic. According to just about everybody, Ryan's orgasmic moan is Oscar-worthy. 'Legendary!' Don says, laughing, clapping David on the shoulder. It is part keening howl, part wailing lament.

Later, David, Don, Chelsea and Ryan sit together in director's chairs, watching the unedited playback on a tiny monitor.

'I screwed up,' Ryan says.

'Where?' asks Don.

'I don't know. This one point. Like, halfway.'

Don fast-forwards. They watch the sped-up footage until they're about two-thirds through. Ryan holds up his hand. Don pushes PLAY. Most of the crew has gone home, having stacked or leaned dividers and tables and chairs against the eastern wall. The warehouse is cavernous and dark. Those remaining keep their voices low, aware of the echo.

In the clip on the screen, Ryan's talon disappears up to the knuckle into BJ's anus. Her entire backside is slick with lube.

'Here,' Ryan says.

On the monitor, Ryan seems to lose his footing.

'That's it?' asks Don.

'Go back,' Ryan says.

They push some buttons, review the footage. Now it's clear: Ryan's right foot slips on some spilled lube, making a barely audible squelching noise. His foot comes perilously close to slipping off the platform. He wobbles for a second, shifts his weight and regains his balance.

Chelsea dabs a towel at her hair, streaked with purple goo. 'I didn't even notice,' she says.

'It's fine,' Don grunts, pressing FAST-FORWARD, eager to watch the finish.

'Are you sure this fucking gunk is safe?' Chelsea asks.

'I thought it was real bad,' Ryan says. His eyes feel as dry as marble. His lips quiver. 'It just seemed ... I don't know ... just long and bad.'

Twenty minutes later, Ryan is the last to leave the warehouse. He uses the washroom again while the others slip out. He tries to hurry, not wanting to linger, then jogs to the exit and steps into the sudden lancing light of the afternoon, the humidity of late July. He walks the fifty feet to the parking lot and his waiting Subaru. Inside, he finds the seat belts too hot to touch.

Once home, Ryan kicks off his sandals and tosses his baseball hat into his closet. He pours himself a glass of water. The kitchen is blue-grey, the curtains drawn over the window to reduce the white-hot glare of the city. He drinks the water quickly, his muscles contracting. He opens his freezer, staring at frozen dinners, leftovers, icy hunks of meat and vegetables. Something still rumbles in his bowels, but barely.

Ryan picks up a bottle of dark Jamaican rum and unscrews the cap. He pours two fingers into a stout tumbler, adds a few cubes of ice and a splash of almost flat Coca-Cola. He grabs a package of cigarettes, opens the sliding door to his balcony and sits on a lawn chair on the ledge, looking over southern L.A.: other apartment buildings, condominiums, and in the distance the reflective glitter of a freeway. Although Ryan has lived in L.A. for twenty years, he cannot say which freeway it is. *It could lead anywhere*, he thinks.

He drinks the glass of rum quickly. He takes long, deep hauls on his cigarettes, then grinds them out into a rusty Folgers Coffee can, over-flowing with other butts. The sun begins to set somewhere out of sight. From where he sits, the sky looks like a mixed palette, a riotous smear of blue and orange and yellow. He thinks for a moment about his dad, whether he's watching him from somewhere in that swirl of colour. It's vaguely beautiful, he thinks: the thought of being watched, however unlikely. He feels as though the sky is following a script, written a long time ago. He feels somehow relieved that it is only vaguely beautiful – that any extreme display would seem somehow embarrassing.

He moves to his room for a better view of the setting sun. He figures there is nothing else to do, so he sits down on his bed with his glass of rum. He stares at his computer monitor, sitting on a coffee-cup-cluttered desk in the far corner. An undersea-themed screen saver pierces the early evening murk with exotic fish and coral and billowing oxygen bubbles. A sperm whale courses by in the far distance, gazing toward the ocean floor as if caught in the throes of a catastrophic sadness. Ryan closes his eyes, thinking back to the afternoon's shoot, listening to his screen saver imitate the ocean.

It was just so weird. That moment during the shoot when he thought he'd fucked up. He thought it was somehow *longer* than it turned out to be – it was just a second of film, but at the time, it seemed like an epic mistake. He'd leapt onto the platform almost laughing, moving with the exaggerated jerks of an animatronic dinosaur instead of the natural movements of something flesh-and-blood. He'd seen enough theme-park attractions and low-budget movies to know how to imitate something robotic. It was all a joke, anyway, he thought. Why not have fun with it? But after several minutes of miming a machine, he could tell he was screwing up – Don kept cutting, trying to get him to act more naturally, more fluidly. 'Like a real-live Tyrannosaurus!' he yelled, as if this were the most natural thing in the world.

Ryan's face felt microwaved in the mask. Sweat dripped between his eyes, over his nose, into his mouth. He hauled in great, ragged belts of hot air, panting, spitting beads of sweat from his upper lip. Sweat gathered and chafed in the crevices of his joints. But though the heat was punishing, and his vision hampered, he was decidedly calm: wielding the fake penis meant he had no need for even the barest prickle of desire. It was as he imagined it would be. He could perform as a vehicle: locked into the suit, going through the motions, obeying commands from the pitch dark, with Don's metallic rasp telling him to 'take it easy' or 'slam it in' from the shadows.

But Don was right. Ryan was messing up his shots. This jerky shuffle was so far from a grade-A performance. And the buzz from the pot wasn't going away, tricking him into thinking he had to sprint to the washroom and empty his bowels at least four times. It was so misty and hot, with no way to know how long he'd been grunting, pushing and squinting through the mesh of the mask, so he tried to recall the way the computer-generated dinosaurs moved on the TV documentary. Those were dynamic, graceful creatures: every rippling breath and heavy-lidded blink was rendered in beautiful, painstaking, CGI detail. So he tried to move his hips less robotically, tried to swing his stubby tail with a more sweeping rhythm. He tried to be more serpentine, to caress and be tender. It seemed to be working: Don quieted down, occasionally clapping when Ryan performed some especially organic manoeuvre.

As he began pushing his finger inside BJ's anus and her sphincter muscle began flexing and relaxing, his thoughts drifted from his present surroundings, the way they could when he was engaged in anything menial. He began to remember scenes from the documentary – specific scenes he thought he'd forgotten. They had done this weird thing, he remembered, where an image of the Earth started spinning backwards. They showed animations of whirling clocks with reverse-spinning minute hands. The narrator asked him, in a thick British accent, *How many nights in a lifetime?* Ryan remembered lying dazed, drunk, trying to multiply 365 by the average 78 (or 42, his dad's age when he died). *How many nights in a generation?* He couldn't compute the figure, gave up trying. They were showing Asians in the next scene – Mongols, they called them – riding barebacked across moonlit fields. They showed a young boy adrift on a raft on the still waters of the Nile. They were suddenly spinning away before Christ, before any cities of Europe, before the pyramids were built with all that ripped skin and crushed cartilage. They showed him the first tribes of Africa, branching northward and eastward, tiny clusters of brown and black peoples that they said *would one day become nations of kings and rich executives, turning life-or-death stone-and-field work into monstrous leisure, satellite dishes, the atomic bomb.* And the porn industry, Ryan thought (in his heart, it was always porn, porno, fuchsia and pink – it would never be adult entertainment). They showed him the first man, an Adam with hirsute limbs, ragged teeth, sloping brow: the bent gait of a gorilla, top-heavy, the scream of his flesh as it was torn by a predator. Then they showed him a family of grunting apes, told him they had *nothing of our imagination, only the seed or spark*, though Ryan saw that they had our eyes – eyes that could gaze forever at a figure on the horizon, terrifying eyes that could be wax in a museum, or eyes that could convince a young girl of many sweet and fatherly things.

There were images of hulking, bleating mammals and shrinking rodents underfoot, the *new dominion* of post-catastrophic Earth, enough oxygen now for his dearest ancestors, the waters finally purged of toxins and radiation. He remembered the digitally recreated meteor impact that would annihilate all life save for that which was small enough to dig and despair, the tidal waves making clean the mountains, the walls of fire that ate away the woods, the rains of yellow sulphur and black bile that poisoned the waters and eroded the rocks. He recalled the last Tyrannosaurus roar, stuck in mud to its hips, calling out to the sky; the last triceratops as it folded into itself, great lungs collapsing from an air made vile and toxic; the last pterodactyl as it plummeted toward the face of one of the great oceans, a Cretaceous sea, boiling with monstrosities, with everyday leviathans with stadium mouths and penny brains. And it struck a chord of sadness, even though they were ignorant beasts, and even though they were CGI and obviously so, and even though it was over 65 million years ago, and even though without their dying there would be nothing to show for humanity. It was still sad. Those dumb eyes rolling up. Those dumb snouts opening and closing, trying to breathe.

He remembered watching the Jurassic and Triassic dinosaurs eat and mate and die, tearing leaves from 150-foot trees with mouths perched on telephone-pole necks, shaking the earth with the lightest, most delicate tread. He watched the landscape spin through millions upon millions of years, each year composed of sixty-second minutes, sixty-minute hours, twenty-four-hour days, thirty-day months, but bereft of calendar or clock, only the slow passing of sun up and sun down, the breathing and drinking and eating of the moment – no conscious acknowledgment of the earth's shifting and reshaping and sailing across the sea to form super-continents, or its breaking apart, forming archipelagos and island reefs, punctuated by the pimple-bursting excess of volcanic eruptions.

The documentary spun the Earth backwards into eras before the first dinosaur. Giant arthropods, the scorpions and spiders of yesterday, battled with amphibious toads and reptilian crocodiles and bizarre lizards. Things seemed to simplify as the years spun away. Suddenly the earth was no longer a jungle, a steamy and stormy mess, but a barren, red-dusted crater. Only enormous insects prowled the rocks and soil and

Martian-like stalagmites. Even vegetation seemed like too much to ask for. Beneath the surface of the blue sea, the impossibly blue, boundless ocean, Ryan watched a computer-generated recreation of the first stumpy leg of an amphibious creature retract and shorten, becoming a pure fin, over millions upon millions of years. Millions of years moving fluidly like water. Gone. A stump becoming a fin. A fin becoming nothing, becoming a smooth curve or bump on a scaly, CGI slug, as it undulated over a ridge of coral. And before the years slowed completely, there were only bacteria, dancing and dividing into complex things.

It was supposed to be a violent, exciting montage, but Ryan, remembering it so clearly in the warehouse, with his finger pushing into an asshole and his eyes half-shut in the near-suffocating heat of the mask, recalled feeling the opposite – felt it unfold as soothing, lapping waves, though they were tinged with that haunting minor chord of sadness. The comforting British accent, the authority of television, the pills and drinks in his bloodstream slowly rocking him to sleep. The Discovery Channel credits rolling over a black screen, the urgent voices of commercials, then oblivion. There was no worry, no dread. He'd let the empty glass fall from his hand, his head back against the soft fabric of his pillow, his mouth open, for there were *dreams* that sent his eyeballs rolling and darting beneath his lids, dreams that welcomed him in his passage to sleep. Swaying in the costume, his gloved hand gripping BJ's hip, Ryan allowed himself to remember. And there! *There!* It was then, watching the documentary, on the verge of passing out, that he had had The Last Dream.

Ryan couldn't believe he was remembering the dream on-set, as two lube-slick women churned beneath his prosthesis and the lights blurred around him. He'd been trying to remember for so long, trying to find that last dream before the end, the final stop and all the ensuing worry. But he could see it now, clear and cuttingly sharp.

The Last Dream simply prolonged his last waking thoughts, his last glimpse and impression of his room, as if he hadn't fallen asleep at all. As if he'd closed his eyes for just a second. Then he was being shaken awake. He opened his eyes and turned to look at a woman lying beside him, close and relaxed, as if she'd been there the entire time. It was someone he recognized, but he couldn't put his finger on who she was.

She was shaking him awake, was kidding him gently about his slack mouth and the thin line of drool that trickled down his chin.

'Should we get under the covers, turn off the tube?' the woman asked, drowsily, her voice and breath so familiar that he hurt with the effort to remember.

Ryan put his arms around her, and she lay with him over the covers of his bed, his fingers wrapped in hers, his nose buried in the scent of her hair. It was raining, cool, noisy, like a tropical storm, water hammering on a roof of fronds and leaves. And the dream continued for only a few minutes, maybe, before everything else faded into forgetfulness, the dinosaurs long gone – he remembered the flickering white and blue of the television, and then the abrupt drop to black as the woman in his arms raised the remote and turned off the set. He remembered the silver light of his dark apartment, his pale reflection in the television screen, his breath rising and falling opposite hers, the rising tide of sleep. The moment, held by light and the hushing sound of rain, seemed to affirm only comfort and erasure. What did anything matter? So much of what he cared about seemed, in the deep shadows and rhythmic water, so laughably insignificant. He thought for a moment of talking about his dad, of telling the woman in his arms his hopes for his dad's second life, beyond the reach of flesh and fear. The moment passed. What did he care about, anyway? He was drifting, falling asleep. He cared about nothing. It was gorgeous.

The Last Dream, Ryan sighed fondly, sweat stinging his eyes. So calm, so relieving and so vivid. As if it wasn't a dream at all. He coasted there in that memory, losing focus.

And that's when he slipped on the little pool of spilled lube and quickly regained his footing. He could see again, and the moment, the fine silver light of the dream, was gone, fading out into the backdrop of brainwaves, the cemetery of all sleep. He glanced nervously at bj, afraid he'd botched the scene. She moaned as before, as if nothing had happened.

And that was that. The rest of the shoot, the triumphant, purple-toned money shot, the buzz through the footage, the drive home. The screen saver, bubbling.

Ryan sits up in his bedroom, blinking. He glances at his television. He can still see his reflection, his slumped shoulders, the near-empty glass of rum in his fist. No shadows, no smudges, no ghosts in the mirror. There is nothing to scare him or make him think that something is haunting his room. No one is beside him. No one is watching him. He is alone. *I am entirely alone*, he thinks. *All the dinosaurs are gone.* Every life went the same way; everything passed through the same turning mechanism, the same coursing water. He feels hardened to this, and lonely, and sad, and deeply wise, and somewhat philosophical even, sitting in the growing shadows of dusk, staring at the television, empty of haunt or threat.

Some minutes pass. His screen saver breaks the silence. The passing animated sperm whale – one of Ryan's closer friends, enriched now by his expansive feelings of kinship and sadness – issues a long, haunting *moo*, like a lone foghorn, a hail and farewell, and bubbles, rising with the release of his magical breath, burst.

ACKNOWLEDGEMENTS

Thanks to the publications that risked bankruptcy and scorn by publishing earlier drafts of some of these stories. Thank you (specifically) to the editors of *Departures* (above/ground, 2008), *Dinosaur Porn* (Ferno House/TERU, 2010), *experiment-o* (AngelHousePress, 2008), *For Crying Out Loud: An Anthology of Poetry & Fiction* (Ferno House, 2009), *Gulch: An Assemblage of Poetry and Prose* (Tightrope Books, 2009), *The Frequent and Vigorous Quarterly, Joyland: a hub of short fiction* (and *Joyland Retro Vol. 1 No. 2: Selections from Joyland Magazine*) and *zaum*.

Thanks as well to the Ontario Arts Council and the Toronto Arts Council for generous support of this project in its hatchling stages.

Special thanks to Alana Wilcox for her belief in this book and for her keen edits. Thanks to the entire Coach House crew – Evan Munday, Leigh Nash and Simon Lewsen – for the tremendous support, camaraderie, enthusiasm and gross fact checking.

Many thanks to my teachers: Trevor Cole for the help in shaping many of these stories into readable format; Jeff Parker for constant brotherly support and wisdom; Rosemary Sullivan for the much-needed encouragement in the fourth quarter; Robert McGill for the excellent advice; Anthony Bright for first and lasting lessons; and Nathaniel G. Moore for putting me over in the main event. Thanks as well to all the patient writers who have read and commented on these pieces and to Arnaud Brassard for the cover design.

Thanks to all my wonderful friends, from Burlington, Ottawa and Toronto. There are far too many exceptional people in my life to list in this small space, and for that I am truly blessed. Thank you for your support during the dark ages.

And lastly, a million thanks to Stephanie Ward, my partner, who traded a country and a home for the sake of us, and thanks to my mother Susan, father Kenneth and sister Emma. All my love.

ABOUT THE AUTHOR

Spencer Gordon holds an MA from the University of Toronto. He is co-editor of the online literary journal *The Puritan* and the Toronto-based micropress Ferno House. His stories, articles and poems have appeared in numerous periodicals and anthologies. He blogs at dangerous-literature.blogspot.com and teaches writing at OCAD University and Humber College.

Typeset in Aragon and Aragon Sans, from Canada Type.

Printed at the old Coach House on bpNichol Lane in Toronto, Ontario, on
Zephyr Antique Laid paper, which was manufactured, acid-free, in Saint-Jérôme,
Quebec, from second-growth forests. This book was printed with vegetable-
based ink on a 1965 Heidelberg KORD offset litho press. Its pages were folded on
a Baumfolder, gathered by hand, bound on a Sulby Auto-Minabinda and trimmed
on a Polar single-knife cutter.

Edited and designed by Alana Wilcox
Author photo by Arnaud Brassard
Cover design by Arnaud Brassard

Coach House Books
80 bpNichol Lane
Toronto ON M5s 3J4
Canada

416 979 2217
800 367 6360

mail@chbooks.com
www.chbooks.com